2

Talk to Strangers

> To Meg,
> who is always inspiring
> and encouraging — I wish I
> had taken your advice 10 years
> ago and gone into nursing —
> a Novel but now maybe I will
> write
> love Susan
> aug. 2012.

by Susan Erickson

4

Thankyou to my family and friends

6

A Fable

Los Dos Perros Blancos

Mi vida es muy simple. Mi casa, comida, familia, libros, el jardín – estas son que las cosas componen mi vida. Todos los días camino con mis perros en el bosque y por la orilla del mar. Todos los días, caminos por el sendero y los perros les gusta el olor de terreno bruto. Y por la orilla – peces muertos, la sal del mar, la marea, y otros olores interesantes. Cuando volvamos a casa, los perros coman y duerman mucho. Un día, más diferente que las otras, los perros tiraron de la correa; ellos querían correr en la reluciente arena donde la arena encuentra el mar. Los perros corrieron por la arena y un arco iris descendió desde el cielo. Una bandada de pájaros blancos fue volando por encima de los perros, y los perros trataron de capturarlos. Los perros quisieron volar como los pájaros. Los perros saltaron tan alto que les convirtieron en pájaros y volaron lejos. Mi historia está muy triste pero, *¿Cuáles son sus sueños?* Yo amaba a mis perros. Pero yo tuve que liberar los perros. Después de eso, yo solo vi los pájaros y escuché el viento. Los perros sonados con volar. Nunca vi a mis compañeros otra vez.

A veces, los sueños que tenemos, puede ser de otra decepción.

Chapter 1

Elena stood transfixed in front of the *bonsai* exhibit. She had once walked down back alleys and contemplated the vastness and organization of the modern, industrial cities of Japan, where useable land was not wasted; where, amidst industry and expansion, nature had not been forgotten. Down every street were small gardens wherever there was enough room, in small pots on window ledges, in greenhouse sheds lined up and down, and on rocks and doorways in every back alley. Elena said out loud to herself and to the ancestors and past caretakers of the *bonzai*: "When the artists of long ago first developed the bonsai, they must have been looking into the future and seen that one day there would only be enough space in the cities for miniature pine trees to grow....*Hai, hai hai, sooo dessku*." She walked around the three hundred year old pine, its knarred thick trunk like an old man's hand and crooked fingers holding up an elegant fan for all to admire. Stanislaw her husband appeared and thought she was speaking to him.

"Elena, there you are. Come quick the dancing is about to start."

"Stanislaw," she said surprised to see her husband, "I was just admiring the display. I haven't seen a *bonsai* since I was in Japan. Aren't they incredible? I wonder how many years a person looks after a *bonsai* before they pass it on to the next person to take care of." Stanislaw took Elena by the hand, and led her away from the miniature forest, and they returned to the ballroom of the grand hotel.

As they entered the ballroom, Elena realized how long she had been gone. The dinner had been cleared away, and the tables had been moved. Many couples were now standing and swaying, rocking forward and back, to and fro, drinks in hand next to the bar. Elena stepped into the crowd and then waited awkwardly for her husband to find them a seat at a table near the dance floor. She stood alone, dressed in a fitted gown made of moss green silk brocade. It had a stain on the front - hopefully it was not noticeable. The dress was one she had sewn herself especially for this kind of occasion. She held her now empty glass in one hand which she balanced in position by resting her elbow on her other arm folded across her chest. She stood looking into the crowd for her husband in the assembly of festivities held for employees and clients, and came to the grim realization that she knew none but him; and that her pleasure, how she survived the evening socially, was totally at the mercy of the guests whereby, like a swarm of grasshoppers to a pasture, they would either notice her or simply surge past her, greedy to make landfall somewhere else. She did see her husband again; he was standing at a table looking over at her and directing a woman in a dark ruffled dress towards her. The sleeves of the dress and the hemline puffed out with so many ruffles that the woman's elbows and knees, in the fashion of an attacking turkey, cut a path in the crowd of suits, or otherwise hens, chicks and barnyard roosters toward her. Out of the gathering, this ballooning woman, with her ruffles like feathers, determined in her gait to reach her destination through the throng, arrived at the surprised Elena. As she stood there, Elena looked down at the cream colored boots, at the pointed toes and spiked heels. They strutted of their own accord, and the toes of the boots were decorated with several small shiny buttons which reflected the overhead lights and served as mirrors for the wearer to catch a glimpse of herself at any time that she looked down.

"You must be Stan's little woman!" asserted the woman as Elena raised her eyes up from the floor. Poor little Elena, she had never been introduced to this woman before, but she surmised that she must be high up in the company, or desired it, if it was not already the case. She was well groomed, almost shiny, and very slick; and she flashed an extraordinary diamond ring which protruded out from her left hand which held her glass.

"I am a woman, if that is what you mean," Elena replied politely with a faint smile, "and Stanislaw and I are married." The creature looked perplexed and then added,

"I'm Alex. I am sure Stan has mentioned me, we work together."

"Oh, yes... he may have," said Elena as she thought for a moment, "I'm Elena." She offered her outstretched hand. "Are you in marketing, then?"

"No, I'm the Chief Financial Officer. I run the show, if you know what I mean. I'm an accountant by profession – Stan and I did our Masters together, that was a few years before I started working for this company. And what do *you* do, Elena?"

"I'm an engineer, a *domestic* engineer." Stanislaw had coached her on what to say to those personal and sometimes rude questions. Miss Alex gave a quizzical look.

"You know, I oversee all the '*domestic*' duties, superintend, direct. But mostly I am a charwoman," added Elena. Not knowing how to receive this unexpected outpour of information, the woman changed the subject, and enquired again,

"And you have children. What are your children doing, right now?"

"Well, I can hardly say, hopefully they are studying hard at university, and saving lives. Our eldest is an emergency room doctor, and our youngest, Clarissa, is at home with her grandmother," finished Elena. Alex suddenly turned aside and looked at the crowd. At this very moment, a loud speaker started ringing, and the Master of Ceremonies for the party announced the band, and began to introduce the musicians. It was impossible to continue the conversation, and everyone had turned one's attention to the stage. It was the polite thing to do at this time. The gathering at the bar moved away to their tables and to the dance floor, and the band began to play, loudly.

"Alex, there you are," interrupted a man appearing with two drinks. He glanced at Elena and words of cordiality were lost in the hammering of the band. Stanislaw appeared next and moved in where the others had left.

"Stanislaw, it is really too loud to talk in here, I'm going out in the hall. Thanks for the refill," she added as she reached for another glass of champagne, and handed the empty glass back to her husband.

"I'll be right with you; I'm just going to tell Charles to save our seat at the table."

He turned and was immediately engulfed by the suits, and Elena left the noise of the ballroom and wandered out, into the lobby. An elegant curving staircase with white marble steps and a highly polished oak banister drew her attention and curiosity. It was impossible to make small talk with people one didn't know, especially when one had to shout to be heard. All nuance of expression and interpretation was sure to be lost even amongst the most attentive or astute conversationalist.

Elena climbed the staircase and ran her hand up the smooth polished banister. When she got to the top, she realized that the staircase led up to the mezzanine. She walked through an arching doorway, and down a corridor until a narrow doorway led her onto a balcony surrounding the ballroom. She looked down on the floor below her. The voices were lost in a cacophony of sound and echo which drifted up together with the colorful dresses and the swaying silk ties. Together they flew up through the huge chandeliers refracting a multitude of color and sound against the high ceiling. The gargoyles and Putti ate and spat out, cried of stomach aches and sensual delights as they danced and stood watch from the ornate, gilded ceiling. Elena leaned over the banister, unnoticed, and when she espied her husband making his way towards the door leading into the grand lobby, probably looking for her, she turned away from the menagerie below her, and lightly on her feet, like Cinderella at the ball, she returned down the great staircase in time to meet up with her husband.

"Love, are you looking for me?" she called to her husband.

"Hey, what are you doing out here?" he asked her in his familiar way.

"I really find it too loud in there, and it is so hard to talk. Let's sit in the chairs by the door for a few minutes, and look at the harbor lights." As they started to walk toward a group of cozy antique chairs with big tasseled cushions, they both turned to each other with a sense of bewilderment.

"I feel something. The floor is shaking," Stanislaw said to Elena, "An earthquake!" As he called out unexpectedly he grabbed his wife's hand and pulled her towards the huge wooden doors. The sound of a rumble and the clinking of chandelier crystals swayed above them. Moments later, they stood outside the doors of the grand hotel and witnessed people running from the building amid a frightful heretofore unfelt sensation. The hotel was old and beautiful, and seemingly strong, but it was unfortified, made out of un-reinforced brick which was vulnerable to collapse. The two stood outside, gaping at the scene, not knowing what to think or do.

"If I die before you, marry someone rich," Stanislaw blurted out to Elena. She grabbed him around the waist and responded in a frightened voice,

"Don't say those words, dear Stanislaw, why would you say something like that?"

"Irrational thoughts in a moment of crisis," said Stanislaw knowingly.

"No one is going to die. I love you."

"I love you too," Stanislaw said as he stared at the scene before him. They witnessed the ivy covered building shake for a minute that seemed like a dream one couldn't wake up from. Through the trembling of leaves, all over the building, and throughout the shrubs and trees on the lawn in front of the hotel itself, the world moved like seaweed under water. There was a screeching and cracking of ancient timbers as a wave of aftershock rippled apologetically. A gargoyle fell from the cornice of the building with an awful thud, and Elena shuddered as she grabbed her husband even closer. They stood and watched as people crawled on their hands and knees, across the sidewalk, and across the lawn, clinging to the ground beneath them. Some felt the cold wet earth on their knees.

"Oh my Lord," was all that came out of Elena's mouth. And then she confessed to her husband, who stood in shock, his arms around his wife, and she said,

"I always wanted to feel an earth quake." And then she ended in a whisper once again, "Oh my Lord." They held each other quietly now, as they stood on the lawn of the grand hotel. They waited for the shaking to stop with the heel of Elena's shoe anchored firmly in the mud.

While the earth stretched and decided to wake up, a thousand people on the ballroom floor fell several feet to the basement floor below as the ballroom dance floor caved in. At the same time, a giant root ball from a century old ivy plant that had taken root under the hotel, burst through the hotel's foundation making its presence known. With a prompting from the earthquake, the ballroom floor had opened up hoping to join in the festivities.

Sirens in the night air were sounds not heeded, phone lines would not connect, and hysteria and uncontrolled sobbing ruled the night. Mother Nature was a humbling entity. There was much confusion and darkness on the streets; and people were dragging boards and rubble from fallen buildings in a desperate attempt to find their loved ones. It was all over so suddenly; but it was just the beginning. It was dark, and it was cold.

Chapter 2

A few months later, Elena was sitting in an outdoor restaurant in a small city n Mexico. The earthquake felt like death on the doorstep, but when she and Stanislaw were at last safe at home, and their children were all found to be safe, people carried on, adjusting to change and new directions. Elena and Stanislaw were to travel to Mexico together, but Stanislaw came home from work one day and announced to Elena that he was unable to go with her.

"I have an important meeting with some clients, Elena," he said, "You'll have to go to the language school without me. Please forgive me, but I must stay here." At first she did not accept the change in plans, but Stanislaw convinced her to travel alone.

"Please go Elena, you'll be fine. You'll have fun; everyone else there will have the same interest in learning Spanish, and you like meeting new people... talking to strangers," he ended slowly. Elena was convinced. But not right away. She didn't rush her answer, it wasn't an instantaneous '*I'll go!*'... She didn't even give it the required, 'I'll think about it' response with a few days of polite deliberation. She waivered for over a week. Her friends would *scrub* for a week and do more! given the opportunity to get away on a holiday. They always tried to encourage her to join their book clubs, or join their running groups, but she never really felt confident on her own, Stanislaw was always there – he and the children were her number one focus and priority. However, after the earthquake, she began to think of her own mortality and Stanislaw's reference to dying and thought, 'I must not be afraid to live life the way I want it to be. My decisions must not be made based on fear – or fear of the unknown. Were not the traumas and tribulations in life the guideposts for refining and narrowing what is most significant and worthy of our time and energy?' As she sat in the café, she thought about all that had gone through her mind before making the final decision to come to Mexico alone.

Someone was looking at her; she could feel his eyes on her as she sketched pretending not to notice. Finally she looked up, and scanned the scene avoiding him until the end, like a resting dog, feigning sleep, waits for the cat to pass by before springing up and chasing after it. Now she looked at him, and he did not run. He looked vaguely familiar, the man in the blue shirt; and he thought he knew her as well. She sat at the table of an outdoor café, '*al aire libre*', thinking about the strange phenomena of seeing someone that looks like someone you know, when you are in a different part of the world. Elena thought she knew the man in the blue denim shirt. She averted her eyes, and listening to the Mariachi band at the far end of the courtyard, she sipped her lemonade through a straw. The square filled up as the sun went down, and she sat and sketched, trying to capture the ambiance of the classic town square, the *Zócalo*. It had a fountain, the wrought iron fence, the intricate yet heavy black iron gate, allowing people in and out of the patio, and the *plumeria* trees, with their dark glossy leaves, filled with their flowers and soft grey mourning doves. She could smell the sweet smell of *frangipani*, the perfume from the *plumeria* flowers overhead, most fragrant at night. The local people believed the *plumeria* trees provided shelter to ghosts and demons, whereas in Polynesian cultures, Elena had read, a woman wears the *plumeria* flower in her ear to indicate her status with men: she wears it over the right ear if she is seeking a relationship; and over the left ear if she is taken. In other tropical cultures, in parts of India, the white *plumeria* is associated with death and funerals, somewhat like the Christian faith associates white lilies with Easter and the death of Christ, and hence white lilies at funerals and on coffins, (although here it is said that the strong fragrance of the lilies was meant to mask the smell of the corpse). But the problem for Elena was how to capture a scent so sweet in a graphite sketch. And so romantic and seductive a scent! She would have been better off writing a poem, the sweet fragrance affected Elena's imagination, so powerful a scent it evoked images of seamen landing on paradise islands, Captain Cook's crew in the Pacific being welcomed by native women, topless but for the *plumeria* garlands which they wore dangling over their breasts, and placed around the necks of the starving sailors. The perfume is so intoxicating and inducing a feeling of serene pleasure, that some people hang a garland over their pillows for nights on end, conjuring up dreams of desires. And then, Elena noticed that there was also the smell of the neatly pruned autumn sage hedge, also known as *salvia greggii* which formed a square within a square in the center of the plaza. There was so much to look at and enjoy: the vendors in their traditional attire – men in white shirts, black pants, cowboy hats and boots, and the children, girls with skirts and embroidered blouses, boys with dark pants and white shirts with big bow ties. And there were birds everywhere. 'You can sit there for as long as you wish,' the Spanish teacher at the school had told the class: 'There is no need to rush away; it is a gathering place for the locals and students from the language schools and universities alike; it is good for business, the proprietors encourage it.'

Elena sat there content to sketch, ignoring as much as possible the man whom *she* was the subject of. Soon the patio lights came on, and though tables weren't full yet, the *Zócalo* was now a banquet hall of activity. She sketched the tropical trees which hung over the square and the mourning doves, with their sensitive, tender cooing, while they flew back and forth across the square, and landed from time to time on the edge of the fountain to drink.

The man in the blue shirt noticed her because she was alone, and her dark hair contrasting with her marble like eyes made her stand out from the rest of the local families and the graying tourists whose shopping bags and large purses were stowed safely on their laps while they sat chatting amongst themselves. He ordered two more drinks for himself, and waited for her to notice him again. Elena glanced up from her work, again feeling that uncomfortable feeling when one is being observed, an aggravation that wouldn't go away, and she saw him staring at her. She looked down at her drawing. Sketching was one way to keep occupied when you really were alone. She felt lonely, suddenly.

The next moment he was at her table.

"Good evening Ma'am. My name is John Lees. Would you like some company?" he asked.

He looked at her intently, but she ignored this and thought that there should be no harm in conversing.

"Hi, I'm Elena Beaufort. I am waiting for someone," she lied, "But you may join me here if you would like." And then she added timidly, "Don't I know you from somewhere?"

"You know *exactly* who I am," he replied self-assured.

"No I don't, you look familiar, that's all," she said innocently.

"Ya, sure, you look familiar too," he replied as he stood there staring down at her, "although the sweater is a bit heavy, too concealing." It seemed as though he had already had a few to drink, as his manner was unnatural, and his speech sounded calculated. However the Mariachi band had started up a new song, and there seemed to be more people at the restaurant now, and there was a lightness to the air, and feeling of festiveness. Somewhat self-conscious and embarrassed, she looked around her to see if anyone was watching them. Everyone seemed to notice this man as he got up and moved his beer and himself to his new spot. Another man, clearly a tourist, was watching, smiling at the scene as he sat alone at a table just two over from them - maybe he even heard their whole conversation. A young Mexican girl now came up to John at his new seat,

"*Hola. ¿Quieres comprarlo?*" she asked him, "Do you want to buy it?" as she showed him a painted leather bookmark. He said something to her in Spanish, as she circled him and pleaded, looking up into his now smiling face, and clasped her hands in humbleness, awaiting his answer. He reached down into his jean's pocket and took out some pesos to pay.

"Thank you John" the little girl said to him in English, beaming. He turned back to his new company.

"Where are you from?" he asked.

"I'm from Canada. I'm here learning Spanish. Where are you from?"

"Take a guess," he toyed with her languorously, enjoying the game.

"You sound like you are from Texas, although I have never met anyone from Texas before."

"Well now you have. What else can you guess about me?"

She guessed to herself that he was quite drunk; '*frunk*' as she called it– that is, drunk and flirty combined. She didn't tell him this though, and she hesitated a moment.

"Guess how old I am?" he continued helping her with the game, and getting comfortable, he propped up his head in his hand as he studied her, and picking up his beer with the other hand, he extended his leg toward her and nudged her calf with his foot. She looked at him carefully. Surely he was intoxicated, smiling, grinning like he had finally found what he was looking for. 'Oh well', she thought, there are a lot of witnesses around, and he seems all right for temporary company, I can handle him,' - she was never afraid of any man. However, at the same time, she dare not get carried away and become too friendly, he may take it the wrong way, and become determined and sentimental at the same time. He was talking like a man who had just had an argument with his lover – angry at women, but wanting and needing them, floating from woman to woman like a sphinx moth to the fragrant *plumeria* flower - always seeking the nectar but never finding it. The waitress came by and he ordered three more beer.

"I would guess you are about fifty four," she replied after a moment, not wishing to offend him by guessing too old, nor wanting to flatter him either with a guess too young for his real age. 'Why would a guy care anyway, what age he looked? Ego, I suppose,' she thought. Obviously he cared about his appearance, he was well groomed – the shirt showed creases in the sleeves where it had been recently ironed.

"I'm fifty six. I'd like to buy you a drink" he said as if it were her prize for guessing so close to his real age. He liked this woman. 'Intelligent. Good looking,' he surmised as he looked around the terrace in comparison. He was always looking. So was she, wondering if she were really safe.

"Thank you, but I am drinking lemonade. Maybe when I'm done I'll have just one beer." She wanted to stay out for the evening; she had all intentions of having dinner here and meeting up with her classmates later. Everyone was supposed to be coming to the *Zócalo* for the evening. There was going to be a *Mardi gras* parade. Although *Mardi Gras* was not really celebrated here in a big way as in Brazil or in New Orleans, however the Catholics had some festivities to mark the date.

"Are you Irish?" he asked looking into her green eyes.

"No, I told you I am Canadian," she replied, her blush hidden under her dark skin.

He didn't reveal his Canadian connection yet - there was time for that later, if chance had its way. He only wanted one thing.

"Did anyone ever tell you that you have beautiful eyes?"

"No," she said indifferently. Although she would have returned the compliment to him, as she noticed that his eyes were a very different colour, a shade of deep blue, like the intangible blue of the Mediterranean Sea, and set off by his blue shirt; but she was on her guard. He was a very handsome man - for his age. He was tanned, his hair was cut short, and it was thick and sandy blond, but slightly graying above the ears. He was tall, muscular and lean - built like a swimmer. And he wore cowboy boots, dress cowboy boots, perfectly polished, and pointed, with decorative stitching across the toe. And they were beautifully hand tooled. Elena told him a little of herself, not indulging too much, just enough to show that she was married and had children, and that she was here in Mexico working on her fluency in Spanish.

"Where are your ancestors from?" she inquired of him politely. She was not ready to go back to the empty house where she and another student were staying.

"Germany," he said looking at her and nodding as though he had reached some conclusion about her.

"Are you on holidays here?" was her next question.

"Sort of. I live here part of the year. I'm a commercial pilot. Retired. Trained in Canada."

"What do you do while you are here?" she asked

"I read a lot, I like Thomas Hardy. And I write."

She liked Thomas Hardy too. They did not discuss *Tess of the D'Ubervilles*; in keeping with the decorum of a woman travelling alone, she did not want to allude to the unsavory characters that Thomas Hardy was famous for. As the two paused in the conversation, the smiling waitress swooped upon them, spinning around like rose petals in the wind, and placed three bottles of beer on the table. John Lees paid, and then he rose from his seat, pushing himself away from the table, and asking the waitress in Spanish for yet another round of beer, and then he left the table without a word of explanation to Elena. He was gone for some time, and when the waitress passed the table again, Elena asked her in Spanish if she knew the man with whom she was sitting.

"¿Conoce el hombre, John?"

"Si, si Señora, todos conocen John," - 'everyone knows John'. She said it in such a way that only one woman knowingly can say to another, with an admonishing look that was taken to mean: 'Be careful; the conquest of women is impending.'

"You're back," Elena said to him as he pulled up his chair again and sat down. The café was becoming more crowded with patrons. Suddenly it was dark. There was no twilight here in the tropics. The sun rose, and then it set – it was hard to get used to. She equated warm weather with very long evenings, as it was in the summer in the North. He motioned with his hand to the guitarist who was making the rounds serenading individual tables of guests. The guitarist was a short, dark Mexican, with dark eyes and thick, black brows. He turned to Elena and began to play a romantic serenade - a few words she recognized – *amor*- love, *cielo*- the sky, and *corazón*- the heart. She was supposed to feel impressed, even enchanted, but it was obvious to her, John saw himself as a romantic and was trying too hard to woo her.

"How long have you lived here?" she asked turning to him.

"Two years. I have a son who lives in Texas, and I go to see him every six months. I drive north until I come to the border. Then I stop in - ." At this point she could not quite hear the name of the town he mentioned as the musician had moved closer to her and was leaning over the chair, still singing. Finally the song ended and everyone was clapping and smiling.

"I have a lot of fun at the border town before I go back to Texas," he continued, "…a lot of fun." 'Get the picture?' he was thinking. Instead he asked,

"Travel much?"

"I like to travel, but I've got my husband and youngest daughter at home," she emphasized again. "Last year I went to South Korea with my husband. He had to go there for work. Have you ever been to Korea?" He looked at her, squinting his eyes a little, as if to determine something cryptic in her question. Then he answered,

"Ya," he said slowly and sardonically. "Ya, I've been to Korea," he added nodding, as if suddenly remembering something. 'Vietnam too, earlier though, much earlier though', he was thinking. "US Marine Corps," he said out loud, "I'm a pilot. But as I said, retired, weren't you listening?"

'Single man hiding out in Mexico, ex Marine, German extraction – sounds like a hardened criminal,' she thought. 'He has that familiar air about him….Can't discern anything about him yet - except that he is getting drunk; and these locals have seen him here before, probably every night for the last two years, trying to charm his way into entertainment for the night.'

"Do you live near here?" she asked wondering just how much of a local he really was.

"Ya, just down that way, toward the river" and pointed with his finger from the neck of the bottle he was holding, and tilted back his head, guzzling half of it down. Then he put the bottle down on the table and smiled over at her. He noticed that she hadn't drunk much of her beer yet, and now his empties were standing conspicuously in a cluster.

"Here, *do* have some more beer," he said pouring some of a new bottle into her glass, smiling and trying now to be charming.

"Is there a river walk down there?"

"No, there is not," he said matter-of-factly.

"What is down there then, is it jungle?" she asked imagining him living out of the way of the city, in a small, traditional villa, taken care of by gardeners, cooks and maids.

There were many historical homes here in central Mexico. This small city, once a 'pueblo', was the weekend retreat of many rich Mexicans from Mexico City, and many expatriates as well. It never rained there, except in the rainy season for a short time, when it poured for a few weeks straight. Otherwise, being located at an altitude of over 6000 feet, the air was thin, and the sky a pale blue and visitors from sea level became lightheaded for a few days after their arrival. The homes were square and upright, with arches and open air decks and covered terraces. She imagined he lived in one of these, built along the side of a steep ravine that wound down to the river. Post and beam and plaster, its interior walls plaster with exposed beams, and its hallways reflecting light from the hot sun overhead. Glossy red clay tiles covered the floors, and here and there were pieces of rustic pine furniture, a hallway bench in the foyer, a huge clay urn, and a wrought iron mirror greeting the visitor. Brightly covered woven cushions were heaped on the living room furniture, and carved chairs, a sideboard, and rustic dining room table were the only other pieces of furniture in a large expansive dining area. An old upright piano stood against one wall in the grand hallway, and its music carried its story upward, toward the transom windows, high above the piano wall. An arched, open doorway of pillars and architecturally structured moldings led outside to a courtyard and garden, where a fountain dripped quietly, and mourning doves cooed from somewhere close by.

He looked at her again, intently, and answered in his Texan drawl, slightly amused,

"Ya, it's a jungle down there. I live in the jungle," he added to himself.

She looked again at her sketch. It was time to put her book away. He wasn't interested in her art. She held it up for him to see. He looked at it without commenting and then looked again into her eyes. She put the book and her pen deliberately and slowly back into her bag. Suddenly he was speaking to her in Spanish:

"*Quiero hacerte el amor - mi casa.*"

"Pardon me?" she asked, pretending that she had not heard, although she understood him.

"You heard what I said," he retorted wryly.

"No I didn't," she insisted, stalling for time while she thought of a way to leave, hoping someone would come along from her class.

"I said *do you want to go to bed with me?*" he repeated seriously.

"I told you, I'm a lesbian. I'm not interested," Elena made up her answer on the spot, a response she regretted immediately.

He leaned back in his chair studying her for a moment, and with a sly grin on his face he said,

"At least that's one thing we have in common."

"What's that?" she asked.

"We both like to eat pussy."

"Excuse me for a minute, do you mind, I need to go to the *baño* – washroom. I'll be right back," Elena said indignantly as her face flushed.

"Don't take to too long, I'll be right here, Helena," he said, as he looked around him, and drank the rest of his beer.

She had to get away from him without him seeing her. Suddenly she had lost her confidence. All her karate training didn't help her now. She went straight inside the café foyer which was connected to a hotel lobby to find the washroom, where alone, she could think of what to do next. There were doors everywhere, some half louvered, swinging on hinges; waiters, chefs, musicians, and tourists alike were coming and going, in and out, like giddy children entering and leaving a 'house of mirrors' at the amusement park. Elena chose the wood paneled door, although they all looked similar, except that this one had a *plumeria* flower carved into one of the squares, and it was painted white with a yellow center. The door swung open easily, and Elena knew she was in the *baño* when she saw a beautiful Mexican woman applying her lipstick in front of a gilt framed, full length mirror. When she was done, the senorita turned and gave a warm smile to Elena, and then left the room, letting the wooden door bang shut behind her. Elena was now alone in the spacious, tile covered room. 'Oh, I like these,' she thought, as she examined the colour combinations along the floor boards and around the sink, 'I would like to buy some tiles here, and re-do the bathroom at home.' There was a large, wood framed window in the far corner of the washroom, and seeing this, Elena remembered her purpose in coming in here was to escape. The window was arched at the top, and had a heavy wrought iron handle holding it shut. Elena opened it and looked out. A tree grew near the side of the wall, and running down the side of the window was a large drainpipe. This is where she would secretly make her exit. She flung her bag over one shoulder, hoisted up her skirt around her waist, and shimmied herself up onto the window ledge. Then, with agility and grace, she reached over to the downpipe, and praying that it would not pull itself out from the wall, she slid down one storey to the lane below. A man was walking along and he shouted something at her in Spanish.

"*Perdón, perdón, gracias,*" she said with her best smile and hurried down the lane. She was behind the *Zócalo* now, down toward the river, where the old market was located, and where empty wooden crates and containers were piled on the cobblestone alley. She could hear voices of men at work, cleaning the market and spraying down the aisles. The alley smelled like fresh guavas and over ripe bananas. A few large rats were running down the gutter. She shuddered and glanced quickly behind her. No one was there. She walked briskly now, clomping her way down the uneven, cobblestoned back alley, until she came out of the dark onto a busy intersection. She hailed a cab and got in, relieved, her heart pounding in her throat.

"*Momento, por favor,*" she told the taxi driver as she dug in her bag for the piece of paper which held the address of the villa where she staying. She handed it to the man in the front seat; he looked at it, and cheerfully said,

"*Si, Señora.*"

She leaned back in her seat. 'That was strange,' she thought, and she laughed to herself at the thought of the Mexican explaining to his friends how he saw a foreigner climb out of a two storey building by way of the bathroom downpipe.

By now her Casanova would be wondering about her whereabouts. He might even be feeling humiliated. It wasn't her nature to provoke ill feelings in people. In fact she tried to treat everyone with the same respect and deference. Now she had to sit alone in her room for the rest of the night. She didn't like that either. She wouldn't be entirely alone. A large stuffed marlin covered one wall in the sitting room. It looked like it was laughing. They were both stuck, pinned down, feeling of no air. She knew the feeling well. She had once had a panic attack, on a boat in Egypt, in the middle of the night. There was nowhere to go. Locked in her cabin, she could hardly breathe. Afraid to open the windows, she lay prone on the floor, slowing down her breathing and trying to relax. Now it was the same again. It was dark, and all the villas were locked behind high stone walls. She lay on her bed and listened closely to the wind outside. It came slowly at first, and then rushed headlong don the mountain into the valleys and ravines below.

Chapter 3

Resigned to her room, Elena lay on the bed momentarily staring at the lace curtains which were moving ever so slightly in the burgeoning breeze, and very eagerly put her hand up to her chest and felt inside her bra for her rings. She knew that they were there, sewn into place with a few strands of cotton thread. 'Why am I lying here? Why should I be punished by seclusion, self-imposed exclusion? What was I thinking? Am I really so meek and afraid that I cannot stand up to anyone? *Don't take things personally - don't take things too seriously* were the advising words from someone, some friend from some time past. Why should I be in bed so early, when everyone else is out having fun in the *Zócalo*? What is wrong with me? Why can't I stand up for myself?' These and other thoughts of self doubt and insecurity rolled around her like the smell of smoke from burnt eggs. Then, as though some rogue mosquito had flown into her lair and startled her, she sprang from her bed and went to the window. 'It was definitely too late to go back to the town. What if there were indeed bandits on the street?' Elena opened her bedroom door and took a few steps into the hallway and looked up. The stuffed marlin on the wall looked down at her amused. There was nothing she could do, here all alone, way up at the 'House of the Laughing Marlin' as she named it, the '*Casa de Riendo Marlin.*'

    She flopped down on her bed and stared at the ceiling once again. The words of her karate *Sensei* came to her, as she pouted about being alone, and missing out on all the social action and activity of the *Zócalo*: "Remember to be alone with oneself is not a bad thing. We must get to know ourselves first before we can truly understand the world. Being alone, one can test what we are truly made of". It was Stanislaw who encouraged her to join *Karate*. He himself practiced Judo in his formative years, and recently he urged Elena to get out and try something new. She found she liked it. It was challenging, mentally and physically, in fact the philosophy of *Karate* was a study in itself, and misunderstood by those who knew nothing about it. People associated it with fighting, but really it was an art, based on specific precepts which were its foundation, the fundamental principles of Bushido and Zen: humility, respect, compassion and patience. And then its founder summed it all up in his credo: "Karate is like hot water, if you do not give it heat constantly, it will again become cold." Enough of lying in bed, "*I all alone, beweep my outcast state*", Elena said out loud to herself quoting from Shakespeare's Sonnet 29 - "Enough of this moping."

She got up again and began to practice her Karate. There was no one there, only herself, with movements like the wind – like the namesake *Shotokan* – *shoto* in Japanese meaning *pine waves*, the movement of pine needles when the wind blows through them; her movements were sometimes slow and deliberate, sometimes swift and sharp. She did a sequence of blocks: down block, set, rising block; down block, set, rising block. The Japanese words echoed her controlled attacks, '*gedan barai*', '*age-uke*' and then '*gyaku-zuki*', reverse punch to the opponent's stomach. She continued thus, memorizing what she thought was her next '*kata*' sequence, and forcing herself to do her push-ups and sit-ups on the floor. For these last exercises she placed a towel on the floor, and when she felt she had given fair time to the exercise of her body, she lay on the floor stretching, slowing down her pulse, and listening to the sounds outside, all the time straining to hear the sound of her returning roommate from across the hall. He did not arrive. They never ate the evening meal at the house. The 'Mama' prepared an authentic main meal at 3:00 pm., and left some food for her boarding students in the kitchen for them to eat when they returned home in the evening. She did not deserve the warm appellation of 'mama'. She was more of a dorm mistress – severe and scary looking. She was there at breakfast and again in the late afternoon, but never at home come evening.

"She gambles," the young pre-med student from Ohio had told her. "She just does this for extra income, so that she can go to the casino at night. She goes out with her friends, all night. She doesn't usually return until very early the next morning."

No wonder the 'Mama' had such huge dark circles under her eyes. Her hair stood up on her forehead and was short and curled, but it curled away from her face and down the back of her head as though it were constantly blowing in the wind. And she had a long and narrow hooked nose, and the skin under her chin sagged in layers. Her large hands had hard fleshy fingertips which where thick, and pointed nails lay embedded in the tips, covered in a shiny, deep red polish – like claws. In essence she had the appearance of an iguana, with beady eyes, waiting for its prey. She was surprised by Elena's age when it was revealed to her. ' I know I do not look my age, but I don't have that ugly habit of playing slot machines or cards in a dimly lit room all night either,' Elena thought. That day from the very beginning had started with ill will. As the Mama was preparing breakfast she noticed out of the corner of her eye, like a crow to something shiny, the glitter from the diamonds of Elena's wedding rings. Sitting down slowly with her bowl shaped cup of coffee, and her dark suspicious eyes peering through the curling steam, she let out a breathy, nasal comment which slid off the end of her long sharp nose:

"You should not be wearing your rings in public. Give them to me and I will look after them." The young Robert interpreted and translated into English her demand to Elena.

"No, thank you, just the same. I always wear them," Elena declared firmly.

"You mustn't wear them here in Mexico, someone will try to steal them from you," and she made a movement with her hand on her other finger as though she were trying to yank the ring off.

"She wants to look after your rings here," said Robert. "She thinks someone might try to rob you."

"That's ridiculous."

"She may be right."

"Put them safely away in your room," Robert interpreted once more. She was not intimidating enough to force Elena into giving up the rings. After breakfast that morning, Elena went immediately to her room and with the sewing kit that she kept in her suitcase, she took out a needle and some thread, and stitched her rings to the inside of her bra for safe keeping. No one said anything more about them.

After her lonely workout, and recollections of the day, including a feeling of remorse for running from her dinner in the *Zócalo*, hunger crept up on her and forced her to face her predicament. "Don't be silly," she said to herself; "You are all alone here, and you are locked inside the villa gates. No one is here, and there is nothing to be afraid of." She left her room tentatively, peeking around every corner, and glanced up once again at the smiling marlin. Then stealthily she glided on sock feet, across the polished marble floor into the kitchen. What should she eat? Nothing looked familiar. There was a tiered wire basket of fruit on the countertop, and in the fridge was some American cheese, imported. She ate some of that, thinking of Ben Gunn from *Treasure Island*. All he desired was a piece of cheese. There was plenty of fresh fruit which she discovered when her eyes adjusted to the dim light, and so she cut up bananas, oranges and a melon and feasted on the fruit salad. It didn't taste the same as it should. After that she heated some milk, and slowly, like at home, drank a large mug of hot milk - slowly. The halls echoed in silence and darkness.

With much discretion, she rearranged the fruit in the wire basket, bananas, guavas, oranges and avocados. But the limes and the bright orange-red jalapeno peppers, the staples of Mexican cuisine, she artfully arranged on the white crocheted doily. It was a fountain of color, from the purple grapes at the top dangling over the black wire basket down to the wooden tabletop. She washed, dried, and put away her dishes, leaving no evidence that she had eaten that night, back at the villa. The table had been already set for the breakfast the next morning, so she moved everything back into place as it was. She could see the bright moon, as she looked up to the roof through the courtyard window. A set of stairs and iron railings curved around leading to a room that appeared to be attached to the top of the house. No light was on there either. She noiselessly walked to the front door, an oversized copper covered door, with no windows. She played with the latch, and then to be sure it wouldn't lock on her, she went outside and closed the door behind her.

She stood alone in the garden for a few moments and then crouched down to feel the grass beneath her. It wasn't exactly grass, but it was green and it was cushiony. She sat down and leaned back, looking up at the sky and the moon. The big dipper was still visible but it was right on the edge of the horizon. And there were other stars unfamiliar to her. Even the moon appeared to be tilted the wrong way. The fan palm, which moved gently in the wind above her, was a silhouette against the sky. There were strange animal noises, and chirps and trills coming from somewhere close by. Although she tried to postpone going to bed, she suddenly felt tired. "I wish I could sleep here under the stars" she thought to herself, but the thought of being confronted by the walking lizard, sent her soon enough back to her room for the night.

Sometime later, after reading in bed for a short time, she fell asleep. There was no candle to blow out, no beautiful tiles shimmering in the light, and no maid, or loving hands to tuck her in. But she imagined that her bedside table was one from colonial Mexico, and here she placed her book, next to the silver candle stick, a half a glass of port, and her watch. She leaned over and blew out her imaginary candle, and fell asleep.

It was some time later that she suddenly woke up not from a dream, but from something else. She lay motionless for a moment, staring at the ceiling in the dark, listening and remembering where she was. There it was again, a noise from the door. Could it be the door handle rattling? It was the door knob to her bedroom door. She lay there frozen. Her heart was beating loudly. It was beating in her throat and in her ears. Was she awake or asleep? She tried to move, to reach over and turn on her light, but she couldn't move. She was awake. She pulled the covers up closer to her chin, and her eyes, straining her eyes in the dark; she could make out the lace curtain. Someone was trying her door knob. She had locked the door, hadn't she? She couldn't remember, but they were trying desperately now to get it open. What could she do? She wanted to ask out loud, 'Who is it?', but what if they could not understand English? She wanted to go over and open the door. She could clobber the intruder with her heavy flashlight, but her legs would not move. Her body was immobilized, but her mind was igniting like a light storm. Who could it be? She ran through each possible scenario. Perhaps it was the medical student, just trying to scare her, 'see just what she was made of' - a practical joke that could be laughed about around the breakfast table. He had heard that there were ghosts who roamed one of the university buildings. It had been someone's home, a hundred years before, and there were stories of hauntings. Maybe now he was playing a trick on her, if not him, then the husband of the house mistress. Was he trying to get in to see her? Maybe he was drunk, and his wife was still away gambling? What would she say if she opened the door and the husband was there? He could speak no English, and her Spanish was not very good – she didn't have the vocabulary to deal with such an encounter. "At what time does the train leave the station- '¿A que hora sale el tren...?' The train leaves the station at five - 'en la tarde'." If it were the house 'Mama', maybe she wanted to steal Elena's diamond and sapphire rings. Perhaps Robert across the hall was not home yet, and she assumed the two students were out together in the *Zócalo*, as planned with the rest of the students, attending the Mardi Gras parade. What if Elena opened the door and she was standing there, the calculating iguana? What would she say to her? Maybe the Mama would club her on the head and search the room for the rings.

    The noise went on, and Elena could not move her limbs. At last it stopped, the intruder had given up. Elena wished she had stayed out all night, out in the open; but she had been afraid. She was afraid that she might become carried away, a married woman forgetting herself, losing herself in the festivities of the *Zócalo*, the Carnival. 'This is what happens when you don't face your fears. You become a victim'. She lay in her bed trembling. She lay, with her eyes open, straining in the dark, until the first of dawn showed the gentle movement of the lace bedroom curtain. It was light now, a rooster crowed somewhere in the distance, and then she heard the gentle plodding hooves of the donkey, and the deliberate step of the his master, the old Mexican, climbing their way up the narrow, winding cobblestone street to the mountain above. Step after step, and year after year, "clop, clop, clop." At first it was two men, one older than the other, now only one, and

the donkey. She could hear them passing just outside the courtyard wall. She was that close to the road which led higher still into the mountains, beyond the city limits.
It was quiet now, and soon, the city would be waking up. Cars would roll past her house, and shouts would be heard from construction workers, and frustrated drivers. With very little sleep, she could move now, and she made herself ready to go into the kitchen for breakfast.

Everyone looked the same. Or did they? They were all there waiting for her, to see her reaction.

"*¿Durmió a pierna suelta?*" they asked her in Spanish. She looked stunned for a moment. "Did you sleep well?" Robert interpreted. "Actually, it is an idiomatic expression meaning something like 'did you sleep as soundly as the dead?'"

"*Si, bien, gracias*." She replied to them all, and stared at her cornflakes, waiting to break the spell. They all know, she thought. Or one of them knows, and I don't. If I say something, it will sound as though I am accusing one of them. 'Better keep my trap shut' as my father used to say. 'Stay out of trouble. Eat up and get to school.' Which she did; she ate her breakfast, barely, and took a ride from the *esposo*, leaning way over to the window on the passenger side with the window rolled down, and her hand on the door handle. She leaned her head out of the window, letting the wind rush through her hair, enticing the morning sun to her face. Looking up at the passing trees, and catching a glimpse of the cathedral, she could hear the comforting bells begin to clang.

Chapter 4

The following day after class, Elena waited near the fountain where the students gathered.

"Mr. Wood," she called quietly to an older man, "or should I say: 'Dr.' Wood, pardon me, I know that you are a doctor of Philosophy."

"Do not worry about that, call me Reginald."

"Reginald then, I don't mean to be rude, but are busy right now?"

"In fact I am thinking about visiting another museum, would you dare to join me?" This was a rather bold statement coming from Reginald. He was mild mannered and gentle, a most unassuming man, and Elena was ashamed to admit that before he even spoke, when she first observed him at the school orientation, she thought he looked like an unrefined plumber. Well, she couldn't be blamed for that. 'After all,' she thought to herself, we all make judgments based on appearances from time to time.' He was rather short and broad across the hips, and his pants slipped down just a little as though his belt was stretched out of shape, and his beard was a little scruffy. However, her impression of him soon changed. He was a real gentleman and very proficient in Spanish. And here was an opportunity. Elena wanted to go out very much. She dreaded the thought of returning to the house and she wanted desperately to share her experiences with someone she could trust.

"I would love to join you. My husband and I like to walk through contemporary galleries together, but we have nothing like the great cities in the way of museums."

They chatted about their classes and about the sightseeing trips they wanted to take while in Mexico as they walked through the grounds of the school and beyond to where the curving cobble stone streets met the busy road.

"What did you do in class today?" Reginald asked Elena with keen interest that only a British accent can show.

"We had to write a fable, in class! Tomorrow we have to read it out loud, so I have homework to do."

"Whatever did you write about? I can't think to write a fable; it would be beyond me entirely", he added.

"It was easy for me to come up with the characters because I have so many pets, and I like animals. I'll tell you briefly. It is about a woman, sort of like me, who leads a very simple life by the sea, taking care of her family, her children, the humble home she lives in, et cetera. But she takes great pleasure in walking with her dogs. One day the dogs, who become tired of walking along the path held onto by their master's leash, tug and pull, wanting to be released to run. The woman loves her dogs very much, but she lets them off to run, and they actually run away from her along the edge of the water. They jump *so* high as they chase the birds, wanting to fly like them, that they actually turn into birds and fly away."

"Oh dear," responded Reginald. "That is abstruse. What is it really about?"

"It's about love, loyalty, duty, versus being oneself. I think. Sometimes, the things we do, who we really are, what we want to do in our lives, may disappoint others, hurt others, even the ones we love. As with the dogs, they wanted to be free to live their own life, not the one that their owner expected of them."

"Well, I hope I shan't be called upon to write a fable, I wouldn't have a clue," Reginald concluded. They made their way now through the din and clatter of street life, onto the main road which led to the center of town. The air was hot and dry; and the sun pierced down through the thin atmosphere, the way it does at altitude, prickling the skin and tickling the nostrils. Once inside the cab, the air rushed in and cooled the couple as Reginald in his fluent Spanish gave directions to the taxi driver. The fable was forgotten but Elena continued to speak, much to Reginald's delight. She related the story of the rattling door, from the previous night, which was still foremost on her mind.

"I just want to know what you would have done in my situation" she asked Reginald in earnest as she finished the story of how she lay frozen in bed with the inability to move.

"Well, I would certainly get up and open the door. There is nothing to it. When someone knocks, you just open the door, or at least say 'who is it?'"

"I guess that is what I should have done, and then I would know," Elena replied glumly.

"Yes - and why not?"

"The cat would know what to do, but then they have nine lives to play with. 'Curiosity killed the cat' as the saying goes, 'but then satisfaction brought it back.'... I am nothing more than a '*scaredy*-cat."

"Well don't be down on yourself. Sometimes in a foreign country we are simply not ourselves."

"I think that describes me. And at home, the dogs would bark if there were strangers around." Elena looked at the professor. "You always seem to be looking down, in a bashful way, and I am not sure you are not indeed mocking me."

"No, it is not that at all. I am just thinking about my own foibles."

"Then tell me why, a person of your stature, a music professor at Oxford, and an intellect, why do you want me for company? – especially when I am not myself."

"There was simply no one else available'" Reginald said in a matter-of-fact way that made Elena go quiet for a moment.

"I suppose I should take this as an insult, but I am too stupid to even know if it is," she finally said.

"Really Elena, come come, we are here to enjoy ourselves and to learn. If you learn about yourself, then you are more of a person. We have to put ourselves out there to learn about ourselves. Besides, I enjoy your company, you are pleasant and I can see that you are of an artistic nature."

"I am not sure where you get that idea from, but I do like looking at art," she responded. While the two chatted about art, the taxi wound its way from the arched entrance of the school and through the winding streets where between phrases in Spanish, like calling a taxi and giving directions to the driver. The couple continued to talk deeply interested in each other's lives. She learned that he was musician, and he that she also loved classical music.

"Do you paint at all?" Reginald asked in genuine interest.

"I like to draw. People I know keep calling me an artist. One acquaintance narrowed it down to the fact that I draw as a hobby. That is a good way of looking at it. I like to paint once in a while when I am inspired to do so. But my father, he is an artist in the true sense of the word. He paints incessantly, and no matter how much we (his children) joke about and criticize his art, he feels he is above us, and keeps on painting. We even laugh out loud at some of his work."

"Is it good?"

"No, not really, in fact most of it is bad. But, it is original. He has never sold one painting in his entire life. I am storing many of them, some I like, and everyone has their favorites of his style. He likes to paint marine pictures and famous and obscure battle scenes. Do you paint?"

"Once in a while I do paint, but I buy art – I own a few paintings."

"Do you have any of Frida's?"

"No, but I have some paintings of contemporary European artists, mostly Italian and Czech."

Elena thought that she would never be able to find the museum again; there were so many twists and turns in the road. And when they finally arrived at the museum of art, she was too distracted to notice any landmarks around her. Some noisy school children on a field trip were being reprimanded from their teachers for playing next to the reflecting pool. Someone's hat was floating toward the fountain, and a swan was swimming elegantly after it. The fear of the hat becoming lunch for the swan was causing quite a ruckus amongst the onlookers. The *Bohemian* couple slipped away from the boisterous school group, and glided into the cool interior. They wandered around the gallery stopping in front of the same pictures together and sometimes moving quietly apart.

"What do you think of this gallery?" Reginald asked Elena after a short time.

There were few people in the gallery. It was quiet and the lighting was dim compared to the glaring sun outside on the white stucco walls of the building. They stood in front of one of Frida Kahlo's self portraits.

"I love it very much. I cannot believe how beautiful her paintings are," Elena said as they looked at a portrait of her with her monkey.

"Let's go around again and have another look, shall we?" asked Reginald.

"Yes I would like that very much. A good painting is always worth the time of looking again. Her work is gruesome and yet beautiful at the same time. I love it."

The two together in their own worlds and thoughts, moved again through the gallery, stopping to look and admire certain paintings and sketches they both really admired.

"Now that I am retired, and a widower," Reginald continued slowly and sadly, "I hope to paint a little bit more myself, and continue to study and collect art."

"Do you still play the piano much since you retired?" Elena asked curious to know how he spent his time.

"I played the Beethoven piano Sonatas for my retirement grand finale."

"All of them?"

"Well, yes, I did a series over a period of a year, and I recorded all of them in between the concerts."

"How many people came out to listen?"

"Oh, I don't know. I couldn't say really. I'm not a smash hit. Many of my former students and many colleagues came out to hear me. My wife was still alive then, and then there were the relatives and locals. I live in a very small hamlet of Oxfordshire, and I played at the local church on Saturday evenings."

"I wish I could have been there to hear you play. I could not be happier than to hear someone play the Beethoven sonatas," Elena sighed.

Once outside they decided to part their ways, Reginald had some shopping to do, and wanted to go alone.

"Good-bye then, Reginald, I'll see you tomorrow." She didn't really want to go back alone, but she must be strong, and face the impending loneliness of traveling alone. 'Be strong,' she thought. 'After all, I do know karate.' Reginald accompanied her a little further.

She wondered what it would have been like to live in Beethoven's time, and see him on the street, and hear him play, as one walked by his home. She imagined walking down a sunny cobblestone street in England where the professor lived. She heard the music, and looked up above a stone wall to see a sheer curtain billow like a ghost to the music and her world seemed complete somehow to know that Beethoven did not suffer for nothing. She wondered if she could have loved a man like Beethoven. From the histories, it seemed that he was unloved and undesirable. He had unruly hair. Apparently he was ugly. But from a place under the open window where the sound of the piano strings echoed against the red stucco walls, the cobalt sills, and the burnt orange of the archways, what did it matter what the man looked like. The music is the man.

They were walking away from the museum now, down the genuine, not imagined, cobblestone streets of the village. The real colors of Mexico shone brightly in their faces. Reginald wanted to walk back to town, whereas Elena, unfamiliar with the countryside, needed to find a taxi. She wondered why he did not want to spend the rest of the afternoon with her. Perhaps he realized there was no real intelligence there, just a surface reaction to external stimuli - nothing too profound. But she was subtle in her reactions, not wanting to give herself away completely, a subterfuge of personality – a Shakespearean fool, where irony can only be perceived by the omnipotent voice. She wished that she had something more to offer to this worldly professor who could speak four languages fluently, was an aficionado on the art of Frida Kahlo, played and composed music, had written many books on the music of the 'Italian Baroque', and on the state of Opera in Modern Italy. What could she have to say to him? If nothing, then could she not enliven him with an element of fun? And he did not even make an advance toward her or give a compliment to her looks. He must be one of those people, those super intelligent who are concerned with ethereal maters. She was grateful though that he had taken her to two museums and enlightened her on the 'Blue House' of Frida Kahlo.

"It is the most beautiful house that I have ever been to", he had told her. But she was too engrossed in the paintings to ask him how or why. She would make that journey to the house another time, and think of him as though she had meant something to him.

It is strange what a profound affect someone has on another, with a few chance meetings, and one thinks about the other person and never knows if that person is thinking about them. It was the eternal quest to be acknowledged and appreciated that drove some.

The taxi driver motioned to her to get in.

"*Por favor, el Zócalo. Gracias,*" Elena said as she hopped in the car, waved goodbye to Reginald, and focused on the narrow road ahead.

Chapter 5

Whenever Elena and Stanislaw went away grandma Sophia came to stay with Clarissa, their youngest child and only girl. Clarissa was used to entertaining herself; when she wasn't in school with the other children - she was reading books, inventing stories from her imagination, drawing or climbing trees. As far as climbing trees, she was like every other child, and she had a subtle habit of picking her nose; but in most other ways she was different from the other little girls her age. Her brothers were much older than her, and not a part of her life. She spent a lot of time around adults listening to their conversations as she sat and drew in her sketchbook. Her drawings covered the walls in the house, drawings of animals and birds. On this occasion again, Clarissa was outside before anyone else was awake. She had her own little tree house, or so it was called. It was a doghouse that had been hoisted up into the tree where the mighty trunk split into branches. Here Clarissa spent many solitary hours. It seemed like hours to her, anyway.   So there she was in her own little world far above the plebeian life of other children. She put her book down inside the doghouse on the gritty, sandy floor, and turned back to look out into the yard. While her mother was away, she had many hours to daydream. She sat and listened to a sound coming from far up in the sky. It was birds for sure, and she quickly climbed down the ladder, which was nailed to the tree-trunk, and positioned herself in the open yard away from all branches. She looked up with her head bent back like the end of a broken stick. Way up high, barely visible was the sound of migrating birds. She looked deep into the blue, where suddenly coming into focus, just at the right moment, were three Vs, of several hundred birds. There was a large 'V', with two smaller ones connected, and upon scrutiny, as the birds streamed across the sky, northward, it was easier to discern their white underbellies and their darker wings. These were the Geese, and they were on their way to their summer feeding and nesting grounds in the north.

"How did they know where to go, and when to go?" she thought. They must have been doing this trip for many years, and yet it is the same every spring. Suddenly, some birds leave, and others arrive. Mostly birds arrive in her yard in the spring. The Robins, the ones calling out lonely, spontaneously gather in numbers to eat the black clumping berries off the ivy. During this feasting, there is much chortling and chirping contentedly, and calling others of their kind to the feast.

"How do they know year after year where the food is? And what if someone got tired of the ivy?" She had heard people complain about the neighbour's ivy – that it grew up our fence, over our fence, through it and under it, and that it blocked the rain and sun from freely falling in my mother's flower garden. She once heard of a sinister root ball from an ivy plant. The ivy was planted around the outside of a famous old hotel, and it looked like what one might imagine the queen's residence in England to look like. The ivy covered the exterior of the grand old hotel, and the root ball grew and grew under the side of the building. It became so big that it began to grow up through the floor of the hotel ballroom. Her mother had been invited to a function where her father and the company he worked for were celebrating a bid success in sales. Many of the employees were women in the marketing department, and of course, as promoters (of themselves and company), they were dressed in elegant and ravishing clothes, with shoes and jewelry suited to their education and status in the corporate world. They paid the right amount of attention to my father, but I often heard my mother confide in my father, that the women ignored her, and never once asked about her. That night, during the dancing and drinking of the celebration, the floor of the ballroom cracked, and up surged a root ball right in the middle of the event. The people screamed in terror, as the now overgrown root ball, and all its tendrils like root fingers seemed to reach up, and catch and strangle the hems and of the lady's ball gowns and even their high heels.

Since then, Clarissa was nervous and afraid to tell her father about the kitchen floor in their own home. At some point in time, while she was sweeping the floor, she noticed that the tiles did not seem to lie flat, and that they felt like a hill on the kitchen floor. Only she would notice this, as it was here job to sweep the floor. As it was, she never saw anyone else pick up the broom, or the bucket with the rag mop to wash it, so someone had to do it. She did not remember since when she had to sweep and wash the floor, but she could see the water run away from the center to the outside as it tracked down through the grout. It may have always been there, but on some days it seemed bigger than usual. She knew that her father would at first be angry, and disbelieving, but secretly later, when no-one was looking he would go with a leveler, and see for himself whether the floor was indeed warped.

Clarissa feared for the Robins. What if a giant root ball was discovered under the kitchen floor, and the ivy had to be torn down, and the Robins still came with their little Robins to feed? What would happen to them after such a long flight, and there was no food at the end of the journey? She decided that she would not tell.

The sound of the birds began to edge their way into her mind again, and she started to notice the lamenting chirp of the Robin. They were always hard to spot at this time of the year, as they perched solitary on the highest branches and called out in a lonely repetitive note – '*chiiiirpuh, chiiiirpuh*'. The long pause in between each call was a quarter-note rest, and she was sure it was the Robin's forlorn forecast of impending rain. The incessant cackling and haggling of the Sparrows too, made her think that they were in a hurry to tweak off as many of the plum and forsythia blossoms as they could before the rain came and chased the birds away to 'who-knows-where'. She could also hear the sparrows somewhere in the neighbour's yard squabbling it seemed, over something in the large and very foreboding prickle bush- or as the neighbour called it, the, *Ilex Altaclarensis*. 'All I know, is that it's a terrible tree for climbing,' Clarissa once yelled at old Mrs. Mc Brew as she chased her out of her yard one day.

Mrs. Mc Brew did not like the neighbourhood children very much, and because she was very fat, and had extra rolls under her chin, and her ankles bulged over her black sturdy shoes, and her nylons were the color of cod liver oil, and she was very mean, the children would provoke a chase from her by knocking on her front door and then running away and hiding, while one of them would try to steal an apple. Her backyard yard was filled with food for several months of the year. There were raspberry bushes and sweet green peas, apple trees, a pear tree, and a luscious cherry tree, which tempted the children at every hour of the day. Some children in the neighbourhood actually had very little to eat at their own homes. Often Mrs. Mc Brew could be seen bent over her vegetable bed, yanking carrots out of the ground, or digging radishes out with a large spade, pressing her foot dramatically on the edge of the shovel, too preoccupied to notice the children sneaking past her, or reaching up for cherries. And through her yard was also the quickest way to the park. The birds also enjoyed the bounty of the cherry tree in summer, and the holly berry in winter; and in winter, many of the neighbours could be seen chatting to Mrs. Mc Brew, with their clippers in one hand and a few berry laden branches in the other, food for the birds, but destined to decorate the dining room table of some house for the Christmas holidays.

Clarissa climbed back up the ladder grabbing her book, and was soon running up the back stairs, through the kitchen, and up to her bedroom. She had heard the red-winged blackbird calling out its spring song: "*Follow the leader, follow the leader,*" enticing her to go exploring. When she heard this call, it seemed there was no time to waste. But it was a puzzle to her, when the Robin sang in its sad song. No English words would fit the melancholy call, or the chortling, chirping voice. But you knew it was going to rain. The Robin always forecast impending rain; like organ music before a funeral service that creates an introspective mood, the Robin issued a somber warning. The mating call of the Chick-a-Dee also conveyed an impression of sadness; it went from a *C sharp* note, one octave above middle C, to a *B flat* note, and said "*Feee-bee*", but that did not mean anything to Clarissa. Maybe the lady Chick-a-dee was a romantic sort of bird and liked a brooding *Heathcliff*-type of suitor. However, the Red-winged Blackbird's song did mean something to her, and she could hear it calling to her as she brushed her hair, and looked in the mirror, and thought about her plans for the rest of the day.

"*Follow the leader, follow the leader*," called out the Red-winged Blackbird, and "*Kill deer, kill deer - not us, not us,*" sang the Kill Deer. Those silly Kill Deer. They lose their way from the beach and tidal flats, and every year they build a nest somewhere in the neighbour's yard. All the cats know about this. It was a puzzle to Clarissa why they continued to nest near the cats.

"Clarissa, it's breakfast time." The call from her grandmother from the kitchen suddenly awakened her from her thoughts.

"Have you been sketching this morning already, Clarissa?" asked Grandma.

"I've been reading up in the plum tree."

"Oh!" said Grandma, surprised by the notion that she did not notice that Clarissa had already been outside. "And did you see any birds?"

"I heard a lot of birds, but mostly I saw the sparrows. One time last year when it was snowing, I was sitting up in the tree listening to the birds in the prickly bush when I heard Mr. Mofit's car drive into his driveway. A minute later a window opened in his house and I saw a man jump out the window into the snow. He wasn't wearing any clothes, and he climbed over the fence into our yard and stopped beside the shed to get dressed. I think he was really cold," said Clarissa to her astounded Grandmother.

"Did you say anything, Clarissa?" Grandma asked incredulously.

"Not to him, I was kind of scared to say anything. I told my friends. Anyway he was in a big hurry and I was afraid he would see me. He climbed over the fence into Mrs. Mc Brew's yard and I was hoping that she would see him and yell at him, like she always yells at us, but she didn't. I think Mrs. Mofit, you know the lady that lives there and is always going shopping all dressed up, I saw her the next day, but I think she didn't see me."

"Well, dear, you are not spying from up there in your tree house, are you? It's not really proper to snoop into someone else's life –my mother used to tell me: 'Mind your own business, live a long life.'"

"I wasn't spying, Grandma, I just happened to be up there. Anyway, he came into our yard, and that's not my fault. Grandma, there always seems to be enough food for the birds; they are always eating, but they never get fat. And sometimes when you think there is lots of food left, like cherries, the birds don't eat them all. I really think they are leaving some for the hungry kids."

Chapter 6

Elena and Stanislaw were away together this time, and Sophia floated in like a real *Mary Poppins*. She played with Clarissa and read to her, sometimes from adult books, and did all the things that grandmothers like to do. When Stanislaw had remained behind, he went to work, and continued with more pressing matters, and Grandma still came to stay. The time before, many months ago, Stanislaw hadn't been feeling himself, and Elena went away alone. A series of doctor's appointments took up most of his time. He didn't want to tell Elena anything then or now; in fact he didn't want to believe it himself that he was sick. He didn't want to scare her, or make her worry. He wanted Elena to become independent and enjoy her travels, to get to know other men; but above all, in the end, he wanted to feel secure in knowing that she would eventually find another man. That was some months ago now and his symptoms subsided. He and Elena carried on life as usual, and Grandma Sophia was delighted to have nothing more to do than spend time with her fanciful granddaughter whenever it was required of her.

Together in the evening Sophia and Clarissa sat in the living room on the old horsehair stuffed chairs covered in velvety black upholstery. Clarissa swung her feet back and forth watching the fire in the fireplace, and the light it cast on Grandma's embroidery needle which floated up and down, and back and forth like a hummingbird in the garden.

"You know my Mommy has died and gone to heaven. She is with the angels, and no one knows who best can take care of me," Clarissa said out loud fabricating some romantic, imaginative storey of her own. She had said this before in the grocery store line up once, but no one responded. Some old lady with glasses and bright red lipstick glared down at her. She thought about this while she watched her Grandmother embroider. She must not have heard her either. She sat with the fabric in her lap and the many strands of colorful thread like rainbow-rivers dangling down over the arm of the sofa. Her hair was silver grey and her eyes light blue, making her somewhat frail in appearance.

"Grandma, are you going anywhere soon?' she asked her, reverting from her celestial stories to the lilting light of the living room as smoothly as opening a door.

"Yes, I am going to New York to see the opera. And why should travel and romance only be for the young? I ask myself. Hah! To be rich and old is just as much fun as it is to be rich and young. Even better, I think,

Clarissa…I am quite sure because I've thought about this before. When you are young there are certain things you can do. And when you are older and retired, or you take holidays, you aren't exactly interested in the same things as the young people. For example, it wouldn't do to sleep in a hostel with the young people. One must do what the older people do – stay in a beautiful old hotel, and sit on the veranda like you see in the movies. Although, that is a good question, Clarissa, it gives me an idea. Maybe someone should start up a chain of hostels for people over a certain age, like me for example, or over, let's say – half a century, and us older travelers could enjoy the lifestyle of the young among people of our own age and spirit of maturity – sort of like the characters in Chaucer's *Canterbury Tales*."

"What are those, the tales?"

"Oh, I will get my copy and read some to you after I finish this bit here," Grandma said as she pulled the thread through the fabric frantically tugging at the cotton string and then resting the stubborn piece in her lap. "I can see beauty just as well as anyone. I can smell the sweet smell of lilac blossoms, taste the warm salty tropical sea, lick the chocolate off a Parisian éclair, and drink champagne in a café in Moscow, just as easily as anyone else. I can sway to the violin of a busker in a Mexican café, or watch the Mariachi Band fawn over lovers." She picked up her embroidery work again, and began to pull apart some dark purple floss.

"What are going to do with the purple, Grandma?" Clarissa asked.

"I am going to embroider lilacs, I think. When I was little we had lilac bushes all along the fence. They always bloomed in May, which in my part of the world was just around the time of Mother's Day. I don't know when Mother's Day began as an official day of celebration, but I used to pick off a bunch of lilacs and give them to my mother. I don't really think she loved them as much as I did, or I do now. I think we are all alone in our wishes, desires, and loves. They are as individual as we are ourselves. No one can know what makes another happy inside. Lilacs made me happy, so I always thought that they made others happy too. I once saw a young man that I liked, walking along the path towards me in a great park in the city. There were many other people walking too. It was a warm sunny May. I could see him coming from quite a distance, as people recognize the shape and walk of someone they know. I thought for a second that we would come face to face and say hello, but quite suddenly he stepped from the path and crossed over the grass to the edge of the shrubbery that filled the landscape. There he reached up and gently pulled down the branch of a lilac bush, and held it close to his nose."

She was as if in a trance, her eyes glazed over looking sideways at the floor.

"Grandma? Grandma then what happened?"

"Nothing really. I don't remember."

Clarissa's Siamese cat entered the room and sat by Grandma's feet, aching with her eyes for permission to jump into a warm lap.

"No, Cleo. Clarissa, could you do me a little favour and cuddle the cat right now for me. Her claws will ruin the fabric here."

"She doesn't want to sit with me, she always goes to you." Clarissa hopped off the chair and reached down for the cat. "Come and sit with me. Grandma," she continued, "why didn't you say anything?" asked Clarissa.

"Say anything, when? Clarissa," replied Grandma.

"When the man smelled the lilac, why didn't you stop him and tell him how much you liked him?" asked Clarissa.

"Well Clarissa, I don't really know, but I have never forgotten the sight and it brings me much pleasure now in remembering the day, as it did then, maybe that was the gift. And your grandfather was with me."

"Did he like lilacs?" Clarissa persisted.

"I think so, although he never really said. Something very funny happened once. I filled the house with lilacs one May, filled every room with their fragrance, and we had company the next day, but after a few minutes, the company had to leave because their eyes had swollen and become itchy and watery due to allergies. What a disaster."

"Grandma?" asked Clarissa again stroking the cat and watching her Grandmother with the needle and embroidery floss.

"Yes?" Grandma asked in that singsong voice of someone wondering what is to come next.

"Grandma, a man came to the door yesterday and asked for Mommy."

"Really? What did he want? What did he look like?" Grandma asked her with a little curiosity.

"I can't remember. He had a tan, and very blue eyes, and he was wearing cowboy boots. He asked for Mrs. Beaufort. That's all. And he looked at my sketch book and asked if I liked to draw. And then he smiled."

"That is odd. I'm also Mrs. Beaufort," she said half to herself. And then again to Clarissa, "Was the dog barking? I don't remember where I was," she said looking askance, thinking to herself she had neglected her duties to the child.

"I don't know. But I told him to come back later. I said if you want to talk to Sophie, you were busy, I knew I shouldn't have answered the door, I knew you had only gone next door, Grandma; but I told him you were busy cleaning the attic, making space for the raccoons and that you weren't to be bothered. He said he would come back later. I forgot to tell you," Clarissa said as she got up and ran outside to see if the food she had left for the raccoons had been eaten. The cat's claws sounded surreptitiously down the hall.

Sophia immediately put down her embroidery, and hastened upstairs to her bedroom. She quickly undressed, tossed her silky blouse towards the bed, but it floated to the ground just short of the bed rail. She glanced in the freestanding full-length mirror. 'What does a seventy-year old body look like anyway?' she asked herself. She had on a tiny, mauve lacy bra and panties that fit around her narrow hips, bikini style, with a broad band of stretchy lace that covered the dimples in her back but rested just below her hip-bone. 'The knee bone's connected to the –hip-bone,' she sung in her mind. Years of ballet training had left her legs, at least, still muscular. She pulled the pins out of her silky, silver streaked hair. She wondered what it would be like to be with a man again.

"Clarissa, I'm getting ready for bed," she called down to her over the banister "and you must come up soon, too, darling, as you have Sunday school in the morning." They both had forgotten about *The Canterbury Tales*, - the Wife of Bath, and The Prioress, and not another thought was given to the man in cowboy boots.

Chapter 7

Back in the city, Elena now stood at the entrance to the restaurant. Stanislaw wanted her to meet the men that he worked with. The building was built on a wharf, and the door was made of heavy wood timbers and hammered iron brackets. She stood for a moment then pulled the door open. It swung open with more ease than she expected. After coming inside from the bright sunshine, the room darkened before her as though she had entered a cavern at the seaside. It took a few moments for her eyes to adjust to the light. She began to move around the bar, through the high stools and round wooden tables. Eventually she saw Stanislaw sitting by the window. He was with two other men, probably stock promoters, brokers, or bankers. One was an older man, around seventy years old, and all were wearing suits.

"You are just in time," Stanislaw said getting up to greet her with a kiss on the lips.

"Why, you mean I am *on* time?"

"No, your arrival is perfect timing, we have just ordered another bottle of wine. Elena, I would like you to meet some of my clients. This is young Bill, and the good-looking guy, Dale." Bill had on a dark suit, and he moved with the jerky movements of an aging buzzard. However, he could be considered handsome for an older man, except for his dyed hair. It looked as though it had been applied with shoe polish. And he licked his lips much too much as he spoke. Maybe they were chapped. Dale on the other hand, was a much younger and more muscular man, middle-aged and showing the signs of an athlete – a nose that was bent to the left, clearing indicating it had been broken more than once. But his suit made him attractive, as suits did for all the men present.

They both stood up and reached over the table to shake her hand. Bill's was sweaty. She had those sudorific qualities, she looked people in the eye when speaking to them; she noticed quite often when talking to men, they were sweating, either across their brow, over their lips, or in their hands.

"Nice to meet you Bill," she said and sat down across from her husband's friend. The two were in the middle of a business negotiation, while the other listened intently, sipping his wine. Again, she could not see, the sunlight outside was now reflecting off the yachts in the harbor. She wasn't sure if she should be paying attention. She was hoping for some lively conversation. As she could not see the faces of either of the men across from her, she continued to stare out at the boats, but 'listened' like a sleeping dog listens to the droning of a fly. Her gaze eventually rested on a luminous yacht whose name in bold black lettering read: "FOXTROT TANGO YANKEE." Its name, the code words for the letters F, T, and Y, puzzled her. Perhaps they described the owner – a swinging American. Meanwhile, her attention jumped back to the conversation at her table.

"Let's say the brothers each get 2.7 million and 2.5 million – let's just call that 5.8 million for them, and if we start at one dollar a share ..." Bill was saying.

"OK. Our target goal is 71 million. We have 21 million," continued Stanislaw.

"Elena, let me explain a little for you what we are talking about," Bill said as he refilled the glasses, looking over at her, "You see, there's this mad scientist guy, and he has invented this indestructible cable. It is steel coated, and if you can imagine a pipe this big,"- here he set down the bottle and made a circle holding up his hands, "and it is filled with five different cables, satellite connection, optic fiber, phone line and a couple of others, and it is surrounded by a gel – 'NASA GEL', a substance which can withstand temperatures of up to 1600 degrees, and this guy lays this cable in every building, it would be a defense against pretty much anything...except a nuclear bomb; and I say well 'Good-bye pal' because in that case it's all over anyway." 'The bees – what about the bees?' she thought, not being able to stop herself she put in,

"What protection is it if the bee colonies die off? What do we use super cable for? We are not going to perish from bombs, I don't believe."

"You see Elena, and again, I want to say that I am no *techie*, and this mad scientist guy has developed this cable, it will be a safety feature that all buildings will not be able to do without. Our problem today is the religious fanatics – the terrorists. That's whom we have to be concerned about. These guys, they are raised with the belief that they are going to a paradise if they die in the name of their cause – their Jihad"

"I'd do it too for 72 vestal virgins," remarked Dale.

"Have you read *The Koran*?" she asked?

"No, but it sounds pretty good."

"What about ONE vestal virgin? ...If I could do it, if you know what I mean," Bill announced.

'You all want to rule the world. Everyone wants to rule the world. Rule the world and have unlimited sex – with everyone, and have the most money,' surmised Elena. She could not make herself a part of the conversation. It was useless trying to get to know them. She was mildly entertained by their banter; but it had nothing to do with her.

From behind the table another group of men in suits were raising the tempo of their discussion, and a jacket slipped off the chair and onto the wooden, planked floor beneath her. Someone got up and interrupted their foursome.

"Hey Dale, how's it going? Your wife here stepped all over my jacket – look at the foot prints on it," one of the business men pointed out.

"May I keep it as a souvenir?" Elena asked.

"Would you like it?' the white shirted man laughed and took his jacket up in his arms.

"No, but I would like your pin. What is the pin you are wearing on your lapel here?" she inquired.

"Ya, why do you guys all have the same pin?" Dale asked.

"It's the National ski team pin," answered the white shirt.

"I'm *Stanislaw's* wife, by the way," said Elena. "Do you know a guy named Harold ----? He's the only one I know from ski racing."

"I know him of course, but I don't care to know him. I'm from the national ski team," the middle aged racer with a tan and too long of hair for his age, answered as he looked up to size up his competition.

"I guess the mountains do divide the teams. The Crown Range, I mean. The teams east of the Crown want to conquer the west. I think I see it now. Are you associated with international competition?"

"We ARE the National Ski Team Federation," he replied emphatically wanting to end the small talk.

"I'm afraid I don't really remember any names from my era – except for Harold," Elena remarked again. They did not want to talk about 'Harold'. She turned away. 'How could an 'ex' national ski team member have such a bad reputation?' she thought. He seemed nice enough at the time.

"Don't mention Harold," said Dale. "Why do you think he left the country and went to Brazil? These guys know him from the Stock Market. It's a small world downtown. You think this is a big place – just look at all these condos and offices." He motioned toward the downtown with his arm.

She looked up again at the blinding reflection from the boats and beyond to the multifaceted glass buildings.

She could just make out the last words of the 'Ski Team' talk: "We've got to be first. Our Mission statement is to be the best….."

Conquer the world. Be the best in your game.

"Everyone knows everyone," Bill said in conclusion.

"Everyone who is in the top 10 per cent of their game," said Stanislaw. "Isn't that right, Bill? Ninety per cent of all the people in the world are vegetables, and then there are the top 10 per cent who actually do something."

"Would you say you guys are in the top ten per cent of your business, honestly?" asked Elena.

"Ya, I would say we are. This guy Bill, he's one of THE leading guys in the business, Elena; I'd only introduce you to the best, my darling."

Bill looked over at her smiling.

"And I'm single! – And very eligible. Do you have any friends who like money?" he asked her full of confidence.

The bar was filling up. Stanislaw was joking and laughing with the guys across from him now. The conversations seemed to crisscross the table until a large figure in a suit and tie came up to the table. He seemed to know Dale, or at least pretended he did, but he wanted to be a part of the action. Most of the work was done on recognition alone. "That guy looks familiar' – or 'I've seen that guy around."

"And who are you?" she asked brazenly, as the wine in her empty stomach turned her into a different character.

"I'm here waiting for my wife," the man in the dark suit answered somewhat amused.

"Are you Dutch?" she asked him.

"How did you know?" the man in the suit asked her loudly, looking down over his chest and smiling the whole time.

"Your accent gave it away." She wanted to show off that she could pick up the slightest of accents and place them.

"Dutch people always talk with a smile," she added.

"Well you are right, I'm Hans Niklaas," he said pulling a business card out from his jacket pocket and holding it out for her to see. He was the in the mining sector, in the top ten per cent income earners, and was the established generation, in his late sixties.

"You know, I am the original St. Nick, with Black George and all that. And it wasn't a finger that the young man put in the dike."

And with that he made his exit, past our table. He was forgotten about, until his large, outlandish figure glided past our table once again.

"Hey Santa Claus, do you have anything for me?" Elena shouted above the din.

He was eager to engage the crowd. He showed his big Dutch teeth and replied:

"I have a pact with my wife. If I indulge, she will kill me," he replied with his huge hands outstretched, palms upward for emphasis and grinning with the attention of all at the table focused all on him. He turned and strode to his own table, as if suddenly noticing the time.

A few moments later, a stout woman in her late sixties pushed her way past our table. She had a determined look on her face, and wore a quilted vest, although it was late May, and the blossoms had since drooped and rotted on the ground. It was summer, where the men wear their jackets open, and pull off their ties as they head to the bars and outdoor patios. Some of the men reveal thick chains of silver or gold. They have to be thick and masculine, but more importantly, the more gold the better they look. What man would wear a chain of no substance? In spite of the warm temperature outside, the quilted woman was on a mission. A woman of substance, and she carried a cane. Dale glanced at her over his shoulder and said in a low voice –

"There goes Mrs. Claus."
And sure enough she sat down across from the ever smiling and obtrusive Dutchman.

Elena showed the business card to Bill to get his opinion. He looked at the company names and one by one gave his opinion 'for' or 'against' in his estimation, the success of each branch of business printed on the card.

"I know this one, and this one, that one humph, phew, hmm…"
He wasn't impressed; or rather he would not let on one-way or the other. He felt a little jealousy perhaps? About the competition he said, "We must conquer the world before they do."

At last, Stanislaw and Elena stepped out into the lowering sunlight. They walked along the seawall.
"How did you like my friends, Elena?" Stanislaw asked.
"I didn't really. I did not enjoy being in there. It's a man's world. No wonder your *Bill* is single. Money doesn't necessarily get one a wife. How could anyone endure that kind of talk?"
"He's probably not like that at home. I think he is waiting for the right woman to come along, and I am sure he has hobbies and other interests. I thought you might have talked to him more." They walked along holding hands. Shadows from the cumulous clouds along the green mountain walls reached deep into the fir forests. On this side of the inlet, the urban flora was made up of deciduous flowering trees like Acacia dripping in white blossoms. A yellow warbler called out and flitted amongst the branches hanging this way now and then hopping to another branch, picking the small green caterpillars from the underside of the bright soft new leaves.
"Where are all the bird's nests?" Elena was asking out loud. Although there were birds chirping everywhere, the nests were nowhere to be seen. "How do the cowbirds find them – those birds, which plant their eggs in the nest of

a warbler? It's strange isn't it, how they say that cowbirds are parasites. I can't imagine a bird being sinister. I guess it's like rats. No one likes a rat," "What are you talking about?" Stanislaw asked her, suddenly hearing her talking. He hadn't heard the birds either, like someone being suddenly awoken from a nap on the sofa, was confused upon waking. He wasn't aware of her talking and he thought about nothing as he walked along.

"I'm referring to the cowbird, which the books say are parasites. The females lay their eggs in the nests of other song birds. They hop from nest to nest throughout the woods or the city parks and lay eggs everywhere, and the host bird hatches them. Their eggs are usually larger, and the other birds get starved out. They actually push out an egg in order to make room for their own. I just wonder what is in it for the host bird."

"I guess the cowbird wants to take over the world," said Stanislaw as he admired the boats along the docks, "and as for pushing eggs out of the nest, it appears there are injustices in nature too."

'Lay more eggs' she thought to herself. 'Lay more eggs …conquer the world.'

The smell of the seaweed on the rocks below the seawall wafted up to her as she turned her attention to the prodigious world of emerald green beneath the surface. The gentle surge of the incoming tide tossed the bulbous shapes against craggy, barnacle covered monoliths, and fish, withstanding the ebb and pull sucked bits of debris into their open mouths casting shadows on the rippled grey, shell strewn bottom below, and bubbles and froth collided like intergalactic force fields against the rocks and the granite wall. Elena and Stanislaw soon came to their car, and drove silently through the city and over the bridge high above the mighty brown river that restored the ocean. They sped past barns and pastures, electrical towers and warehouses, leaving the city behind like the furrow behind a boat. Eventually they caught up with the second growth forest that protected the suburbs from the world of stock markets and law makers, bankers and businessmen.

Chapter 8

Spring begat summer, the days were much longer, and Elena stood at the kitchen sink staring out of the window. It was after 7:00 pm, and had it been a clear day, it would have been very bright in the kitchen; however, the clouds were low in the sky and the summer drizzle made her thoughts turn inward. She loved the rain in summer. Summer rain: sometimes it came in torrents, and other times, it was a fine mist, but it was always warm. It was still twenty degrees Celsius outside, and the French doors were wide open to the brick courtyard. This could have been anywhere in the northern hemisphere. The green acacia was dripping with leaves. Every day the courtyard patio needed to be swept, not unlike what she had observed while visiting an orphanage in Mexico where all the children had a chore to do and had to contribute to the running and cooperation of the orphanage. The older children could be seen in the evenings sweeping the courtyard with large, long handled brooms, sweeping and sweeping the purple petals into the purple sunset. Here the acacia's yellowed, curled leaves, coated the ground, and turned into hills by golden corn brooms, and filled brown paper bags, day after day. If she did not sweep up the leaves, they would look messy and become thick and slippery. She remembered the day when she and her sister, two middle aged women, got into trouble; one with an idea, needing someone to help her. Elena had spotted an acacia sapling in a vacant lot, all over grown with blackberry brambles and long, tapering field grass. She had always wanted one in her yard; to commemorate the oldest tree in Paris which was a three hundred year old Acacia given to France after the Louisiana Purchase. However, no-one could tell her where to buy one. 'This one was well neglected and no-one would miss it,' she thought. It was filled with the sound of sparrows roosting and rooting amongst the arching, prickly branches of the blackberry. There was enough noise to hide the sound of a truck, and so the two women proceeded to dig up the dainty, four-foot sapling. Out of nowhere into 'no one cares', bellowed the voice of a very distraught Mr. Chatsworth, the president of the Property Owners Association.

"Hey, what do you think you are doing?" he yelled. "You can't do that - that is someone else's property. People think they can do what they want with someone else's property."

He wasn't making an impression on the women except to help speed them along in their task.

"Hurry, grab it by the stem. I'll dig around the root and you pull," one sister frantically told the other. The acacia was released from the ground to the silent cheers of a man's shaking fist and angry stares. He had been struggling with the latch on a high gate in his yard. As he emerged from the gate hollering and moving towards them, the women had enough time to shove the tree into their waiting car, roots sticking out the window.

"Hey, that's stealing!" came his rasping voice again like the sound of a table saw ripping a plank in two. The two women ran around the sides of the car, each jumping in; and the instigator floored the gas pedal as the car peeled away and screeched down the back lane. They could see the exasperated Mr. Chatsworth in the rear view mirror shaking his fist and hollering like one whose masculinity has been brought into question. All was lost in the sound of laughter coming from the car.

Now the tree stood higher than Elena's house. It was the epitome of summer. It was an outdoor cathedral, an oratory where conversation or solitude freely flowed without judgment. The shower was over and the sun now shone through the trembling leaves and cast disks of light, like the reflection from shimmering sequins on a Hindu bride's gown, across the red bricks in circles and streaks. Back in the kitchen, she washed the crystal glasses carefully by hand, and gazed into the dancing courtyard. Her husband, with a cough, entered the room.

"Those acacias," she told him, "come from somewhere down in the southern states, as far away as Louisiana."

"Oh," he said, a little distracted from the conversation by his own thoughts.

"The birds have helped them to travel all the way here," she continued. "Apparently there is one in Paris that is over three hundred years old. It is said to be one of the oldest trees in Paris".

"It's a 'pseudo' acacia, isn't it?" her husband inquired knowingly.

"Yes, as a matter of fact it is a *Robinia pseudo acacia*, named after the British Botanist who brought it to Paris. I am amazed at the life in that tree – and when the blossoms come out, the whole treetop is swarming in bees. I'd like to tell that guy about it, the one who yelled at me. But he doesn't appreciate my motive. I set that tree free."

"It is called stealing. Does anything justify stealing?" asked Stanislaw.

"You could say that I broke the law, but if he had taken the time to inquire as to our actions, maybe we could have persuaded him in our favor. There is no arguing with people like that. Besides, they have since bulldozed the lot, and *all* the trees are gone now," Elena added with the sound of regret in her voice.

"Are you going to the property owners Association meeting tonight? It's tonight isn't it?" asked Stanislaw.

"I am not going back there. The last time I was there everyone was yelling at each other about some issue, and they wouldn't let me vote because I was late with my fees."

"You paid them didn't you?"

"Yes, I paid my back fees, and the ones for this year, but they still wouldn't let me vote. They are against everything anyway, no matter what it is. They want everything to stay the same."

"They are against development, so long as they already have what they need. True politicians – they know what they want."

"Well the *majority* thinks they are right, they are the ones that come to the meetings regularly, and they think that that gives them the right to make decisions, even though we pay our dues. Then when there is an important vote to be made, they find reasons to denounce other members as 'members not in good standing'. The *majority* is not always right. In my mind they are the mediocre masses, who, although they may be educated, they are ignorant and selfish. I believe that the decisions should go to the minority, the few who are probably the only intellects in the crowd. And that Chatsworth, - conservative, circumspect stickler to the rules – no wonder he limps and his hand is all crippled in a knot. These people simply cannot open a book, but they must begin at the publisher's *Preface* so they know what to think."

"I thought that in the end you did get a ticket to vote, did you not?" her husband added rhetorically.

"Well actually I did, I'm a liar as well as a thief. But it wasn't until later. I did in the end after a lot of arguing with Mr. Chatsworth, the now *past* president, but I decided not to vote. Then looking remorseful, satirically, I told him that although I was late with my fees, I believed he was doing the right thing not allowing me to vote, because we couldn't run a democratic association with rules and regulations changing all the time just to accommodate the *Johnny-come-lately*."

"Did you get your ticket to vote?" her husband reiterated.

"I told him how I felt. In spite of the lineup behind me; I said that only those who really care about preserving our community ever come to the meetings, and they are all like minded with the same values of keeping things the same, and keeping our beach for the private use of the locals, instead of making it easier for those from elsewhere to come and litter our beach. I said only us who live here can truly appreciate the beauty of this area, and by putting in more parking, or more washrooms, would only increase the traffic from people living up the hill. I said to him, 'You should really be running for mayor; we need people like you to protect our interests down here. Have you ever thought of that?' Then he laughed and said, 'How long have you been a member?' And when I said that I had been paying my dues for fifteen years, and that I would continue to support the property owners association in the future, he looked at me and said, 'Here then, take your ticket.' With all the flattering, he warmed up to me." Elena pulled the apron strings behind her back and folded the poppies printed on her apron into a drawer in the pantry. "Besides, he's the community spy, and I wouldn't want to be caught by him sneaking around with my dogs on the beach after dark – apparently he reports all unusual behavior. Now I'm off to karate class, my darling," she said as she looked into her husband's eyes, and with a quick kiss, hurried out the door.

    She arrived before the other class was finished, but this she did on occasion in order to see how it was done. The class filed out and she stepped into the dojo and waited. The Sensei was answering questions, and when the last of the students had left, he turned to face her. Slowly he stood in front of her. They had only met once before, but she was not afraid of him, or timid, or retracting.

    "I don't know how to tie this," she said as she held the belt around her waist.

    "First of all, it's left over right," he said adjusting the front of her white cotton *gi*.

    "Yes, you told me that."

    "Now, you take the belt like so," he said as he took the belt from her hands. "You hold it in the middle." And here he balanced the belt delicately on one finger, with his large muscular fist turned under, letting the belt hang naturally to the floor. "And then you start here." Suddenly he put the center of the belt at the front of her waist, and quickly, as if lunging for a punch, he ducked to one side, under her outstretched arms and put his arms around her waist, crossing the belt at her back, and synching it in tight. She pulled in a quick and surprised breath. Then he drew the loose ends around to the front of her, and began to explain about tying a reef knot, 'left over right and under, right over left and under'. When he was done, as though thoroughly exhausted, he straightened up, looked steadily at her with his grey-blue eyes, and then left the dojo without another word. Another black belt began to organize the class. The class lined up now in belt order and bowed in. They began with a warm-up, running around the dojo. Elena tripped suddenly and landed on the floor on her hands and knees, with everyone running past her.

The much younger Sensei organized a sparring activity to begin the training. Elena felt the anxiety of a bird caught in a cage about to be released into the wild. She was matched up however with another white belt, who was equally nervous, someone one fifth her age and half her height. 'This is about me and my learning' she reminded herself, 'and 'it's not about competing against children.'

During the sparring or *kumite* as it was called in Japanese, the language of the dojo, the old Sensei came in to observe. He was still wearing his *gi*, and now and again, he stepped in to elaborate on a teaching point or to demonstrate a move. His large fist came so close to his opponents face, the students could feel the air moving out of the way. He didn't need to shave his head, there was just enough white hair left on his balding head to show his age, but his fist was like granite, and his steady look was inexorable and impassive.

"Elena," he said as he moved off to the side of the dojo to be closer to her, "I think you would benefit from tournament fighting. You will learn month's worth of training in one single tournament. It's like anything, put yourself in an uncomfortable situation, and you will learn and grow. It's like falling off a cliff and suddenly realizing that you can fly. I know you can do it, Elena, don't be afraid. You are strong. You know karate. Do you know what *intrepid* means? Believe me."

Chapter 9

There were days when Elena had to work which gave her as much anxiety as entering a dojo – she never knew what she would come up against. She looked up from the desk as the students began to arrive. They treated her with indifference. She wore her hair in a pony tail at the nape of her neck and wore bifocals perched on the end of her nose. And she always wore the same vintage suite that was forty years old, but fit her perfectly. This was her idea of the respect and tradition which should be paid to education and learning. Her shoes were of the latest fashion though; small healed, and pointed toes, (with a little tassel on each toe) and made of the perfect soft black leather which made her sing as she walked. Her job was mostly to walk around the room to ensure that everyone had something to do in class. On this day, it was sewing class, and some of the girls were making swim suits, while others were sketching fashion trends, and one Chinese boy was sewing a beautiful, tailored man's white shirt. His workmanship was impeccable, the stitches even and straight, the seams pressed exactly, and with precision. It was made of pima cotton so smooth and crisp one would hardly dare to wear it. 'I would buy a shirt from him any day,' she said to herself.

"Why does it cost so much to buy a swimsuit?" Elena asked the class in general.

"How much does it cost to make one?" she asked a student directly when no one replied.

"It is all about design. It's the same for everything. You pay for the name; you pay for the design. Jewelry, handbags, cars – everything." Elena thought about it for a few minutes.

"What are you working on?" she asked another Asian student. This time it was a young woman. She had dark, black hair, shimmering, straight and long – unusually long. She wore a short white eyelet top with appliqué roses on it where one might wear a corsage, and she wore jeans, with a flare at the bottom – like most of the young girls of the day.

"I am just looking at my clothing sketches. We have to hand in some of our designs. I want to be an architect though, so I don't really have many fashion drawings."

Elena picked up the three sheets of paper. The designs were of original substance, except for the recognizable ballet tutu, which her sketch showed to be layer upon layer of tulle, with an intricately embroidered bodice.

"Can you make any of these clothes that you have designed here?" Elena asked her.

"NO, - just the ballet one," she added in an impudent manner, as an afterthought to sound deliberately rude. It seemed to be the most complicated pattern, with an intricate embroidery design on the bodice, and whale bones for support, and more acres of tulle than she had ever seen.

"Are you a ballerina?"

"No, but I used to dance, in Beijing, when I was little," she replied curtly.

"Is the ballet in China anything like the ballet of the western world, such as the British style, as in 'The Royal Winnipeg ballet?" Elena asked her wanting to connect with the students and genuinely curious.

"No, it's much more difficult. We have to raise our leg up onto the ballet bar, and bend at the waist, and put our chest on our leg. We must hold it for thirty minutes. After the first ten minutes, your leg goes numb, and then you can't feel anything anymore. Then we have to do that with the other leg."

"Do you think that outside of ballet there is any practical application for being so fit? – I mean being able to stretch like that? – Is it good for you?" Elena continued to ask.

"Yes, just in case you find yourself inside a box," replied the Asian girl, exasperated.

"*Inside a box*? What do you mean by that?" another student asked. To that the girl did not reply. What came innocently enough to Elena's mind was *"Chinese torture chamber"*, something that children used to threaten each other with on the playground when she herself was in elementary school. But these students mistook her for an unlearned dimwit. She used to be child once too. And she had found herself in a box before, in Mexico, when, like a frightened little bunny rabbit she ran back to the villa to hide from the beguiling cowboy. She did not enjoy the solitude of the box back then. Where was her courage when she needed it? Now she thought about Wordsworth's sonnet. Perhaps the sewing students had not read the sonnet which she had committed to memory, 'by heart,' to remind herself that discipline releases a certain amount of freedom. She began to recite the poem out loud, loud enough for all to hear, as though she were making an announcement to the class about some important test:

> *"Nuns fret not at their convents narrow room,*
> *And hermits are contented with their cells;*
> *And students with their pensive citadels;*
> *Maids at the wheel, the weaver at his loom,*
> *Sit blithe and happy; bees that soar for bloom,*
> *High as the highest Peak of Furness-fells,*
> *Will murmur by the hour in foxglove bells:*
> *In truth the prison, unto which we doom*
> *Ourselves, no prison is: and hence for me,*
> *In sundry moods, was pastime to be bound*
>   *Within the Sonnet's scanty plot of ground:*
>   *Pleased if some Souls (for such their needs must be)*
> *Who have felt the weight of too much liberty,*
> *Should find brief solace there, as I have found."*

When she had finished, she went back to her own desk, and sat down to observe the rest of the class. Some were talking; others were sewing as though still listening to her. One boy walked around the room looking at everyone else's work. Elena stared out the window for a few minutes at the blue mountains in the distance. The bears would just be coming out of hibernation now, they would be rummaging around in the newly melted alpine fields for berries and young supple green twigs to eat. They would be putting their great black snouts in the air, sniffing for danger or something to eat, and they would be smacking their cubs with a powerful swat to send them up a tree, or to warn them to pay attention to the grubs in the log.

"Teacher, where can I put this until tomorrow?" a student asked her coming towards the desk with a half finished garment in her hand.

"Put it somewhere where you can find it tomorrow," Elena answered her exasperated with the meaningless task of sitting in where she wasn't needed. And then she added sarcastically, "Where do you usually put it?" knowing that the student would not bother to answer her back.

Chapter 10

As soon as the week's work was done, Stanislaw and Elena, returning to the pastimes that interested the husband, went in to the city to see a baseball game. Here they could relax and forget about life's little aggravations. People flowed into the stadium like the incoming tide over sandbars. The night was hot and still. Vendors called out to the crowds: "Peanuts, popcorn, ice-cold beer. Get your program here!" The myriads of people were dressed and decorated in a menagerie of color and styles. Some carried souvenirs, while others wore hats, face paint that looked like woad from the ancient Briton tribes, and others, outlandish, like grunting oxen, displayed team t-shirts stretched across their hard and protruding girths. Some may have questioned Elena's interest in the 'spectating' of sport, but she was not above the predilection for raucous, sensuous, jungle entertainment. As Stanislaw became deeply engrossed in the game, Elena left her seat at his request, to get for herself and her husband some drinks.

It was difficult to move up the stairs, as the spectators were at the same time, seating themselves or moving about, coming and going, getting up and down. She happened on a crowd in the ramparts above the seating, and standing for a few moments she looked into the crowd in the foyer around her. There were all manner of people; but the commonality between them was their smiles and seeming indifference to the confusion around them. She left the action of a the game a few minutes ahead of the end of the inning hoping to avoid the line-ups, but it was just as much an event on the stadium field as around her. 'Excuse me, thank you, and hi' were all she managed to say as she pushed her foot first and then her shoulders through the vertical obstacles toward the vendors.

"Hello," was a voice beside her, "Are you enjoying the game?"

"Yes but I would be more, if I could get my beverage and get back to my seat," she replied to the stranger.

"What are you drinking?" he asked her unheeding her last statement.

"I am drinking beer, but I am on a mission to get wine for my husband, and I see now that they are at two separate booths."

"Where are you from?" the stranger asked, swaying with the motion of the crowd.

Elena looked beyond the man out to the field. The inning was over and she noticed a woman clambering over the seats towards the two of them. Her gaze was focused on Elena, if one could call it focused. She did not realize the woman was actually headed her way. Her long, unevenly cut hair, was swingy madly across her face, and her bangs afforded Elena a view of some very fierce, narrowed eyes. She was staring and puffing so earnestly her thick black eyelashes outlined the shining eyes of a dragon. Elena's response was nullified by the surprise encounter. The woman out of the crowd jumped onto Elena, and with her hands on her victim's shoulders, the two fell mercilessly to the ground. Elena's fall was softened by the legs of many bystanders.

"Stay away from my husband," the woman yelled into Elena's face.

"I assure you, I don't know him" she gasped.

"Molly, get off of her. I was just talkin' to the lady," said the stranger to his wife.

"I know you," was the hysterical woman's cry to Elena.

"I am not the one. I do not know you. You've made a mistake," Elena managed to say as she rolled the woman over and hastened to get up as other men in the crowd pulled her up by the arms, and the husband bent over his wife trying to calm her and bring her to her feet. They turned away and the man put his arm lovingly over his wife's shoulder. The crowd was startled and Elena stood there, as staring people walked past her and around her.

"Are you all right, can I help you?" asked an older gentleman in a strained voice. Elena could not reply. She was escorted back to her seat by the gentleman, and she sat down empty handed next to her husband.

"Where's my drink, didn't you bring me back anything?" asked Stanislaw surprised. He rarely got angry; he was calm, his dark brown eyes inscrutable, and his swarthy face ruggedly handsome. He had musculature like the statue of *David;* in fact he was a god, a Roman god - Hercules. Elena always felt safe with him, no matter what happened.

"No. I can't believe what just happened to me," said Elena shaking her head and explaining the random occurrence.

"Married men, Elena, didn't I explain? Women are very jealous. Stay away from married men. The woman was a lunatic. Are you sure you are alright?"

"I'm fine… Intrepid, I know karate," she said to herself as she brushed off her pant leg, looking out at the baseball diamond.

It was a very dark night when they left the stadium; the long stretch of unlit highway was interrupted only by the headlights from the sometimes cars that passed them, and from the infrequent vehicles coming from the other direction, and the moon itself, rising swiftly, full round like a bubble on the horizon.

"Did you hear," Elena began to Stanislaw, not wanting to speak of the incident that had occurred at the stadium, "that ridiculous rumour about Mars being closest to the earth than it has been in centuries, and that it will not be this close again until some date three hundred years in the future?"

"Yes, they were talking about it on the radio. Of course the rumour was started and circulated, but it is a hoax – the eclipse of the moon is tonight. Remember how it turns a reddish brown color? I am sure people think it would look like Mars."

"When I heard it, I knew that anyone who knows anything about the stars and the universe would know that if Mars were to come as close to the earth so that it looked as big as the moon, the gravitational pull of the two would send Mars and the earth crashing together. People accept so much without question. No wonder superstitions and fear are born out of ignorance."

"Maybe people don't know about the sky because they aren't interested in it," said Stanislaw matter–of–factly. "You know, not everyone is interested in the same things as you are. Why doesn't the moon get sucked into the earth's gravitational pull anyway?" he ended. Elena didn't exactly know the answer either. It was something to do with centrifugal force. That much she remembered.

They were now home. A few hours after they had gone to bed, Elena got up and went to the window to look at the eclipse. The floor was cold under her feet. She reached for her housecoat at the end of the bed and put her arms through the sleeves-one at a time like most people, but loved the feeling of the heavy terry towel fabric wrapping around her. She stood in front of the window, and there was the moon, full, sweet and extremely bright. It seemed brighter and larger than most full moons. There was no sign of the earth's shadow yet. She went back to bed and fell asleep for another hour. She woke up again at 2:00 am, and then again just before 4:00. Each time she looked at the moon. At last in the darkest hours before sunrise, she saw what she expected. This time she put on her thick housecoat and a pair of pants, and stealthily descended the staircase one noiseless step at a time. It was still warm outside, but the dew on the grass was cold and wet beneath her bare feet. 'I must get some slippers,' she thought to herself. She looked up through the slowly moving branches of the riverbirch tree. There it was, just as big and beautiful as she had expected. A full round moon was there, the colour of the skin on a sweet potato, eerily hanging in the sky. The Cat's Cradle was slightly darker, but on the rim, around 11:00 was the slightest sign of light. 'I must hurry" she thought and quickly returned inside where she slipped on a pair of shoes. Tonight the housecoat seemed like the one she imagined to be worn by Beethoven while he composed his *Moonlight Sonata*. Quietly, without disturbing the dogs or the cats, she opened the door again soundlessly and closed it behind her. She found the handlebars of her bike, and rode off toward the beach, southward, with her eyes on the moon, her beacon of mystery.

The warm air slipped past, and she could hear her own breath, so acute were her senses, and alert her mind. No one else was about. The night was clear, the stars shone bright with Cygnus, Aquila and Hercules watching. Alone except for these and the moon, Elena stood with her bike by the beach, and listened.

"Come closer, I want to kiss you" was the voice she heard. She gripped the handlebars of her bicycle, unconsciously. "Who is it?" she asked in astonishment at the moon, "I can't see you."

A tall, shadowy figure rose from the sea grass to meet her, as she stood on the bank by the shore now trembling, from fear or from cold, she could not say.

"I want to swallow you up," the dark figure said.

Elena's heart began to race, she recognized the voice, but did not know from where. She turned in a panic, her feet finding the pedals, with a miss at first, but then she had them securely under her feet; and she rode off, turning down a street with lights enough to help her. The man left on the beach laughed to himself.

"What did you just say to me?" her husband asked as he rolled over, waking up from a dream.

"I said 'the moon spoke to me'."

"What did it say?" her husband eventually asked.

"It said, 'come closer, I want to kiss you'. And then I said, 'I want to swallow you up because you are made of cheddar cheese'"

"It's Swiss isn't it?" he asked quite alert by now.

"Not tonight. Tonight it is orange cheddar," Elena answered. She moved closer to her husband and put her arms around his shoulders and her hand around the back of his neck. He felt hot.

"Come closer," Stanislaw said to his wife; he held her close, and began to kiss her passionately. Outside, the birds were just beginning to chirp. The wind picked up the sand and the seeds, and the chimes began to sound.

Chapter 11

The long summer nights were decorated with colourful parties. Night after night, and well into the night, voices and laughter drifted, and hysterical screams and swearing came from street corners and backyards, like the sounds of sea lions and seals joggling for a place on the rocks. Elena lay in bed and stared out at the sky. The bedroom window was a 'picture window' with no curtains, a frame into the sky. However, at some point in time in the life of the house, shutters in the style of the Venetian's were installed to give some privacy. They could be folded wide open, or just titled open by means of a wooden handle attached with metal wire. When one pulled the handle, the louvered blinds opened up enough to illuminate the room. Just by *slightly* tugging on the handle, one could tilt the blinds on an angle enough to see out, without being detected from the outside. One was able to 'spy' on the neighbours, or watch someone walking by. It wasn't used for that purpose very often, however. What Elena had in mind when installing the blinds as opposed to installing full length drapes, was to have an opening at the top with which to view the stars at night and the fluttering leaves of the River Birch in the early morning – the birch branches covering only a small corner of the sky view.

She lay in bed and stared out at Jupiter. It was the only body visible in the sky, as it was too light to see the other stars, and just dark enough that the sun still reflected its light back from the *Giant* millions of miles away. 'Jupiter - what a beautiful sight you are,' she thought. Stanislaw lay snoring. They had been out earlier at a party, and continued into late in the night with the telescope which they had set up at the end of the street. The party was at one of the best situated houses on the beach; and the host was the latest of self made wealthy men, a businessman. He had many friends and made many more when he wanted to throw a party. It was the land of the beautiful people – and everyone was usually dressed in his summer whites – white linen shirts, white linen jackets, white fedora hats with black satin trim, white tennis shoes or white brogues; a sea of white and a wisp of perfume filled every summer party. And everyone was somehow connected to everyone else there, even someone's wife, who did not go to the party at first, but who came later, with a broom in her hands, showed up looking for her husband. He, by the way, was just going to stop in to the party "for a few minutes to say 'Hi', but once inside, the enticement to stay was invigorating. There it was almost impossible to hear what anyone was saying.

"What are your favorite movies?" Elena asked a total stranger.
"Oh, I am excited to say that I have so many. Have you seen '------'?
"I'm sorry, what did you say?"
"Have you seen the movie.........it came out a few years ago?"
She had not heard him the second time either but she answered.
"No!" Almost shouting, she carried on, "I didn't get a chance to."
"Well you should see that one," he replied.
"Oh No! She wouldn't like that one," someone interjected.
"What else did you say you liked?" she asked the man again, who was holding his glass close to his chest protecting it, in order not to be bumped. He pulled a serviette from the counter and asked:
"Anyone have a pen? I'm going to write out for you my top ten favorites."
"Excuse me for a minute while you write those down. I need to replenish my glass," Elena said loudly, and she discretely and politely ducted away through the crowd.
"Hey have you seen my wife?" someone asked her. She made motions with her mouth as though she were answering back and the stout man with a bottle in his hand said 'Thank you", as he lifted his glass in a gesture, and sloshed wine down the front of his protruding belly. She caught snippets of people's conversations while she tried to find some pleasure amongst a rambling bunch of idiotic drunks.
"We are going to visit my family's castle in Scotland. They had to sell it during the war. Now it is a bed and breakfast….."
"Oh, Mike, you remember meeting …."
"Did you see the home run? I couldn't believe it when……"
And on it went, no one was listening to anyone else, and no one could hear or understand a full sentence. She shut herself inside the washroom and waited for a few minutes examining herself in the mirror. These were her husband's acquaintances and their wives – Elena hadn't spent much time with this crowd socially, she had her family, many interests and hobbies, not to mention her work. And all that she had, if happiness could be calculated, was due to her belief that all things she loved or created were the result of hard work, including her marriage. But she wasn't the typical wife, if there ever were such a thing. Some women would say to her, "You are *so* lucky." She never considered herself to be lucky, she always counted her blessings and was tenacious in her goals and values; but what appeared to be huge success by others standard's was her ability to remain optimistic, and make the most of what she had, in spite of her shyness around strangers.

One of Elena's greatest challenges was dealing with the jealousy of others. She looked at her dress and pulled at the straps. Perhaps it was the color that caused women to look over at her but not to comment. Perhaps it was that it was hot pink, crocheted, and very tight; or was it her bright turquoise stockings? Or was it that she did not wear white, or that her skin was a mysterious colour. Her grandmother, it was said, was a gypsy foundling, and as a child Elena was tormented with thoughts of being kidnapped by the gypsies. Her skin and eye colour were possibly a genetic throwback. And she harboured a feeling of never quite fitting in. There were women's voices now close to the outside of the washroom door. She leaned toward the door and rested her ear on the wood to listen.

"She has been after my husband for years," was a woman's voice.
"She's always travelling by herself. I think it's weird, you know what they say about couples who go on separate vacations."

"She used to be so much fun."

"I cannot stand the way she is always whispering to her friend."

"I saw her with another man, walking and talking, and then I saw her come out of his house one day."

"You won't believe this, but my husband saw her get in a fight with another woman at the baseball game. She takes Judo or something, it was a *cat fight!*" One of them said with a "*Mee-oow*" and a laugh. This was reason enough for the other sirens to gloat; it was just what they wanted to hear.

Elena turned on the taps to create a shower of noise, and flushed the toilet to let the gossipers know the door was about to open. When she opened wide the door, three women stood looking agape, and then were all sweet and smiling with their '*Hellos*'.

After the party, she noticed the silent sky again, and blocking out the din and laughter of the friends walking home, she focused her gaze on the end of her street. There, suspended high behind the barn and poplar trees, like an eagle in an updraft, was the rising Jupiter, glowing in the southeast. The group of friends stopped in front of Harry's house. Harry was an entity on the street, the British guy on the corner. He spent many hours on his front lawn swinging his precious golf club - and commenting to and generally haranguing the neighbours as they passed by. He and his wife were both experts in English grammar. He came by it naturally as he was from Britain, but his wife Nancy, she was a teacher. As she always said, "Those who can do, teach." She lunched with the ladies and always remembered exactly what had happened at any time; she was a source for local history. She relied on her excellent memory, perhaps that is how she came to know the grammar rules so well. Everyone was else was stuck in the vernacular.

"I'll be right back, everyone. I'm just running to get out the telescope. Let's have a look at Jupiter. Have you ever seen it through the telescope?" she asked the group as she ran down the street.

"How about 'Uranus'?" someone shouted after her in the dark. There was some banter amongst the men.

"Are you speaking of country matters?" Harry's voice was heard above the clack of her heels on the pavement. "Those are the only ones that count, aren't they? Let me get a better view some time," he continued. The barrel-chested, ruddy faced, bulldogged neighbour was still shouting from down the street. With that comment lingering, she ran inside to get the telescope.

When Elena returned, a few remaining neighbours gathered to have a look at Jupiter and his four largest moons, or captives.

"Those moons are Ganymede, Europa, Callisto, and Io," Harry informed Elena.

"Really? How do you know that?" she asked surprised. "It is interesting how I look at them and see them all the time; and you know their names, but have never seen them!"

"That is a paradox," said Stanislaw as he adjusted the focus on the telescope. "Here, it's ready."

"Harry, you know their names, but did you believe that they actually existed, could you believe they were there if you hadn't seen them before?" Elena asked him.

"I know many things that I haven't seen," he replied with a grin, "Would you care to show me some of them?"

The group gathered around the telescope which Stanislaw had enthusiastically set up. With patience and a steady hand, each of the curious bent forward to have a look through the small eyepiece attached to a much larger cylinder on a tripod. There they were, the moons of Jupiter, four small bright discs in a straight row, lined up like bride's maids before the bride, floating adoringly next to the eminent more brilliant celestial body.

"There - the beautiful maidens floating in the sky next to their captor – although one was a boy; Ganymede was the young man captured by Zeus to be his cup bearer. I can't remember all the details– Jupiter, or Zeus, as the Greeks named him, was the great seducer, was enamored with them all, anyway," Harry said after he had gazed through the tiny opening of the telescope out into space.

"Who is Zeus, and who is Jupiter?" asked someone in the group, unable to keep up with the conversation on account of the wine which he drank from a bottle. After Harry had finished looking, he stepped aside to explain the difference.

"Listen up, just for a moment; I'm going to give you all a brief lesson in Greek mythology." One of the neighbours with his wife and a friend had joined them now, hearing the noise from their patio, they came out onto the street. "Zeus was the Greek god, god of the sky and ruler of the Olympians. The Roman god, the same god, was called Jupiter. Now Zeus was married to his sister Hera, and according to the legend, and ladies don't be angry, Zeus was a seducer of women..." Here his wife broke into the conversation and said to Elena,

"Elena, didn't you meet a seducer in Mexico that you called the 'blue Zeus'?"

"I don't remember that conversation, don't remind me now, I had almost forgotten about that cowboy."

"Hey, listen, let me continue," chimed in Harry again, "as I was saying, Zeus was having love affairs with goddesses and mortals alike, and he tried all sorts of tricks to hide his infidelity from his wife. And *Europa* was a young princess, and one morning when she was gathering flowers by the seashore, Zeus saw her and fell in love with her. He then disguised himself as a beautiful bull, and when Europa climbed on his back, he ran off to Crete, abducting her, and she bore him two sons. Io and Callisto were also beautiful maidens of some sort; but *Ganymede*, now here's where it gets interesting, gentlemen cover your ears. Ganymede was a handsome young Trojan prince, and Zeus fell in love with him also. He was strong and young, the epitome of an athlete, sought after by all."

"Ah, those Greeks are like that," said the neighbour who was standing and listening, waiting his turn to look through the telescope.

"Zeus this time disguised himself as an eagle, and flew down and snatched up poor unsuspecting Ganymede from amongst his friends, and flew him up to Mt. Olympus where he became the cupbearer to the gods."

"And there they are today, floating around in space, two thousand years later," said Stanislaw.

"Who saw them first, was it Copernicus?" asked Diana. "That's the only astronomer I know," she said as an aside.

"Galileo discovered the moons with the telescope he invented. I guess that is not news, but imagine, they had been there all along, some undiscovered treasure," said Elena.

"But he didn't name them," corrected Harry gently.

"Who did then?" asked Stanislaw, happy at the chance to learn some new interesting fact. The conversation was sounding a bit like silly season, illogical and punctuated by giggling and meaningless talk.

"Some other astronomer, I can't remember his name," continued Harry. "He knew of the ancient Greek literature that told of all Jupiter's escapades, and how he fell in love with all these young women. Then, so that his wife wouldn't find out, I mean Jupiter; he changed them into different animals and hid them amongst the stars so that he could still see them. Its kind'a confusing, as the planets are not stars, but that's the story."

"Sounds like Ganymede has been pouring too much wine for *you*, Harry," stated Diana, who was herself named after a goddess. She was the sister of Elena and was always ready to join in the hunting outings, or so they seemed, just like her namesake.

"Who was his wife, anyway?" asked Elena.

"Are you talking Galileo or Jupiter?" asked Harry.

"Was that a bat?" asked Diana feeling something pass by her head.

"It's a star, *twinkle, twinkle little bat how I wonder what you're at…*" someone started to sing mimicking the Mad Hatter from *Alice in Wonderland*… "Up above the world you fly, like a tea-tray in the sky. Twinkle, twinkle-"

"Stanislaw, let me have another look," said Diana, "I'm going to figure this out. Which are the banished lovers?"

"All right," he said relenting, "One more, then I'm putting it away. It's getting too cold," said Stanislaw. Suddenly it occurred to him that almost everyone of the original party had vanished, slunk away like a possum when it is not noticed anymore, trying to call it a night without having to admit being jaded from over-indulgence.

Finally, what seemed like only a few hours later, the first light of dawn was beginning to show through the lacy white curtains of Elena's bedroom. The star so bright, the sky so pale behind; the time alone, and the slow, trepid, waking voice of the first robin was heard calling out: "Wake up, wake up, come dance, come eat." Elena lay awake remembering the previous evening. Jupiter was fading from the sky. Stanislaw was lying next to her, and still sound asleep, rolled over with a grunt and a snort. It was still too early to be up. He said something out loud. It didn't make sense to her, although the subject was typical – it was something about work "Get it straight. We need to roll this one together." She ignored the outburst.

When she fell back asleep, she dreamed that she was at the retirement party of her Sensei, but it was in the school auditorium, and was really a *funeral* for her Sensei, and only she knew. There were many people lined up waiting in the rows of chairs in the auditorium, waiting to have a word with him. He was a man of some renown. There were men, women and children of all ages there, waiting to greet him and pay their respects. "I should not be here," she thought to herself. No one knows that I know him. They will wonder 'Who is that woman? Why is she here? She didn't go to this school'. Then there was silence and all the audience were staring, although she was invisible, because only he could see her. She held out her hand to him, and in slow motion he came towards her, ignoring the others.

"I want to congratulate you on your retirement," she said as she put her small hand into his very large one. "I did not realize you were done teaching. I did not get to know you, and I had looked forward to the classes very much. Will your son be taking over?" She was reluctant to let go of his all enveloping, radiant hand. "I'm sorry I won't be seeing you much anymore. I will miss you, I think."
He looked steadily at her, with unwavering pale eyes.

"Yes, I know you will" he said and turned to greet the other guests and throngs of parents waiting to share their appreciation for him- for all he had done. For a moment it was only the two of them, her hand in his hand, his steady silent gaze holding her own. The noise of the crowd had gone silent. Next she seemed to be floating on a raft, and she was all alone. Surrounding the raft were wolves, dog-paddling around the raft, their mouths red, showing large white fangs warning her of death, but they disappeared. The raft was swirling around and now floated towards a cliff. When she arrived at the shore, she could see people staring into a cave. A big black opening revealed, on closer examination, stalagmites and bats. The bats were changing positions, flying here and there, from place to place, and a group of hikers, were making notes in their booklets. Then her Sensei was there again. He hadn't died after all. This time he was wearing his *gi,* but it was more like a Roman toga. He turned to Elena and said, "I'm retired! And now I am a *spelunker*!"

The dogs barked once, arousing Elena from her dream, at last, signaling that it was morning, and that it was time to get up. She thought of waking up Stanislaw, to tell him her dream, and ask him what he thought, but instead, she jumped up from the bed, trying to shake the dream memory from her thoughts. She hurried down the stairs, around the corner, and into the sunny kitchen. The Borzoi was already at the door, waiting to be let out, her nose pointed straight into the glass, her curling fluffy tail fanning the air with anticipation. The Airedale, on other hand could open the door when she wanted out. She learned that trick from the Siamese cat when she was just a puppy. Every day the cat would jump up on the coffee table near the French doors, and reach up and pull on the door handle until it popped the door open. "See how easily it is done?" she would turn and say to the terrier before hopping down on the floor and slipping outside. After watching this for some time, the dog jumped up against the door on her hind legs and also pulled down on the handle with her paws and, *"voila"*, the door opened for her as well. The Borzoi never learned this trick. Perhaps it was not due to stupidity as some were wont to believe, but rather to the way in which she viewed the world. The Borzoi always looked beyond the door; her sights were, so to speak, always set on the place in which she wanted to go, always looking into the distance.

Elena opened the door, and the dogs now greeted her before they went out. They always showed their appreciation – rubbed up against her legs and tried to find her caressing hand. "Now get out," she said trying to act annoyed for having to get up, and then with a gentle push when she had had enough, she sent them out of doors. She turned her attention to the kettle and filled it with water, and ran back upstairs to get dressed while the kettle rose to a boil. When the kettle began to whistle, Stanislaw got out of bed, and came downstairs with Elena. She made the tea and prepared the breakfast, and they went outside to the patio, where they sat, sipping their tea, and admiring the garden.

"I had the strangest dream last night," Elena began to tell her husband. "It was about the Sensei. He was in a bat cave, but then there was something before that." She paused for a moment trying to remember.
"Oh ya," Stanislaw responded, "Continue, I'm listening." Knowing how tedious it was to listen to the ramblings of someone else's dreams, she decided not to continue.

"Oh, it doesn't matter, it was nothing," she said. But she pondered it just the same. If her Sensei died, who would help her with self amelioration? She poured more tea into her Paragon china teacup and added a glistening spoonful of honey, as though it were dripping fresh off the acacia; and she devoured the cinnamon buns, then added more milk and honey to her tea. She heard Clarissa calling now from within the house. She promptly forgot about the dream.

Chapter 12

"Can we go to the library now, Mommy?" Clarissa asked her mother as she took the plates from the table to the sink where Elena stood.

"Oh, yes, that reminds me, tomorrow is the fishing derby and I wanted to look at some books on fishes." It was still raining but the light penetrated the clouds interrupting them and casting faint rainbows amongst the trees. They drove to the town center in their little convertible with the canvass roof up. With the rain pelting down, it sounded as though they were walking under an umbrella. The new library was built in the town center, behind the grocery store, where Elena liked to go sometimes just to read the latest fashion magazine for free or take at peek at the Sunday New York Times. As they drove along the straight road overhung with dark evergreens, they talked about the new library.

"Mommy, the library isn't much bigger than the first one, and it is not as nice," began Clarissa.

"People made such a fuss over the new plans and the cost, and so many people wanted a say in the procedure that the city ran out of money. There is a place in Spain called Cordoba, where, in the year 900 where the ruler at the time, Abd-al-Rahman the 3rd loved beauty and art so much that there were seventy libraries in his city alone. Now people fight and argue about having one in our neighbourhood. Anyway, in the end the city planners just had to build something to house the books."

"What about the graveyard that was discovered under the library? Didn't they find the bones there of some people?"

"You're right, that was part of the problem. There was a problem a long time ago, over 150 years ago when the European settlers were building the roads through the Indian territory. They killed many Indians who stood their ground and who said 'this is our hunting grounds and our sacred burial site'. The men in charge of the road building said 'we will show you whose land this is', and they killed the Indians who complained and threw their bodies into a mass grave, and covered it up. Then they built their road and put up a trading post over the gravesite, and eventually a library and a general store where there is the grocery store today. When the ground for the new library was being excavated, the elders from that same Indian tribe came forth when the construction for the new library began, and wanted to rebury their ancestors properly. All the work that was in progress on the new library came to a sudden halt, until an agreement was made between the tribe and the city. The ground had to be blessed and the remains moved to another spot, with a proper burial ceremony. It all took time, and now the new library is much smaller than the original plans, but the field beside it where the foxgloves and ferns grow is where the original sacred burial grounds are."

"Mommy, I talked to a ghost once."
Elena had by now parked the car in front of the field beside the library.

"When did you see a ghost, Clarissa?"

"Once when Grandma took me to the library, I was sitting in the corner by the window, where the rock wall and arching window were. Someone came to see me, and he kneeled down on one knee across from me." Clarissa looked down at the floor remembering something very important. She began again slowly, a little bit afraid, just above a whisper. The rain was hitting the windshield hard, and surrounded the car like an army carrying spears. "He showed me a book, and it was open to a page with a picture of a hill with a rock wall around the top with Indian warriors with spears and bow and arrows. He said 'I was there when it happened.' 'What?' I said to him leaning over and looking at the picture. He smelled like musty smoke. He said, 'Look at those people, those are my people - we are a good people, men of strength, medicine, and law. We carried the silver box, a symbol of our people, inside were the bones of our elders, our past chiefs and our mothers. But they wanted the box, they wanted our land and so they pursued us on horseback with their horses and guns, and we climbed as high as we could, to the top of the citadel. There, high above our pursuers, we began to throw rocks down on them. All the time I carried and protected the silver box. Soon our men were falling down dead; we could not win. We only had rocks and bows and arrows. The enemy had guns. Our people wanted to fight until there was no one left, but I wanted our people to live. I yelled to our men, 'Give them the silver box. Give them what they want. Three hundred years from now, we will get it back, and it will be our turn again. They did not want to give up, they did not listen to me, but I flung the box over the stone wall in desperation. In the box was the secret to our culture, our ancestors, our land.

The killing suddenly stopped. Their leader clambered up the hillside and hoisted the box high over his head in the line of fire for all his men to see. They sent up to the heavens a cry of victory, but it is our heaven too. Our lives were spared, but my people's bones are here, right under where I am sitting now.' And then he put his hand on my head and got up, and then he walked right into the bookcase."

"Clarissa, you have such an imagination."
"It's true Mama, I was afraid to tell anyone."

"Have you seen anything since? Why didn't you tell me?" Elena asked her daughter.

"Now it all makes sense, the library is filled with ghosts from the past. We better get inside before it closes." The two got out of the car and Clarissa walked around the car through a puddle and held her mothers hand, swinging her arm back and forth.

Once inside the library Elena suddenly did not want to be there anymore. She looked around the stacks for a book on fish and started toward the front desk, needing more help.

In front of the information desk, Elena recognized a face from the beach.

"It's William, isn't it?" she said as a way of getting the man's attention.

"Yes, Elena," he said bending toward her slightly and pointing at her face. He was a large man, but very fit, the muscles in his calves were hardened by age, running or weight lifting, and his torso was equally tight with muscles covering an expanded chest – most likely he was breathing in deeply at this moment, with his chest like a competitive swimmer getting ready to dive into the pool. His stature, over six feet tall, was topped by very short, spiky white hair that made him look more like an indignant seagull, than the Biology professor that he was. His eyes were stern and piercing and his sharp beaky nose was enough to scare off any 'excuse making' students.

"Dr. Wright, you are just who I'm looking for. Have you heard of the Blue Water Swimming Club?" The answer was a squinting of the eyes and slight shake of the head.

"Well, there is the swim club at the beach, and they have fun events for the children – one of them is the fishing derby off the pier. The kids come down with their rods and bait and fish for bullheads. I was wondering if you would like to come down tomorrow evening and help identify the various types of fish that the kids catch."

"Are you joking with me? Do you realize that you are killing fish with such 'fun' as you call it?" His voice was filled with vehemence and his words were spitting out like an eel on fire. Unprepared for this sharp retort, Elena took a step back from him and explained that she was genuinely interested in knowing about the fish population, and that the derby records have been kept since the derby began over thirty years ago. She thought that it would be interesting at the very least for this newcomer to the beach to observe.

From around the stacks came a woman dressed in a bizarre outfit of outlandish colors. She was a short middle aged woman, with a multicolored long sleeved knit top, with gathers of swirling, purple, orange and magenta material hanging in folds from under her arms and gathered at her small waist. The rest of the fabric draped down to her ankles to form pant legs.

"You are talking to the wrong person," the interlocutor began. Before she could continue, the professor took a step to the side.

"Elena, this is my wife, Matilda," said the doctor of zoology. "Matilda, I'll just be a minute with this young lady. She needs to be enlightened on a few things." His wife had an armful of very large books on art and museums, and her mouth though wide and full, sagged at the corners in a broad grimacing expression. Her hair was short, and dyed a reddish-brown colour which also stood on her head spiked upward.

"We were just having a discussion on the merciless killing of *sculpin*," the professor continued, "and she is asking me to offer my expertise on the subject and to condone it."

"Our derby is *catch and release*," Elena argued back; "we measure the fish and then we throw them back into the water. I thought that by being there you might be able to help educate the kids on what is found in our local waters. That is why I asked you to come and take part," she concluded. The professor was inexorable and he added his well thought-out aphorism:

"There is no such thing as catch *and release*. I know as well as you that those fish don't survive after their guts are ripped out, and they have been manhandled like that by shrieking children. You are going to be convinced, and be on my side."

"We are very careful; they all seem to swim away," said Elena. There was no arguing with the prepotency of the biology professor.

"They swim to the bottom and die. There should be a stop to that derby. And you are the person to initiate it," Dr. Wright ended triumphantly. His wife now stood silently, gaping, agreeing with her husband as indicated by the nodding of her head, and the pursing of her lips from time to time, and by the unusual widening of her eyes as if in punctuation of his every word.

"Well I just meant that by educating the children and their parents on the diversity of the marine life that they might notice more about their surroundings, and then maybe appreciate more the beauty of what they see."

"My dear," began the professor's wife, "Dr. Wright has been studying the conservation of marine life for years, including the phylum 'Chordata," subphylum 'Vertebrata,' class 'Osteichthyes', order 'Perciformes,' family 'Cottidae' – commonly called sculpin."

"Or bullheads," added the professor. "You see, I am a doctor of biology and zoology, and you can't convince me in a single sentence that what you are doing is right."

By this time the whole library was listening and the librarian at the reference desk raised her index finger to her lips and let out a loud "Shu-shsh,"- the guise of every librarian everywhere. Elena humored the Doctor of Philosophy in biology by relinquishing a point to him,

"I suppose I need to seek further advice from you, the expert. I do see your point now." And with a sidelong glance and sympathetic smile to the librarian who wasn't convincing in her plea to have law and order in her library, Elena said her courteous goodbyes and left the library with her books and her daughter in hand.

"Mama," said Clarissa once outside, "why didn't you tell him to *stick it*?"

"Clarissa!-"

Chapter 13

The next morning the sun floated through the white lace curtains like dandelion seeds parachuting to a secluded and deep green valley. Elena awoke and quietly before the rest of the household was awake, she rode off on her bike across the dike and down to toward the beach. She gently pulled at the bell on her handlebar with her thumb as she rounded a blind corner. There were always people lurking around the bushes with dogs on a leash, and the last thing she wanted was to be accused of was reckless driving on a bicycle as she startled some passerby unexpectedly. Sometimes when she rode along the dike road, she would jingle her bell quite loudly, and people would scowl because it was too loud. Other times she would purposely wheel over a small bump so as to shake the bell just a little bit, and that seemed to irritate people as well.

'I love a bell,' she thought; 'and the little kids walking or riding along the path seem to understand the language of a bell. They always look up and move aside. I think they too enjoy the sound of something useful and meaningful'. As Elena rounded the bend that day, there was someone there on the other side. It was an acquaintance from long ago who had just recently moved into the neighborhood. Elena expressed all the polite cordiality due to someone of easy going nature- a former colleague, and teacher of her nephew, in fact. Although his hair was graying, he had a youthful appearance that lingers in teachers, and he wore shorts and knee socks and runners as though he were ready to play basketball at any minute.

"Good morning to you sir, we haven't spoken since that infamous night last summer."

"Oh, hello," he replied, looking askance down the lane.

"Stanislaw and I would love to have you over. We've been meaning to call you before now, the winter seems to go on and on but then before we know it, it's summer again. Perhaps you and your wife could come out on the boat with us one evening. It would be interesting to see your new place from the water. There are also some really good coffee shops around. Would you and Loretta like to go out for coffee, or come by for tea and pie with us sometime soon?"

"That would be nice," replied Andy looking wistfully up at a house on the hillside and then over to the silver tide pools in the bay.

"We don't know the area very well at all yet, although I used to spend some time here in the summer when I was a kid."

"I'd like to show you our favorite café; it's a great little restaurant up the hill."

"I heard there is going to be another annual 'Welcome to Summer' party at the McQueen's place on the beach down here," Andy reminded her.

"Yes, I know," she said, "are you going?"

"Quite possibly." He seemed anxious to continue his walk, taking a step in the other direction. "But Loretta has never really forgiven me, - or you for that matter for intruding on our privacy last year at two in the morning. She is a very jealous person, and views other women as competition. In fact I know that she does not want me to associate with any of those people any more. They are all a bad influence – well, truth is, I am in trouble because you came knocking at our door."

Elena sensed the constraint in his words. It seemed that he wasn't as free to live his retirement by his own natural tendency. He and his wife were renting a house on the beach, 'the front beach, on the water' – meaning, they weren't two streets back off the shoreline; they actually had waterfront *view* property. Elena wanted to leave off on good terms.

"May I just ask, before we part, what you are doing in your retirement now?"

"There is enough to fill the days; looking after grandchildren, entertaining friends on the porch, and wintering for as few months in the Tropics. I can plan out every day. Loretta and I enjoy being close to the beach. I like to work in the garden; Loretta likes to sit in the sun. Loretta shops for the groceries, and I cook the dinner and clean up. I like to watch the news and Loretta likes to make the evening cocktail for the two of us. But you know, Loretta longs for the privacy of her former home, and doesn't care to mix and mingle with the people that I talk to over the fence. She feels it is an invasion of her privacy to have throngs of people walking past her house, staring into the window as she sits there naked, as she is wont to do, drinking her coffee." He stopped speaking suddenly.

"What are you looking at?" asked Elena as she noticed Andy had turned his gaze upward.

"I'm wondering… where this rezoning is happening - trying to see if that property is going to be up for sale. Anyway, I can't be long, as Loretta is out walking and I don't want her to come across us together."

"Why is she still angry with you? I apologized to her for waking her up that night, what else does she expect?"

"She says she would like a serious talk with you. Not only did you wake her up demanding to see me, you also woke up the neighbours. You caused quite a stir," he said half to himself with a little smile.

"Which neighbours did I wake up, the ones on the left or the right of the house?"

"Both. And they complained to Loretta the next day."

"Clearly I had had too much to drink. And it seemed to me that at the party *you* were fully enjoying yourself and the generous hospitality of the host's open bar. The party *was* a bit on the wild side," Elena continued remembering the party from a year earlier. "But you were convinced it was too early to end. You were inviting *everyone* back to your house. Anyway, I know both of your neighbours. Tell the widow that my father went to school with her; he was just talking about her the other day. And the other neighbours, well, I am acquainted with them too. They can't possibly hold it against me. It was my first misdemeanor. Tell them we were at a party to initiate the tennis season, and they will understand. After all Andy, it was *I* who was invited to the party. *You* were the party crasher".

"You have to understand my situation, Elena," was Andy's retort. "My Loretta is a very jealous person; and you coming over and pounding on the door at two o'clock in the morning caused *quite* a stir. You see, she thinks you may desire some sort of intrigue with me. It sent her into a rage; she spoke ill words about you."

"Why didn't you tell her that you had *invited* me and some other people over? It wasn't just me at the door. Why would you not tell her the truth?"

"The truth is, Elena…I had an affair when we first moved here. Loretta is not over that – we were going through a difficult time then anyway; it was a tough time for both of us. Loretta became listless, unhappy, she refused to enjoy anything; even this beautiful place was not enough to shake her from her despair. She longed for the lifestyle she once had and was unhappy with her current situation. And this turned to jealousy; and whenever I went out, suspicion. The truth is she was overcome with acedia, and I in turn found solace in the company of one who praised God and nature, in all their glory. The lady I'm referring to just happened to be a local Sunday school teacher, and that made the situation a scandal."

"I am married Andy. And *I* don't intend on being the cause of any scandals. I am sorry to hear of all your marital problems. No offence to you, but you can tell Loretta that if I were to be interested in another man, I certainly wouldn't go after a sixty year old retired teacher," she added indignantly. "You can tell Loretta we have already had our serious talk in the form of my first apology." The two then parted in a disgruntled air. Elena soon forgot her uncomfortable encounter and before long, like a child with a new toy, was engrossed in her own thoughts and plans for the day ahead.

Chapter 14

If everyone had a habit, good or bad, it wasn't fair to exclude Elena. Upon awaking, her routine was to lie in bed and say a prayer. Most people said their prayers before they got into bed, but hers were said upon waking, before she got up. She would be too shy to talk about her spirituality in public, but her prayers were always thankful and reverent, her blessings liberally bestowed. She never wanted to be counted as one of those – *the Bible Thumpers*!!! - Something from her childhood made her afraid of the thumpers and the *Boogie-man,* and so she tried to live a modest upstanding life.

Particularly in summer, as on this day too, Elena walked or rode her bicycle, every morning along the path, through the woods and down to the shore. She often whistled to herself or spoke to her dogs - or even herself if she were alone. "When I close my eyes I can hear the clitch, clitch of my shoes on the fine, crushed gravel path, and the sound of the wind in the poplars which line the dyke road, the soft panting of the dogs in the warmth, and the distant "*roo-roo*!" of the cargo train. When I open my eyes the sun reflects off the upturned dusty white leaves of the blackberry, the silver underside of the poplars, off the every ripple of the incoming tide, and off the collar of the Kingfisher posted high in a dead tree, waiting to dive into the lagoon." And so ran the merry thoughts of Elena as she walked along with a cushion of joy under her feet. In this early morning, little fenced-in bit of paradise, one could be sure that this was the best time of year. And so many blackberries! They climbed up into the wild apple trees just beyond a mere mortals reach and made her wonder, "Just who are they for?" Those that took the trouble to carry a ladder for a quarter of a mile would surely reap the rewards of this black, illustrious bounty. The scene enraptured her but she had an engagement in the city in the afternoon with her sister, and so she turned abruptly off the path and back on to the street that eventually ended at her house.

The drive into the city was uneventful, and she soon found a place to park her car on a curving side street and under the shade of a tree. It was an older part of the city where the store fronts were preserved in their original stone and brick facades, and the view of the cupola of the art gallery was visible over the tops of the low rise buildings.

A loud whistle flung forth from her four fingers. On a crowded street downtown she would have expected many people to turn round, but only Elena's sister stopped in her rushed walk and turned to look.

"How did you know it was me?" Elena asked her sister as the two came close enough to speak.

"I also use a whistle to get the kid's attention. It sounds as familiar as my own name," she replied smiling.

"I love what you are wearing," Elena said as she glanced up and down at her sister's long white linen dress - dazzling in the sunlight like a waterfall in the forest.

"Your skirt is beautiful too; you look well put together with the orange shoes and the green jacket to match."

"Thank you. This skirt is linen too, and I can wear the plaid with so many things. I call these my Frida Kahlo shoes. They are sort of from the fifties; the cork sole is really comfortable. I dressed up as Frida Kahlo for a party and put flowers in my hair. I penciled in a moustache, and drew a unibrow. Diana said I looked just like Frida. Stanislaw went as Diego Rivera. He wore work boots, as did Rivera, and a cowboy hat, white shirt with suspenders, and black wool dress pants. All the women kept remarking to me on how good he looked, and how handsome!"

"Did anyone know who you were?" her sister Louisa asked.

"Only a few, but someone mistook me for Hitler's lover."

The art gallery was over crowded. Only a week was left in the traveling exhibit, and art students gathered around the paintings while their teachers explained the significance of each piece. The light played off of Monet's paintings as though there was a hole in the wall of the gallery, and one was looking out at the real landscape beyond, at the wind and the sea at play.

"On closer inspection," the sister in white linen remarked as she leaned forward over the wire barrier closer to the canvas, "Monet captures the light with white highlights. You can see much better with these." Here she held the one arm of the reading glasses over her nose. "They are broken, but I use them as magnifying glasses. Look, you can see every brush stroke – it looks three-dimensional." She turned and handed the broken glasses to Elena to try, as though there were no one else in the gallery.

"Monet celebrated color I think," said Elena feeling it necessary to at least add some comment that sounded intelligent. The art teachers seemed to find a lot to say.

"Look at the brush strokes with this – here, I have a magnifying glass. I carry it with me as well. It has a leather cover, on one side is the magnifying glass, it is good for reading charts in the boat, and on the other side is a compass," Louisa interrupted Elena and continued to instruct her to be sure she got the full effect of the canvas.

'How handy,' thought Elena, and she proceeded to inspect the brushstrokes, 'what felicity!' More than interpretation of the art pieces Elena was stimulated by emotion. Whereas a Monet painting gave her surges of joy, and spoke of fresh air and sunlight, the Frida Kahlo paintings she had seen said to her "Modern art, Powerful modern art."

"Notice how Monet differs from the Van Gogh that we just looked at," said a gallery guide, now standing next to Louisa and Elena while waiting for her group of students to gather around. "Come in close,' she continued, until her voice was not audible and was lost in the muffling of shuffling feet and coughs that rose up to the high ceiling and disappeared into clouds of vibrations. The group dissolved itself and the two sisters had room now to move onto the next painting. The solitude lasted but a brief moment, broken by the sudden wailing of a small child; the gallery seemingly became more crowded again and the air suffocating and hot. People stood and stared, looking at paintings for whole minutes at a time as though they were really thinking intelligent thoughts - contemplative serious people, studying, staring, and motionless.

  Elena unwrapped the silk scarf from around her neck, and parted temporarily from her sister - profound thoughts eluded her. Scanning the masterpieces from Monet to Picasso and passing briefly through the post war realists, she cut a path through the dense closet of people, coats, bags and hats and landed with a sigh of relief upon a velvet covered bench in the grand hallway. Here she sat and waited, having nothing more to do or think about than to wait for her sister to appear through the gallery door. She waited as the continuous chomping of caterpillars on green leaves, leaf after shimmering leaf, gnashed their way through the paintings and out into the main foyer, dispersing among the columns like leaves in an empty forest. Sometime later, Louisa emerged from the crowd and Elena sat up like a dog recognizing its master and got up with a smile.

"I'm so hungry," Elena said relieved to see her sister, "shall we eat upstairs?"

"That would suit me fine," replied Louisa, equally appetite consumed. The two left the exhibit engaging in small talk as they climbed the marble staircase to the café, their words lost in the rafters and the echo of voices in the hall.

Once outside the art gallery Elena had to push her way through yet another crowd of jostlers. There was an impending election and protesters had chosen the steps of the art gallery as their point of convergence like crows gathering for the fall migration. Elena could not wait to get back to the quiet of her home, away from the traffic and the stimuli of the city. There were things she wanted to accomplish. She parted ways with her sister, and zigzagged her way back through the streets toward her patiently waiting car, where yet another impediment presented itself.

Directly in front of her, tied to a lamp post was a dog on a leash, sniffing the air and wandering back and forth across the sidewalk. Elena kept her eye on the dog. The lampposts had been placed decoratively in the middle of the sidewalk, as the storefronts were set back from the street. Here someone had tied his big, beastly, furry, black dog to the lamppost and, someone else had placed a dish filled with water in front of the dog, some three feet from the post. Because of this, the dog had to stretch to the end of its tether in order to reach the water. As Elena walked observing all of this, she came face to face with a man who was coming in her direction from the other side of the dog. She hesitated a moment, gauging which way she should go to get around the dog. She looked at the man, and then he bent down immediately to pat the dog. She thought that the dog was his, and that he was going to untie it. Instead he looked up at her and said,

"You should vote for this dog for council. Next election, vote for this dog."

Elena, somewhat good- humouredly said that she would, and laughing to herself, she circumnavigated the man, the dog, the leash, and the dish, and turned into a coffee shop with some relief to buy herself a cup of coffee, before going back to the country.

Sometime later, as she left the café, and thinking of nothing in particular, she stepped out onto the sidewalk and came suddenly face to face once more with the man who had talked to the dog. He looked straight at her, and it took her a few seconds to recall their last encounter.

"Hello Angel," he said to her as though he knew her.

Elena looked him in the eye for a moment – alas, that was all it took to give him the confidence that he needed.

"Tonight at the Shoreline Inn," he began, "all the dogs in the community are assembling there, I've called the mayor, and I've told council, but they won't believe me. All the dogs will be there, and there's a bird, a Myna bird that's going to translate the 'bow wow wow'. He's going to translate it into English. I told the city what the aliens told me, and they wouldn't believe me. I told them that the world is going to blow up tomorrow, and now I'm going to have to press a button tonight, and all the guns in the world are going to melt. And then council will have to clean up the mess, because they wouldn't believe me." He reached over and grabbed her gently by the arm and looked at her in a desperate struggle of infirmity.

Elena looked at him speechless. He needed someone to talk to. At least he was on the right track. He loved dogs; and melting all the guns in the world was a good idea too. Elena noticed his jacket wasn't done up right, and that the faux fur on the collar was discolored. She did not say a word, but turned with that jerk that set her loose; and she rushed in the direction of her car like a wind up doll with stiff, swinging arms. "Why me?" she asked herself once safely in her car. She pressed the button to lock the car door. Someone indignantly pounded on the trunk of her car as it rolled slowly out of the crosswalk and into the traffic. People began to file out of buildings, clumping like dust from the shaken bottoms of heavy wool mops. Grey suits and black suits streamed into the streets, and election issues surged amongst the derelicts and the decrepit ones.

Chapter 15

Elena was thankful that it was the weekend, free of all distractions and otherworldly concerns.
"I can't spend the rest of my life mowing the lawn," Stanislaw said out loud, as the two of them sat on the back of the boat sipping a glass of wine, and devouring the cheese together. He started to speak and then changed his mind, not ready to say what was really on his mind. His talk of lawn mowing was incongruous with his situation.
"I thought that you said that you weren't hungry," said Elena noting his appetite.
"I'm not really, but a man's got'ta eat when he sees the food."
"I would have brought more, but we can go out for dinner later."
"This is perfect. This is enough for now. It's good," he said smiling with the nourishment brought to his attention.
"Why do you want to retire then, if you can't see yourself mowing the lawn?"
"I do and I don't. I want to make some folding money, some serious money, and I want to make a name for myself - and then I can retire, go boating, go traveling with you," he said warmly as he looked over at the woman who looked after his needs, " I need to set you up, set the kids up."
"You are *not* going to want to go traveling. And we already have *more* money than anyone needs. What will you do when you retire?" she said half to herself thinking, and studying the cliff behind the boat. "I don't think that you have enough to do, - hobbies I mean," she added gently. "You will always want to work, no matter how much money we have."
He took it as an insult; maybe it was intended that way. Someone without many hobbies, who has spent their whole life working to accumulate a certain amount of money, doesn't have time for hobbies. Work is their life - but he always saw himself as a man with many interests and hobbies.
"There is plenty to do. I'd like to paint the house for one thing," he said, "I find it relaxing."
Elena leaned back into the leather seat of the boat, and gazed up at the tall hemlocks which grew up the steep slope of the riverbank. 'Why should I worry about that?' she thought. Some people are very happy working- their whole life. But to her it wasn't about just working. It was about doing something really useful, masterful. Like Frances Perkins. Few people knew who she was. She had ideas, and through hard work, luck, circumstance, friends, believers, all that, she seemed to be pushed to the top, to the top of

the political ladder, and doing great good for the common people the whole time. She was an advocate for decent work week hours, making the drudgery of the complacent middle class bearable. All they wanted was to have a little extra time for entertainment and a little extra cash with which to do it.'

"You know what I think? I think the middle class have just enough of a sample of affluence to keep them all happy. They have just a taste of luxury to satisfy themselves without working too hard to acquire more. And those who are unhappy with their situation console themselves with thinking, 'I could have done better had I had more encouragement; I could have been like him had I had better teachers, coaches, - councillors; I am as good as the next person; but my life is satisfying enough because I know someone who met someone who actually knows someone famous.' It is all right *there*, just within their reach, if they really want that – the exotic life, the bigger house, the house with the pool, two houses even, both empty because they don't have the time to be at home. The Striving, it's like some great monster, always running and working, and chewing and swallowing; a machine, a river, a comet burning up space in its race past its contemporaries, burning out, sometimes in the view of its counterparts. I would like to do something great, rather than make money for its own sake," she continued almost to herself as her husband was busy wiping off the navigation panel with a serviette, "but it may be too late – or is that a defeatist attitude to say my time has passed, a cop out? But, on the other hand, maybe I should be content. Maybe I have achieved my potential. I really am content though. I consider myself to be very lucky." And she concluded with thoughts to herself: 'It is so beautiful right now. I count my blessings.'

"You are right," Stanislaw agreed suddenly speaking again. "Each person measures his own life by his own standard. We have to focus on our own good qualities and do our best, and the rest is out of our control."

"That reminds me of that man that I met on the train that year. Do you remember I told you about the man with the story about staying focused? He told me the story of *Secretariat* the race horse. I was seated in the dining car of the train across the table from a gentleman who was about sixty years old. The most prominent feature about him were his large, round, brown eyes, whose irises were enhanced and made larger by the very thick glasses that he was wearing. The lens had the effect of making his eyes appear innocent and childlike. He was also conspicuous by most standards because he was of grand physique and proportions, and on top of his head was perched a cream-colored Stetson, like a bird with outstretched wings, which he wore at the dinner table. He also wore a cowboy shirt, which was navy blue with white stitching and mother of pearl buttons. Bob was a horse breeder. He had on his ranch at any given time at least twenty-five thoroughbred horses, which he bred, raised, sold or raced himself.

'Them horses are bred to run,' he told me, 'just as a dawg is bred to herd sheep, them horses are bred to run and will keep on runnin' even if they have a broken leg. Them other horses will try to run with 'em and they'll keep on runnin' until their hearts burst.'

'They shouldn't breed them like that.' I said, 'that's awful.'

'Do you remember *Secretariat*?' he asked me. 'Everyone knows Secretariat. Well that horse just looked 'round for two years at all the other horses and didn't do anything. Just looked at what was goin' on around him all the time. They were going to shoot him. Somebody said, "Let's try blinkers." And from the day they put those blinkers on, the horse had FOCUS. It's all about focus. Secretariat never lost a race after that, except for one time, and that was when he had an abscess tooth. We can learn from the animals,' he said wistfully. I then asked him where his ranch was.

'Ah, well, I've just retired,' he continued. 'I sold the ranch, and I have an old farmhouse in Montana, which is where I am goin' now. I can't wait to put the Christmas lights up. I'm goin' to put them up all along the fence, and I've got these icicle lights to hang from the eves. And then I have some of those, what do you call them... they sort of drape down. Ah, I've got all kinds to hang up.'

I told him he was going to have to get a ladder.

'Oh yeah, I've got a ladder all right, that's why I'm headed out there now. I want to get the lights up before it gets too cold and icy.'

We all turned and focused our gaze out the train window at the snow coming down in October.

'Well you better hurry,' I told him. 'What about your hat?'

'Ah well, I like to dress up. I have about thirty of these outfits, includin' tuxedos, and I have thirty pair of boots.'

I asked him where he was going to wear all those boots.

He responded again in a sort of southern drawl.

'I used to wear them to the races in California and Arizona.'

'I guess your new house has a lot of closets. Usually those old houses don't have any closets. You'll have to make a museum for all your outfits.'

'Oh, it's got closets all right. I'm keepin' my clothes.'

And then in everyone's mind we saw him lining up thirty pairs of highly polished, hard shiny cowboy boots of all different colors and stitching.

As the train rumbled its way slowly through a prairie town, Bob stood up, put his hands on the back part of his hips and stretched a bit backwards.

Then he straightened up again and let out a low whistle, as he gazed out the train window, down the street of the town to where he noticed a buxom woman getting out of a car and walking over to a mailbox. He adjusted his Stetson, and thought once again about the miracle of the blinkers..."

"Here comes the train now," Stanislaw said. As he listened to the story, the horn of a nearby train sounded faintly in the distance like a sonorous bassoon tuning up. The herons heard it too.

"It was so quiet for a Friday night, now listen to all those squawking herons up there," Elena motioned, turning her head once again to the riverbank. High above the marina was a flock of great blue herons – *Ardea Herodias*. One must have been startled by something, for it lifted its great expansive wings high over its plumed head and let out a loud raucous 'kraaaak'. This set the others stirring as well, a great commotion was beheld up in the dark and windy evergreens, high above the marina. The train's horn blasted its presence annoyingly over the trestle and announced itself like a crack in the night with the rumble of the steel on the tracks. 'Perhaps this is what set the great birds in motion,' she thought.

Looking to the West, they decided it was time to go for dinner. "Let's get back to civilization," Elena said, "Now I am really hungry." The ducks were returning to the ditch for the night. The ditch was man made, but the bank, planted with a row of pines and wild roses, perfectly protected the habitat from harsh winds and rough seas. The lush grass on the banks was flattened in circles where the ducks had made a nesting spot, and the shallow saline water was abounding in dabblers and divers, the water rippling with swirls and splashes, foraging and flirting, courting and flipping metallic speculum, white downy throats and underbellies, and the bright white rears of the generally dowdier, less colourful female ducks. The majority of the fowl were mallards, ubiquitous most of the year; their emerald green shiny heads and wing feathers were made almost common-place by their numbers. But everywhere interspersed between flocks of the mallards, retreating from hunters with shotguns, were the American Wigeon, and Teals as well, their browns, greens and purples blending in with the landscape. There were white and black Canvas Backs with their elongated gossiping bills, and Buffleheads with their stubby round faces and small prim bills, and the American Coot, with its white bill and orange eyes, daintily stepping around on the shore, its unusual long feet that were green like the grass, but were designed to keep them balanced on top of the mud. But the most beautiful and rarest of these was not a duck at all; it was the bird that came to sing in the morning.

As Elena and Stanislaw emerged from the thicket, the pier in the distance came into view, afloat with people, some fishing, some crabbing - a sometime city on the beach. And as they walked along a young couple was meandering in their direction, seemingly waddling down the path like the ducks, a woman with her arms up over the man's shoulders.

"I think that is Daniel from work" said Stanislaw surprised, and he slowed down to greet the approaching couple.

"Hey Stan, how's it going?"

"Daniel, good to see you. Did you just fly in from Hawaii?" Daniel looked as though he hadn't been in the tropics. His skin was white, and he wore small round, wire-rimmed glasses, and no hat, revealing a thin and receding hairline. He was wearing a short-sleeved business shirt and lightweight wool gabardine pants. The woman accompanying him wore jeans and a bright green belt that fit tight on her wide hips; she could easily have been wearing a pannier, the hoops worn over ladies' hips to expand the skirt at their sides, such was the effect of the wide belt. 'Like *Little Bo Peep,*' thought Elena, except that her blouse just barely reached her belt line so that one caught a glimpse of her midriff. It wasn't tanned either, but the gold stud pierced into her naval reflected the sunlight.

"Ya, I just got in last night, and Dallas and I came down here to check on the project she's been working on. It's actually our anniversary."

"Congratulations," both Elena and Stanislaw chimed in together. Dallas broke into the conversation without delay,

"Stan, it's great to see you. How's your boat? Did you get out in the boat much this summer? Dan and I haven't had a chance to go sailing as he's been away for six months and I'm now working with another company here. How *are* you anyway?" she asked with great animation, pushing the hair away from her eyes as the wind caught it from behind her, and pointing at all the boats in the channel she added, "We should be sailing right now. You have a power boat don't you?"

"Oh yes. We've been out a few times," he replied feigning indifference.

"So, how's it going with the new company?" she continued.

"Dan can tell you, Hawaii went real well as you know; who wouldn't want to live in Hawaii? It's going good." Stanislaw turned to his own wife and introduced the couple to her. He was waiting for a break in the small talk.

"Elena, you've met Daniel before, and this is Dallas. She was in marketing at Fellowes when I worked there."

"Hi, nice to meet you. Hi Daniel," Elena greeted them both as Daniel smiled, hands in his pockets, kicking at the gravel on the path. Dallas looked at Elena, seemingly aware of her for the first time -

"Elena, how *are* you?" she queried, "and the children?"

"Our children? I wouldn't exactly call them children. We are well thank you. The older two are busy with their friends, work, and university of course. We still have one younger one at home," returned Elena politely. Dallas was not really listening to Elena's answer and she could not think of anything else to say.

"Do you have children?" Elena asked hesitantly, not sure how long the conversation would go on for, and wondering at the same time if she needed to know all the details of this person's life.

"No, no children yet, and I've been traveling too. I was down in New Zealand - well Stan, you know the story," she said gleaming, and turning her attention once again to Stan, "I went down there with Arnold and Zack, you know, we went down scouting out property for development, but - the rest is confidential." She shrugged her shoulders and laughed, "I've moved on to work at Port Place - we have so many exciting projects. I'm VP of marketing- Stan, don't you think I'm the *perfect* fit? ..." *Quack, quack, quack*, she seemed to go on incessantly. Elena noticed she wasn't talking at all now, only making the noises that the ducks make. After some time Elena focused again on the conversation just in time to hear the end.

"...yes, I've heard about them," continued her husband abruptly. "A guy from my MBA class was working for that company. Anyway, we've gotta go, we're just on our way to dinner. Catch ya later." And then as they were walking away, Stan called over his shoulder to the couple,

"Hey Daniel, are you going to be in the office on Monday morning?"

"Ya! I'll talk to you," he shouted back.

Elena and Stanislaw at last continued on their walk, Elena deep in thought. 'Women seemed to postpone having children until well into their thirties; or decide not to have them at all, and of those that did, even fewer wanted to stay at home and look after them themselves. And yet, in some countries, women were forcibly limited to the number of children they could, or worse, women were subject to seeing their children suffer from malnutrition or disease. When we consider all, there seemed to be so much injustice. So many modern women said that staying home and looking after their own children was too boring! Why look after a child for next to no income, when you could pay someone else next to nothing, and you could go out into the business world and make money – to buy more, and to go on more holidays with your children?' She had heard many women say that they were bored at home. 'Women who stayed at home were only bored if they had no imagination,' she thought. 'Consider if there were a war. I wonder how many women would like to go off to war with the men and kill other men and women and leave their children at home in someone else's care for the sake of working? Would working and having someone else take care of your children be as appealing?' She thought about this aspect of work, and of women wanting to be like men, of the separation of the family – the relationship of men and women, working, and raising children. Everyone does what one must – it was individual - and very controversial. There did not seem to be an answer as to what would be the most natural, most suitable, the most 'humanistic' way to live. And people became so defensive in their argument about working over staying at home and looking after their children. 'Why were people so judgmental? Why are the women who choose to stay at home considered less in society by society itself? What would the little children say if they could talk? My children are almost fully grown,' she thought, 'and I am thankful that I had the opportunity to raise them myself. I suppose I owe a lot to my husband for this.'

They continued their walk, now turning down one of the little neighborhood streets that ran in from the beach. The sun was just about to set itself on the edge of the sea, its light made golden by the low angle, that part of the spectrum when light is refracted to yellow and orange. The gardens around abounded in moisture and honey, and the rays coming through the clouds set the wet leaves shimmering and they hung like glistening lollipops wrapped in cellophane. Eventually Elena and Stanislaw came out on to the main street where rows of shops and restaurants receded behind trees and shrubs and stone planters. Stan, like the gentleman that he was, opened the door to what was a very lively restaurant and bar.

"After you, my love," he said. The two stepped inside, glancing around for the familiar faces of their neighbourhood.

Chapter 16

The restaurant inside was steamy and noisy. In the far corner, a trio was performing, - a vocalist, a keyboard, and saxophone smoothly issuing forth as on the waft from the kitchen, the genteel elixir, "Blue Moon". They made their way through the tables into the other dining area, and looked around for a free table. Patrons raised their heads as they passed, to glance at the new guests. There she noticed seated at one end of the bar facing into the performers, was a man whom she recognized from somewhere. He was looking right at her, expressionless. Perhaps he did not really see her at all, although he held his gaze long enough for her to notice that he had blue eyes. The Hostess came into the dining area from behind the bar.

"Do you have reservations?" she asked.

"No, but I see someone we can sit with," Stanislaw answered matter-of-factly, and pointed to his brother-in-law and sister sitting at a table for four.

"Hey you guys, come and sit with us", the brother-in-law motioned with his arm. He was the convivial sort.

"Great. We couldn't have planned it this way."

"What an unexpected pleasure!" Elena said never really surprised by coincidence.

"I suppose you expect me to pay for you too," the brother-in-law teased. "What'll you have to drink? We're drinking wine."

"That's fine with us, as long as your pay'n," Stanislaw joked. The two men always flipped a coin for the bill when they were out together. The couple seated themselves, just as the waiter came back with menus. In a distinctly Quebecois accent he announced the specials of the evening:

"Good evening M*esdames et Messieurs*, I would like to tell you the specials we are offering dis evening. (And here his voice rose at the end of evening) We 'av lobster in season, prepared in tree different ways, for your enjoyment – first, as a starter, we 'av the lobster bisque with a hint of cloves, it is very nice, next we 'av the a steak and lobster main dish, the steak of course prepared to your liking, and de lobster tails are grilled and served wid a melted boottair, side dish, and we also 'av de fresh prepared lobster linguine which 'as been poached in ah fish fumet, and served wid a brandy, wine tomato sauce. I will give you all a few moments to tink about it, and I will be back. Would you care for some wine or something else to drink?" he asked as he looked at the new couple.

"We'll start with a bottle of red wine, please, whatever your house wine is will be fine" said Conrad wiping his shiny red lips with the serviette. "Are you guys ok with red wine?"

Everyone agreed. They had already drunk a bottle at the boat. The music still sounded from the trio, and there was a bustling of people just arriving at the restaurant and getting seated. Elena looked again toward the bar, curious about the man with the blue eyes. He had on a blue, long sleeved shirt, and jeans, and he was much tanned. He looked in his mid fifties, streamlined in build, and had short, straight, dirty blond hair. His foot was propped up on the rungs of the bar stool next to him, showing off his shiny black leather, tooled, cowboy boots. He was leaning on one hand with a mug of beer in the other, and staring now at the band. She looked away from him to the saltwater fish tank which was situated at the far end of the bar. Here the bubbles competed for attention with the bubbles of music flowing up and popping out of the saxophone. The colors swirled around and flitted behind castles made of sparkling golden sand; and treasure chests and ship wrecks lay half buried in the rocks at the bottom. Beautiful, graceful and elegant angelfish floated effortlessly, and then snap, their tail fin changed their direction as if on a tack, and then darted to another spot, and hung undisturbed in a private corner.

"I'm thinking of getting that boat," continued Conrad, he was spreading butter now thickly on his bread as he spoke, and biting off pieces, leaving the butter slightly melting and dripping from his ever wet lips. "I think the '30 foot' is the better deal. I like the fact that it has a furling main and jib, and the inside is just beautiful, all teak. I want something that I can handle myself, basically. I just need you to come down and check a few things for me. I have no idea about the motor, and the broad who is selling it is a nut case. She is playing this dominance role with me, but is coquettish, flirty." And here he was thinking: 'This broad wants me and my money. She probably wants to get me aft on the double bed where she can hit me over the head with a club, dump me overboard, and sail away to the Bahamas with her lover."

"I can come down any weekend, you set it up, and then call me," replied Stanislaw.

"Why do you say that she is a 'nut case'? - the owner of the boat" Elena asked.

"Ya, she doesn't really know anything about boats, it was her husband's," said Conrad.

"They used to race it, and he changed all the rigging, and she doesn't want to part with the boat, so she is not making it any easier. She's just bitter about the whole divorce thing and has this thing against all guys, I think. She's manipulative. She's a bitch. I hate her."

"Maybe she is hermaphrodite – like those angelfish in the tank there."

"What?"

"What are you talking about?" her husband asked, as everyone laughed at such a ludicrous statement that didn't really fit into the conversation.

"Well, like those Angelfish in that tank over there, when the dominant male is removed, a female will turn into a functional male. Maybe she really wants to take over now and run the boat, so she is trying to ward you off."

"I'm going to get the mechanic down during the week to inspect it, if you could come with me Stan, it would be good."

"What are you thinking of getting?" Elena asked her husband as she tried to concentrate on the menu. "Has anyone ever had quail before? It is served with quince preserves."

"That steak and lobster sounds *reeeal* good," Stanislaw said putting down the menu.

"Kay, what about you?" she asked her sister-in-law.

"I'm thinking of going with the linguine special, I've never had it with lobster before," she answered with an emphatic smile. "Have you ever had fresh lobster?"

"Yes every night that my husband offers it."

"What are you saying? Are you drunk or something?" asked her brother-in-law, this time laughing.

Her husband looked over at her, anticipating her answer.

"Yes I have had it, a few years ago in Toronto, in an affluent part of town by the lakeshore. Stan's office had a year-end party to celebrate the sale of the new development, and they shipped in fresh lobster from the Maritimes and boiled them up in big metal vats outside on the patio. It was a beautiful warm humid night in June, and the sun did not set until after ten o'clock. It was down by the lake. I remember the lobsters going into the vats - giant creatures with huge claws. The meat was very juicy and sweet, and firm, very firm, the meat from the male is 'especially firm' when it is fresh, - according to the 'Joy of Cooking'. I remember it very well. It is an experience. I can taste it now, getting my mouth around it, and biting down, sliding my tongue around the outside, licking the butter off, and chewing."

"You are lewd," said Conrad, "Now I will never be able to eat lobster. You ruined it for me. You're the hermaphrodite, talking crudely that way."

"Alright! A piece of tail has taken on a whole new meaning," added her husband elatedly, and then, "give her more wine, I'm looking forward to the lobster fest tonight."

The waiter returned shortly and took their orders. She of the lewd ways did not order lobster in the end; she ordered simply a beef steak, as she too had an appetite. The two men ordered the steak and lobster, and it was negotiated between the brothers-in-law, that Conrad would buy the dinner to thank Stanislaw in advance for the help he would give Conrad in accompanying him for the boat inspection. He was not a true voluptuary, although judging from his turgescent complexion and tendency to grow heavier every year, one wouldn't think so. However, he showed true restraint and moderation in his choice of wines and lived a private life reading and edifying, and showing discretion in his choice of entertainment and restraint in his spending. He spent most of his time at home with his family, watching TV and reading books on famous politicians and business gurus. And his wife portrayed in public, and sometimes in private amongst family, an obsequious personality, that was very often described as 'genuinely nice".

Conrad was particularly boisterous this evening, and dominated the conversation. He had a mission to accomplish, that being, he had to buy a sailboat. The speedboat could only be used for certain things, and sailing was so peaceful. He loved the sound of the furrow on the hull after the motor was cut. It was more acute when compared to the drone of the small motor as it pushed the sleek boat against the chopping tide. The two men began to talk about the details of the sale of the boat, and what had to be done to it to get it ready for winter if they did buy it. Also there was the powerboat to discuss. Sometimes when Elena looked over, she noticed that the man at the bar was looking at her. Maybe he wasn't really seeing her. She looked away and began to inspect the paintings on the wall. The plaster walls were painted a deep gold color, and rustic, exposed beams and posts framed each painting. A mermaid floated through long curving strands of thick green kelp, exposing her bare breasts to the onlooker. Other vibrant swathes of color floated in and out of her long dark hair, which flowed down over her heart shaped green, scale covered fish shaped body. Her eyes were aglow, with servitude and longing. It was as if she were saying 'someone please buy me and take me home, I will do well for you, and I will please you.'

When the dinner arrived it was as luscious as the paintings. The array of color and the magnificent beast, the lobster, plunked on the plate. It was a lobster party- straight out of a still life. The table now resembled a work by a 17th century Dutch Master, like the ones in the Wallace collection in

London where Elena once stood transfixed imbibing the bounty. Each little dab of white reflected light as though there was a shining object, just there beyond the wall. There were fruits, and meats and wine glasses half full of shimmering ruby colored wines, and candles and sometimes a book, all laid out on dark velvet table coverings. A pheasant was amongst the works, its silky plumage intact, its broken neck draped over the table edge. They represented the ephemeral and transitory, but earthly pleasures! But the paintings survived – they outlived the era they rang to represent.

The conversation turned to other topics: first was about football, then baseball, then the boats, and so on.

'What about athletes?' Elena thought. 'People always talked about athletes. They were the 'peoples' heroes. Almost everyone had played sports when they were young. People could relate to athletes, but now it meant something more. To be an athlete meant the potential to make a lot of money.'

"Why is it that no-one can name a famous athlete out of his time? Can anyone give me the name of an athlete from a different era? …Say from a hundred years ago?" she interjected into the conversation. Stanislaw thought for a moment. Then collectively, a few names came up of contemporary, retired, famous athletes, but they weren't from the last century.

"In one generation we forget the names of people we worshipped. But musicians, writers and artists, and that includes architects, are not forgotten, their influence is felt and known for thousands of years," Elena said.

"So, what's your point?" someone asked.

"I'm just thinking how we worship athletes, but they are quickly forgotten."

"I don't agree with you," said Stanislaw. "Athletes inspire people in their own time, but the collective memory of strength, youth and prowess lives on. And athletes usually overcome more than the physical to become outstanding. I can give you lots of examples of that. And then there are the ancient Greeks and Romans, those we can name like Hercules, Atlas, and Achilles, the famous legends. But there are many more to show how society praises athletes. Many ancient Greek athletes were immortalized on Greek jugs, and have survived from the 5th century B.C. - remember the Greek wrestlers in the Uffizi gallery in Florence? There were others too, immortalized in bronze and marble. And the discus thrower," he added as he remembered the marble statues. "And then there is the bronze statue of Roger Bannister. Wasn't he the first man to break the four minute mile barrier?"

"And the bronze statue of Michael Jordan in Chicago," added Conrad, "have you ever seen that? It could last 2000 years too."

"I believe you are right," Elena confessed. "We do celebrate famous athletes over time."

"And then there was Paul Bunyan, and Beowulf, they were heroes and athletes weren't they?" asked Kay.

"There are religious leaders too, whose names survive history. And philosophers, and politicians, great leaders" added Conrad.

"You are right. The names of intellects and thinkers survive time, but overall I think individual athletes are forgotten. I suppose they all have something to offer, but the inspiration and wonder that an athlete creates in others is ephemeral. I guess I have no point; it is just an observation," ended Elena, and her thoughts turned inward: 'One can't go to a dinner party and expect to have discussions that require thought. Dinner was the time for quick-witted axioms, and stories of local happenings and sensational personal experiences – or those of someone we know. Someone else can do the talking. I wonder what is really on people's minds. Should we say what we are thinking? Or do we risk becoming boring? Above all, keep the dinner talk to happy thoughts and everyone will be safe. Don't mention 'controversy', whatever you do. Just talk about what happened down the street'.

The man in the blue shirt was leaving. Elena had forgotten about him. She thought she knew him from somewhere, but just couldn't place him. The dessert arrived. Always they ordered '*tiramisu*'.

"What is *tiramisu* exactly?" asked Conrad.

"It is sponge cake with custard and alcohol. I think it means 'pick me up.' Or does it mean 'lift me up'?" she asked. "It is Italian, whatever it means". She would have better luck with the Spanish coffee heaped high with whipping cream and topped with a maraschino cherry. Always after such dinners out, she paid penance by eating porridge for breakfast and cabbage soup for dinner the next day, to remember those who weren't as fortunate as herself. She remembered her childhood, how hungry she always was, how the bakery filled brown paper flour bags with the crusts of bread from the slicing machines, and left them at the back door of the bakery. She never questioned why they were there; it seemed as though they were there for her, as one would put crusts out for the birds. She knew the very day and time that the bags were put out, and she was there, with other children, gathering handfuls and filling their mouths with the tasty, soft dough, encrusted in brown chewy dryness. There was so much injustice, but as a child she never viewed it as that. Now she was grateful, but always mindful of her happiness where others still suffered. The waiter arrived with a platter balancing the four hot coffees and the desserts.

Chapter 17

A few days later, Elena took an early walk with dogs. All the locals had gone back to work. It was truly one of those summer mornings - the picture of perfection, everyone's ideal. She headed up toward the dyke. The dogs knew which way to go. They yanked and pulled, catching the lingering scent of a long gone coyote. And it was warm. Not a hint of dew, nor a breeze from the north, from some high, glacial slope of winters and millenniums past, intruded the magic morning air. Today, yes today, there was none of this chill, to spoil her solitary morning meander. Only the dogs knew the presence of other creatures, always invisible, but ever present in the air. Her Borzoi, named Laelaps, was always hunting, and always watching, and protecting her. And then there was the Airedale, a constant companion and playmate for both, walked briskly on the leash, on the left-hand side of her master, prancing and bouncing at the end of her leash, stirred by the scent of the elusive and unseen. There were many people with dogs here by the shore where civilization meets the windy wild of the sea. Usually people referred to a dog and his master as 'the lady with the two large dogs', or 'the man with the little poodle.'

This was a peaceful morning. In the distance Elena noticed someone walking her way. It is very awkward to walk towards someone on a lone path, without saying something, and without turning or looking away. She looked at the man, focusing her gaze on him for the steps until he came up to the point of passing, then she suddenly stopped as if to make way for him, and sat her dogs. He stopped too, a few feet from her, and smiled, his hands on his hips.

"I know you, don't I?" she asked him forthrightly.

"I think so," he said looking her up and down. "I thought that was you the other night in the restaurant."

"Do you live here?" she asked him, "I thought you were from Texas."

"I am, but I live here too, sometimes. My mother owns a house here. I should say, my late mother."

"I am sorry," Elena said.

"Thank you, I came here to find solace."

"I am a little confused. You were in Cuernavaca when I was there studying Spanish a year ago," Elena said intrepidly.

"Ya, and you left me in the lurch, didn't you?"

"I was the one in trouble, if I remember correctly. You had had a little too much to drink, I think. Actually you were quite rude. I don't care to be addressed in such a manner."

"What about undressed?" he quickly put in.

"Ha. I should be affronted. This is a joke. What do you take me for? You are a total stranger." She spoke with a little more civility than would otherwise be called for, because this was her neighborhood, and she felt comfortable.

"Ya, same green eyes, and a little temperamental, aren't you?" he laughed. "May I walk with you?"

"I am going this way, towards the beach, where you have just come from."

"I know, I am on my way back," he said as he turned around and looked down at her dogs. "Tell me something, whatever brought you to San Miguel?" he asked.

"I study Spanish, and I heard that it was a nice place to visit. And I was very pleased with the university and the classes. It has a very good atmosphere – maybe because of the altitude, I don't know."

"What about the people you met, what did you think about them?"

"You mean you?"

"I spent my summers here as a kid," he said changing the subject. "My father was a brigadier general, and after the war, he was stationed overseas, and we came here and lived in the house down here on the beach that was my mother's family summer home."

"So your mother was Canadian."

"The house is left to me, and I have some things to straighten up. My sister and I might keep it, but we won't be making any decisions just yet. It is a very sad time for me. Your parents still alive?" he asked politely.

"No, sadly they are not. What was your Mother's name?"

"Same as mine – Lees," he said as he looked at her sideways smirking. 'As if she doesn't remember,' he thought.
The name did not mean anything to her.

"Which house did you say it was?" she asked as she bent down to pick some wild flowers with her free hand. The dogs stood patiently waiting, side by side.

"It's down at the end of the beach, a big brown house, 'Seelen' it's called. It's a play on words in German, 'See' meaning the seaside and 'Seele' or '*mit deiner ganzen Seele*', meaning with all ones heart."

They came through the opening in the grotto; the dogs were tugging at the end of their leashes, smelling something, probably a rabbit under the thick cover of the blackberry brambles.

"Come on, dogs," she said irritated, as she yanked them back onto the path. "Sometimes they can be so annoying and stubborn, and a sudden lunge into the bushes hurts my shoulder." He wasn't paying attention to the dogs. As they came out into the full sun, a woman jogging with her two husky dogs was coming their way. Elena had never spoken to her. Her Borzoi was protective of her; she never knew when it would cause a scene by lunging and barking at other people or their dogs. The Airedale, on the other hand, wanted nothing more than to be set free to frolic with anything on four feet.

"Hi", she said to the woman.

"Hello. Jasper, heal. No bark," she replied as she tugged on the leash of her dog. She was frail looking, and didn't look as though she could manage two dogs, although one was off leash and followed just behind her. She always wore shorts in the summer, and a sweater, and Elena noticed her thin legs. She wondered how someone who walked so much could have such thin legs. They continued walking. She tightened up on the leashes and the dogs passed without incident.

"Do you know that woman?" he asked her, looking back at her as they passed.

"No, not really, I have seen her a lot though. I try to avoid letting the dogs stop to say hello to everyone else's dog. She lives just at the bottom of the hill before you leave the beach. One day she shook her fist at me, as she was trying to cross the road, but I was driving down the hill and I didn't really see her in time to slow down, so I try to avoid her now. Some days I just like to be by myself. There are some people that I see frequently who I just don't care to acknowledge. I usually veer away from people and their dogs if I do not know them. But this woman, I am acquainted with. She taught Sunday school at the church where I used to attend. The men like to talk about her. There is some rumor that she had a child when she was a teen, and that she was forced to give the child up for adoption – of course no-one knew any of this at the time. You know how society was in those days; and she ended up getting married much later, but the couple had no children of their own."

"You seem to know a lot for someone who veers from strangers," he said cynically.

"The reason I know all of this," Elena continued, "is because her husband died recently in a plane crash. And just last year her daughter, who is now in her thirties, found her, as she was looking to reunite with her birth mother. It is such a weird story, but for many years that woman sat on the stage of the church talking to the children with her legs folded to the side looking like a mermaid, and all the men would go to church just to see her. I am not making this up. These are the facts as I heard them from the ambulatory."

The Texan started to laugh out loud, but he kept his head turned in the direction of the Sunday school teacher as she jogged down the path, her blond ponytail swinging with her step.

As they struck onto the path that led around the beach, a slight offshore breeze met them, but it was warm and wonderful, and smelled of the sea, and seaweed. The tide was running out, and the tidal pools reflected faraway cumulus, puffy clouds. Her borzoi dragged her in the direction of the hard and flat, shimmering, silver sand.

"I am going down to the sandbars. This is where I let the dogs off to run. Of course I know in the summer we should not be here, but it is very early and I'm taking them out to the edge of the water."

"I'll walk with you then," the Texan agreed.

She felt as though she knew him. If his mother was a summer resident at the beach, then he must be OK. Chances are they had many acquaintances in common.

"Do you believe in the afterlife?" he asked her suddenly.

The question came as a surprise.

"You mean do I believe in heaven?" she asked, interested in the topic.

"Well, heaven or the afterlife, whatever you want to call it."

"No, I don't. Why do you ask?"

"Because my mother told me when she was ill, that after she died, she would come back in some way, give me a sign, or come back in some way to show me that she was still alive. And she didn't. That bothers me."

"I really don't believe in the afterlife, but it must be very difficult to lose someone you love, whether it is family or a friend. And places could be so meaningless after someone dies. But I believe in something greater than an afterlife. Mostly I live in the here and now."

They stepped across tide pools, all the while walking and looking at the sand scattered with the myriad ribbed brown and tan cockle shells, the giant white horse clams, bivalves missing their other half, singly scattered, the thousands of purple clam shells, and the bleached white sand dollars, money but not. John Lees was lost in thought. What had his life become? The endless search for pleasure, the loss of friends, and now the loss of his mother plunged him in to existential thoughts. He felt so alone, so achingly empty.

"Sorry, what was that you just said?"
Forgivingly she replied,
"You were asking me about the afterlife. Don't you participate in the 'Day of the Dead' celebrations in Mexico? When I first learned about that festival, when I went to Mexico the first time to study Spanish, I was really moved by the tradition. It is hard to know if that is celebrated by all Mexican people, or if it is just a cult, a tradition amongst the indigenous peoples, but that point is irrelevant, you probably know better than me. What altered my feelings most though, - at first I thought it was weird, sort of idol worshipping, when I saw all the pictures of these skeletons - but on the night of the 'Day of the Dead,' we visited a graveyard, late in the evening. Our bus driver dropped us off, a little way on the outside of the village, as there was no room to drive through the narrow, stone walled streets. So we walked together up a hilly climb toward the cathedral spire, and into the graveyard. The smell of marigolds and guavas wafted towards us before we could see the massive crosses and '*offrendas*', or memorial monuments to the deceased, made entirely of luminous, orange marigolds. And the graveyard was lit by candles; and families and individuals sat around talking softly together and drinking liquor from small ceramic shot glasses. And I was trying to step around the fresh mounds, so as not to disturb the dead, and a small old woman, only four feet high, reached out her hand from under her dark wool cape, and she took my hand to help me over the mound, and our eyes met in the dark, candle lit, moonless night. And she looked into my eyes and smiled a toothless smile; and her hands clasped together over the top of my hand. And I marveled at the time at how soft, how silky and soft and warm it was; and she just held my hand and I looked at her small face, and observed how wrinkly she was, brown and wrinkly all over, but how beautiful and old she was, and still able to smile, and even laugh with me, because she understood the humor in the situation, of me and the mounds. And I've never thought about it since until now, until you brought the memory back for me."

"That's quite a description"

"I don't remember much else, only that, how bright and alive it seems, although it was dark at the time, and it was all about death. But it gave me a better perspective about death, and I think that culture is so wonderful for that, if nothing else." He stopped and looked at her, but he could not speak. He wanted to grab her and kiss her, but he dare not. He wasn't that much of a cad. She was married after all. Some men would walk away, thinking 'too deep for me'; I just want to get laid. But he was like her in many ways - an intellect can have many interests.

"So, if you don't believe in the afterlife, why the visiting to the gravesites?" he inquired.

"It's for those remaining, I think, to celebrate, get drunk, have a good time, and remember the dead. It was fun out there amongst the tombstones. I was in Egypt once. It really changed me. The trip is for me, a reference point. Things either happened before the trip, or after. It really changed me. We toured many temples, including the underground tombs of the 'Valley of the Kings'. Our guide showed us many columns and walls of hieroglyphics, and he would stop in front of some and read and interpret what they said. Each letter of the hieroglyphics is a piece of art. Most of these were from 3500 B.C. Just the age alone filled one with reverence. But I noticed that each temple, from Cairo to Aswan, seemed to me more beautiful than the last. When I confronted my tour guide with what I was experiencing, he said: That's because 'the more you learn, the more you notice; and the more you appreciate.' The written word as art – as beauty - I am still thinking about this."

"That is probably true for just about everything, I would guess, the more you learn, the more you appreciate."

"But back to your afterlife question. The Egyptians painted 'still life' on the inside of the tomb, they painted all the things that the Pharaoh would need in the afterlife, even in Pompeii, which I know was 79 A.D. when Mt. Vesuvius erupted, - in Pompeii a fresco survives of a 'still life' on the wall of a home; it's a bowl of fruit and a vase of flowers. There was one other thing in Egypt that was truly beautiful. One of the Pharaohs who was a woman, maybe the only female Pharaoh, had made an obelisk to herself, carved out of a single piece of rose granite, and it is still standing after thousands of years; and it is completely carved in hieroglyphics. The top is a pyramid shape, and it was once covered in gold and silver. The inscription, it is said, was to her lover and husband, and she tells him, 'Gold, so I will be with you in the day when the sun shines; and silver so that I may be with you when the moon is out at night.' And she lives on lifelike, for all to see and appreciate." He was listening intently now, and that feeling came over him, the sudden heating of his face and stomach, and goose bumps down his arms. His mother had told him, 'I give you the memory of the beach, remember how beautiful it is, how golden the sun shines by day, and how silver the moon by night.'

They had reached the end of the beach where the path turns into a lane.

"I am turning here," she said, and called the dogs to leash them.

"And there is my house. Now that you know where I live, come by for a drink sometime, if your husband will let you," he said. "I'll be here for a while yet; we can practice speaking Spanish together."

"Thank you. How long are you here for?" she asked blinking in the sunlight.

"I'll be back and forth for the next few months."

She turned away without saying another word, but all the time she was thinking, 'There are two kinds of single men, no, maybe three. There are the ones who only want sex; there are the ones who don't have that on their mind; and then there are the polite ones who may be thinking about that while they are talking to women, but they are too polite to say anything and risk being shunned for good. He was the first, she thought, and accepting an invitation to visit may give a man the wrong impression. Her husband and she had an intimate relationship, based on a mutual, affectionate understanding.

Chapter 18

John returned to his house, and as it was still very early, he put the kettle on the gas burner to make some coffee. For him, ones of life's pleasures was breakfast after a long early morning walk, and the time to sit on the porch, and drink coffee with the newspaper in hand, and to survey the view of passing beach walkers, and think over the conversations of the morning. He had many chores to do later, but for now, quiet contemplation and reflection like a thousand scents filled his head. Unlike in Mexico, one had to relish the privilege of relaxation, for there was always something more be to done, and here, there was no help for domestic duties. He had to mow the lawn, take care of some paper work, repair a leaking faucet, and other such duties that come with the benefit of owning a home. These he was pleased to do, as there was some new interest in his life, which kept his mind very preoccupied. He passed the day in this way, in and out of the house, a drive up to the grocery store, frying up some chicken and rice for his dinner, and then once again, he sat out on his porch, in time to watch the sun setting, and rewarding himself with a bottle of ice-cold beer to drink.

It always took some time when one was on holidays, or just returned from a trip to find old acquaintances, or meet new friends; but he had a cousin who still lived locally, and before going out for the evening to the pub at the marina, he would call up his cousin.

They decided to meet at the pub. Yacht clubs were the same all over. If one belonged to one, usually members were welcome anywhere. You walked into one, noticed the trophy case, maybe some pictures, and usually the wooden helm from some old yacht. You made your way past the front reception, and into the lounge, where tanned and glamorous, or scruffy and boisterous boaters sat in groups or alone, enjoying the sunset. This one was no different. He waited patiently, drinking his rum and coke, with lime, and looked around the bar. It was easy to get into a conversation – 'How's the sailing been', or 'Are the fish biting yet?' He sat at up at the bar, making small talk with the bar tender. She was a nice looking woman, slim, attractive, and all smiles.

"Would you mind changing this drink here to a double?" he asked her politely.

His cousin finally arrived, "Good ta see ya, John. Sad news about your mom."

They gave each other a strong embrace, "Ya, good to see you too, Ben."

"How's my nephew Josh?" enquired Ben.

"He's doing great. He's in his sophomore year."

"How about his mother, did she ever remarry?"

"Oh ya, about eight years ago," John said with much pathos, and then added somewhat good- humouredly, "Bitch." The two men spent the evening together and the bar filled up as the sun went down and boaters came in from the bay.

After the bar shut down John wanted to walk the long way home around the beach. He needed to clear his head.

"Ben, it's time to head out," said John getting up and extending a handshake to his cousin.

"Hey cuz', now that you're in town, call me if you need anything, come over for dinner."

"Thanks, Ben. I appreciate the offer. Talk ta ya soon," said John anxious to go.

He walked home along the gravel road. He could hear the distant sound of teenagers laughing and talking, and loud music coming from somewhere echoing across the marsh. He looked up at the clear night sky, the air was still warm, and there was that smell of moss roses, and wet bark. He walked along silently, and out of the blackness from the north came the faint horn blast of the train. 'What was he to do now?' he thought. He knew what he wanted. There was no rush. He was retired, single, his son established at college, and his sister happily married. He deserved to enjoy the rest of his life too. He had served, and he had worked hard. The trip with his mother and sister, brother in law, his nieces and nephew to Hawaii, was his last responsibility toward his family. It was an emotional trip, and in hindsight, the last trip he would have with his mother. Being back in Honolulu was elating; it brought back the memories of his stop-over to Vietnam on his way to the war. This second time there, after so many years, invigorated him, like youth, like being in love, like going off to war again. He loved his nieces and nephew. He needed to be around happy children. And he knew that his mother was ailing. That was hard on him. They cherished their holiday time together. He had no regrets. Everyone had been living their lives to the fullest, in the best possible way they knew how. He lived his life in Texas, flying for the airlines, and on holidays he wanted to spend them somewhere else. His mother understood. She had a good life too, with all her friends, and charities, and her connections with the military.

He took his time walking home in the dark. He could hear a few crickets now, always hushing as he got just within their vicinity. He trudged along, slowing down and even stopping and smiling to himself, 'I wonder if

I'll meet the Sunday School teacher - she was kind'a cute for an old broad. She looked interesting.'

The train had been grinding its way down the tracks toward him but he didn't notice it until it was upon him, over-head on the dyke. It had just chugged its way slowly across the trestle, and now was gaining momentum. It was so loud at present that it smothered his very thoughts; steel upon shrieking steel, and the noise and the blackness crashed up against him, and pummeled his thoughts into nothingness. The engine up front let out another lustful boom on the horn, this time lasting for several seconds. It was deafening, penetrating and all consuming. And then it was gone, like a giant in the night, marching across some miniature landscape, trampling the craggy rock-strewn escarpment as though it were only soft, dry grass.

John flopped himself down of the sofa. He could hear the waves slowly rolling in. It had been a little windy during the afternoon, and as the tide came in, the wind lifted up the crests gently onto the breakwater. His mind was spinning, and his head reeling with emotion. He thought about the various people whom he had met that day. Why Vietnam?

The bar he supposed, resembled something he had visited while in Hawaii on his stop- over to Vietnam; and the recent trip there with his family had brought back the experience. He didn't want to go there in his mind now, but it was cruelty to deny the memory, it wanted life too. His first time in Hawaii was the start of the Vietnam War, but the tropics were a new sensation, like his first sweetheart, his summer love. He didn't know what he was getting himself into; only fear and anticipation mingled in youth. He was a Marine, on his way hurling through space. It must have been the music playing in the bar on this particular evening that brought it to life, a show on the stage. Every time he heard *Touch Me* by The Doors, he was moved by their depth of experience. That song rang in his head for many years. And he was swallowed up with it, just as the train had enveloped him earlier. Vietnam made him grow up in a hurry. It turned him into a man. And when he returned, all he could think about was the glorious array of nubile young women who had no idea of what he had been through; women who would provide him with the necessary distraction that he felt almost certain that he was entitled to - and a man knows the beauty of a woman's touch.

He lay on the sofa remembering... the ship in Honolulu. It was warm and windy that day. The guys filed into the bars in Waikiki like sand running through an hour glass. He downed a few Mai Thais, and then some more, until he didn't remember when night turned to day. He didn't remember getting back to the ship either. But he did.... The alcohol had gotten to him tonight. Perhaps it was the rum, it wasn't his usual drink. Soon the gentle rhythm of the waves outside lulled him to sleep, here and as with there, then as with now.

Sometime later he awoke abruptly, staring at the ceiling, and listening to the pounding waves. Hawaii, no... Nam,

"Where am I?" he called out as he starred straight up toward the invisible black ceiling, his heart thumping hollow in his chest. He awakened from a terrifying dream, a terrifying heinous act. In his dream he was in a helicopter, and he was looking down over what appeared to be the plains of Africa, the Serengeti, where he could see herds of Zebra and antelope running in one direction and then another, charging ahead of the sound of the *helo*. The animals in a stampede would suddenly turn and charge at a ninety degree angle from which they were running, simultaneously, instinctively, communicating only with the pounding of their hooves, and the steaming sides of their muscular, impervious bodies. They would be lost momentarily under the canopy of trees, and then emerge under full power, with dust at their feet. Then, from a semi-arid landscape of browns and blacks, the scene changed to jungle, and the deep colour green which hid the animals, started losing its layered canopy under the invisible spray of Agent Orange. Now instead of Safari animals, it was people who were running, running and scattering, trying to hide from the onslaught of bullet spray from the M16 rifles...*Rat-atat-tat*...the rattle of rain on the roof, like the sound of bullets, kept his dream going. A mere whimper emersed from his throat.

"No, No, Stop!" he was screaming silently in his dream "those are people!"

That was when he awoke. His heart was racing, his breathe shallow. Those were the kinds of dreams he suffered. Those were the souls of the Vietnamese villagers coming back to haunt him. He used to wake up more frequently, when he was married, and young, and he would reach over to find the hand of his wife awaiting his. She would comfort him, and reassure him. 'They forgive you, John,' she would say to him. 'Go back to sleep, I love you.' But he would reach over her realizing she was awake, and he would put his arms around her, his animal inclinations taking over, and he would be lost, lost momentarily. There in her, he would find some solace, and all the worldly sounds would disappear; only color, rainbows and color, bright bursts of color, reds, purples and greens would explode in his inward eye. And the pounding in his chest would subside. When he had exhausted himself into a crumpling mass, he would cry and fall back asleep.

But he suffered. And he was terrified to be alone at night. He tried to work himself into exhaustion during the day, to ensure that, like a child, he would sleep soundly at night. In his college days after the war, it was football; then it was golfing, or running, and work; and then finally, it was the drinking. He had never been back to Vietnam since; but he was there, almost every night, in his dreams. 'It is time,' he thought,' to face my fears. The battle of atonement is with me.'

Mexico was dry and sunny. It rarely rained, and the people there were happy. You couldn't say '*Hola*' without smiling; and it was as far away as he could get to be at peace. But he knew he could not hide out there forever. He raised himself up from the sofa, steadying himself on the back of a chair, the squall had now subsided; and with only the moonbeams to guide him, he climbed the narrow, creaking staircase up to his bedroom that overlooked the whispering, washing sea.

Chapter 19

Elena rounded the bend of her favorite corner, under the arbutus tree, and just before the massive branches of the grand fir extended themselves out over the pathway, harboring eagles so far up that their size was lost, minimized by the back drop of the infinite blue sky above them. This was a great day, a great morning. And it was Saturday. Everyone was out on the beach. She walked along and smiled at people and their children and their dogs. She glanced over at the house where her new acquaintance lived. 'What do you say?' she remarked to herself. There he was mowing his lawn. His head was bent down and he looked determined. She walked up to the fence to get his attention. It was just her way to be friendly. He was coming directly towards her, the wheel of the lawnmower just to one side of the previous tire markings in the grass. He was looking at the ground beneath him, concentrating on maintaining a straight line. The lawn seemed very thick and long as though it hadn't been done in a while, and clumps of grass lay strew across the yard like large animal droppings. But they were a rich, dark green, and they looked wet which suggested that the grass was too wet and long for just one mowing. As John pushed the machine towards her, he must have sensed that someone was watching him, as he spontaneously glanced up. There, in the fire in his eyes, she beheld the tears. He was clearly crying, and the tears were rolling down his cheeks. The tears and the red made his eyes stand out electric blue; she did not look away out of curiosity, though embarrassing it was for her, in her jovial mood, to be intruding on some else's privacy. His look was one of confusion, and she decided not to turn, and run away.

"I am sorry to disturb you," she called politely.
He didn't speak at first; only he looked at her steadily, as one in a trance, not unlike their first meeting where he stared her down in a café.

"John," she started to say again, "excuse me for intruding."
He wiped his eyes with his sleeve, and turning off his lawnmower, he came over to the fence and said,

"Come here for a minute, I want to show you something, do you have a minute?"

"Well, I just wanted to say hello, I'm out for a walk and my husband will probably be waiting for me. What is it? "

"Come inside, I am a bit out of it. I need to sit down. I've been preparing something for you." He wiped his eyes again, and he looked at her, unfaltering. Sweat glistened on his forehead. He waited for an answer.

"Something for me?" she asked surprised.

"Ya, sure. I've been thinking about you. I know how you told me you liked music, the opera and all that. Well, I found some of my old piano books here, my sister and I used to play a bit in the summer. Would you like to hear me play? I've been playing more since I am retired."

"You play the piano," she said to herself. And then she mused, 'How it is that it some people have so much talent, so many attributes, and that they are willing to share, they desire to please. 'I like this kind of person,' she concluded.

"I would love to hear you play. Just one piece though, I can't stay long."

"What makes you think that I would give you more than one?" he said to her dryly.

"Because I could listen all day, if you were good. Music needs to be heard, and those that can play should share their talent, to bring joy to others. If you can play, that is. So, naturally, I would love to hear you play. I am feeling a little awkward that you have been thinking about me, and practicing for me. I am married you know."

He adored looking at her and listening to her prattle. He attributed this nervous verbosity in a woman to the effect which he had on them. However he answered her in an equivocal aside,

"I'm interested in someone else, dummy. I'm just using your good judgment as my sounding board, so to speak." At this remark she felt a little hurt. OK, so she was married, but it was flattering to think that another man was interested in her, romantically. He turned and led the way up the steps two at a time. She followed him into the house, up the broad wooden steps, their footsteps echoing across a wooden porch, and into the old house.

"Humph," she said as she sat down on the large, sagging, chesterfield.

"Have a seat," he said as he pulled out the piano stool and sat down. He adjusted the pages of the book and without a glance back over his shoulder at Elena; he began to play at once.

"Wait a minute, before we begin, what is it?" she interrupted him immediately.

"It's a Chopin piece, the C# minor waltz. Do you know it?"

"I recognized the beginning. I love Chopin," she said wistfully. His music brought her such joy, such pleasure. She listened, not even thinking about the performer, but loving her good fortune, of running into this depraved Texan with admirable, cryptic talents. She had at first found him creepy, and thwarted his advances. But now that she was in her own natural environment, she was no longer afraid. Her spirit soared, truly as those eagles circling above his house. When he finished the piece he turned around on the stool, and still seated and leaning with his broad hands on his legs, he smiled at her, a genuine, soulful, smile.

"Did you like it?" he asked.

"Thank you very much. It was beautiful," she said clapping. And then he stood up, and came towards her slowly.

"Now, just a kiss for me?"

"What do you think I am? I think that you have the wrong impression of me, and my impression of you was right the first time I met you," she argued in response feeling as though her genuine friendliness had been taken advantage of again. "I am truly affronted that you would put me in this awkward situation. Not to seem rude, but I am going to thank you, and refuse."

"Just one little goodbye kiss?" he insisted pointing to his lips and smirking again.

"I have to go, and I am married. I think you are interesting, and maybe could be a friend, but kiss you I cannot," she said tentatively as she pushed herself out of the soft sofa, and rose to go.

"I find you interesting, and attractive. I am attracted to you," he acknowledged.

"Have you ever read any Gandhi?" she asked.

"No, can't say that I have. Why, are you going to protest by not eating? You are already thin enough; doesn't your husband feed you?"

"I am talking about his desisting in feeding his *sexual* appetite. To put it bluntly, he stopped having sex with his wife. But it was not until after he had indulged in his lusty appetite for many years. He was, I think, a self-proclaimed sex maniac. Maybe his wife was happy when he stopped lusting after her. His desire was still there though - right up into his old age. But he thought that sexual activity drained a person of his full potential, and that humans, like animals, should only mate for the purpose of procreation."

As she had gotten up and was making her way to the door, he was right behind her and he grabbed her by the arm, and tried to kiss her cheek from behind. She turned the other way, and moved over to that side.

"Maybe you are easier from this side," he said behind her ear as he tried in vain to kiss her again.

"I am not easy from any side" she replied and turned and faced him. He was over her like a hawk on its prey. She ducked away from him and turned to him incredulously.

"You are a spoiled, selfish man," she said as she recovered herself.

"You need me," he said. "I am like honey. I will stick to you. You will come to me like a fly to honey." And then he added knowingly with a smile, "you'll be back."

With those words, she turned and boldly walked through the old wooden screen door, and forcibly slammed it on the way out, walked out into the sunshine, and dared anyone to mock her or say anything untoward. He called out to her from inside the house: "I don't want to get you in trouble. But if you do get hungry, I'll be here. I'm a good cook. I'd love to make you something to eat some time. Keep it in mind," he called cheerfully, not believing she was angry.

As she left, her heart was pounding. She could have kissed him easily. But that time she got away safely. Of course she felt attracted to him. And it wasn't just his looks. Life had brought them together, and it was there for her if she wanted it. She was perturbed. 'What music though! Think of the music. Think of Chopin in Majorca, composing. The music was uplifting.' These were her thoughts, as she set out down the path in the glorious sun, amidst the beach visitors gathering in front of the ice-cream parlor. She was smiling now, forgetting everything, enjoying the sights, families setting out their blankets, and fathers and little boys and girls learning how to fly kites. 'What is this?' she thought as she studied a familiar figure with a rope in hand, wrapping it around a log close to the tide line.

"Hello George! How are you?" Elena asked the oddity of a man on the beach.

"Great!" he said as he looked up from the log with the end of a rope in his hand. "Good... Good gracious! What a beautiful, marvelous, delicious sort of day. I haven't seen you in long time," he said enthusiastically, pulling on the straps which held up his lederhosen.

"What are you doing George?"

"I'm building a raft."

"Oh," was all she could say to this smiling middle-aged man. He was stout and stogy and resembled a turtle, drooping eyes, a pointed sharp little nose, and a balding head with a ruff of hair left that circled the back of his head from ear to ear.

"How are you doing?" she continued to inquire.

"Not good, really, but really good on account of it. My wife, the bitch, she kicked me out. Just like that. I have nowhere to go, no place to hide. I know she will come looking for me."

"That's too bad, why did she kick you out?"

"She says I drink and smoke too much. She hates the smell of cigars. I took off and went to stay with a friend on the island; she is a pirate friend of mine. She doesn't hassle me. Sorry, sorry, sorry I should be, I stayed away too long. Obviously I came back too soon. She didn't miss me enough."

"But George, you have children. What about your *children*? They need you. Maybe you should stop smoking and drinking and help to look after them."

He looked up at her squinting in the sun and smiling as though she didn't really understand.

"Well, maybe don't give up the drinking; I liked the beer you used to make. But surely you can live it out together until the children are grown up."

"Nope, I'm done with her. I'm manic, and right now I'm up."

"Where are you living then?" was Elena's next question.

The waves lapped gently at the log he was lassoing, and he turned toward it and said:

"I'm going to live on my raft, of course. Could you help me with this please? Just hold the rope here, while I go and get some more logs." And he started to walk towards the water away from her.

"George, I really must be going, I've been gone all morning, and I need to get back. George, you will have to find someone else to help you. Here, I am dropping the rope."

"No don't do that" he called. "Wait, I will tie the end to some rocks!"

"George, I insist, I must be off. I would like to help you, but I can't. Good luck with your expedition," she said and dropped the end of the rope and started for home.

Chapter 20

That was a very unusual morning. Elena did not mention to her husband *all* the details. When he asked her where she had been, she told him the story of meeting German George on the beach. Stanislaw was aware of the village residents in general; everyone seemed to know of everyone else - if you weren't too busy with your own life - and their discussion led to one on the benefits of living in a small village such theirs. A homeless person could not live on a raft in the city. Society and rules would not accept a person of lesser advantages or capacity, or be kind to them, or give them empathy or a chance to blunder and start again. In the big cities, the street people and homeless people are nameless and anonymous. They are ignored; their day is a void, and their nights without form. But here, in this neighborhood, or maybe it is bigger than a neighborhood, if you had a problem in your life, someone would know about it, and there would be help, or at least someone would keep an eye out for you. There were so many little cottages or carriage houses, sheds with heating and a hotplate, where single people on low incomes lived, there was a place for everyone.

The weather was really changing that day; over the past few weeks people kept saying wistfully that summer was truly over; a second bloom on the clematis vine, and a bumper crop of blackberries was pushed into submission by the stronger winds which edged into the area at night, and pushed summer out by morning. In spite of this change, Elena spent the rest of the afternoon preparing for the boat excursion which would take place later on. By the evening of the second weekend in September, the hearts of the people were ready to let go of summer and begin to think of nest making and nut gathering like the many squirrels, or plan to go south like the fleeting ducks, who gathered along the shoreline, vociferous all night long.

Indulge them for a while longer, the rustling reeds seemed to say, "- stay awhile, stay awhile, we're lonely". But that evening on the boat, a blanket was needed for legs and shoulders. The colors of summer swirled past the summer gleaners, four friends, Elena, Stanislaw, Rosie and Roman. The latter were married for 20 years; they moved and spoke like two instruments in an orchestra. She was the lead violin, as she spoke, her long dark hair, with shiny bronze streaks, swayed and jumped in abrupt movements like the bow of her instrument, accentuating her every comment. She had a *button* nose, as some called it, and her eyes, round and large, and changeable as a cats - so people would often ask her, "Where did you get those eyes?" to which she would reply, "China town." And her husband, then, would be stand-up bass. He was a prominent figure, broad shouldered and perfect posture, always handsome, attractive; and his Black Irish hair hung straight down, framing his tanned prominent cheekbones. He was perfectly in tune with his tuxedo, or so it seemed he was always dressed, just right for every occasion.

"I love your shoes, Elena, where did you get them?" Rosie asked Elena looking down at their feet.

"Oh, these I bought in Mexico. They are almost like yours!"

"Mine are made in Spain. We both have the same ribbon, except mine are more like ballet shoes, tied around the ankle. But your skirt has the same ribbon!"

"I made the skirt to match. I bought some ribbon as well when I was in Mexico. The fabric shops there are amazing; I bought yards of ribbon and lace, a seamstress can never have enough!" exclaimed Elena, holding the hem of her skirt and examining the lace. The ladies were never at a loss for conversation, they could talk about shoes anytime.

As the motor took them slowly and smoothly under the train trestle-bridge, and out around the point where the chop from the waves met the serenity of the river, the sudden movement toppled the bread and cheese and sloshed the wine up one side and then the other of the wide bottomed tumblers; the boaters smiled and made merry as though it was their last day ever on the river. What this boat really needed was gimballed glass holders, and so did its crew and passengers. We all needed to be gimballed to help keep us steady on our feet, horizontal, and right side up. We all needed a little and help and kindness from others at some point in our lives, when our lives became rough and chaotic. Security and stability from both sides: two arms, two hands to grasp, the gimballed sides of ourselves supported by others.

Now out of the marina, and after some time on the open bay, they reached their destination in a quiet cove, and with turned-off motor, they drifted about aimlessly, enjoying the freedom. A seal silently pushed its head out of the still water and swam in a line parallel to the boat observing the passengers. A craggy knoll on the side of the cliff waved its bleached silver fronds at the lagoon below, and a misshapen, Garry oak gnawed at the sky, beckoning the winter winds. A kayaker paddled near the shore in the distance.

"How is Stewart doing, since he's gone back to university? Is he still going out with that gorgeous young woman that he took kayaking in the summer?" asked Rosie.

"No, actually he's not. He's doing great at school, and playing Rugby. I can't understand how young people can be in love with someone for a year or two and then suddenly, they are not in love anymore, and a young man, or woman, is lamenting with a broken heart. They date so intensely, and then where they start to differ in their interests, or when they see the other's foibles, they are gone, scared or something. It seems like a waste of time. I don't really understand it, the heart break of it all. I just don't see what good can come out of it. And they may all eventually end up marrying someone, why not just stay with the first person? What is it all about?" The boat rocked gently and peacefully and the two women sat silently for a moment staring out at the water, perhaps remembering a first boyfriend from long ago.

"But that *is* what it is all about. They are finding out what true love really is. They are learning," her friend responded with deepest feeling. "What sort of advice will you give to Clarissa? Are you going to do anything different with her?"

"No, I suppose I will talk to her about all the scenarios, she reads a lot, there are plenty of romance novels to explore – *Jane Austen's* to begin with; to quote my favorite line from *Pride and Prejudice*, Charlotte Lucas says 'Happiness in marriage is entirely a matter of chance...' that part I agree with. But I also firmly believe two must work hard to stay one. Anyway, I don't want to talk to Clarissa about growing up just yet. At what point do you tell a girl that a man may be abusive, or be a womanizer; or have some terrible addiction? We could dwell on the horrors, I am sure the list is endless. Let us talk of love and nature."

"I guess you are right....Look at that!" exclaimed Rosie. A seagull with a purple starfish stuck in its beak had just landed with perfect timing on the bow of the boat.

"What about us," Stanislaw said suddenly joining in the conversation. "We have been together ever since we met."

"I love this story, I was there too," said Rosie.

"I saw Elena from across the room at a banquet, and immediately I fell in love with her. And she walked past me, in that pink gown, and looked at me too, and I spoke to her, my voice urgent and trembling. We have been together ever since, and I love my wife more today than ever."

"– and they met when she was just sixteen – cradle robber," said Roman finishing the story.

"It is what so many would wish for, but some are just not capable of such love. Some can only *imagine* a romantic, beautiful beginning," Stanislaw added poetically.

Elena reached for the wine bottle and filled the glasses. The men were now contemplating the seagull, which had flown off to a floating log, with the starfish still stuck in its beak.

The conversation changed course, as abruptly as a school of minnows, and the discussion of whether to keep drifting or not was interrupted by "Whoa!" and the "Hang on to your drink!" All of a sudden, though not unexpectedly, as all boaters know happens on water, the wind and the sea had changed, and it was getting too rough and too cold to be comfortable.

"I see rain on the horizon, look over there. A squall is coming," the skipper informed everyone as he looked into the distance at the foreboding of a dark cloud on the horizon.

"Let's go back, I'm getting cold anyway," said Elena.

The guests wrapped themselves up together in a blanket, and the skipper pushed the throttle forward, with upturned face looking into the wind, until they were bumping and slapping the waves in the direction of the harbor, the landlubbers among them in secret anticipation.

The hull hit the waves with a whack, and the prop lilted up and down, a gurgling sound as it rose to the surface and a smothering blubber as it sunk back down into the darkening green waters. As they neared the shore, they could see stragglers picking up their belongings and walking along the promenade, and the many on the pier eagerly watching the returning boats, and waving gleefully and spontaneously, as though at marching bands in a May Day parade. It was much calmer as they rounded the jetty at the end of the channel; and they cruised into the mouth of the river, calmly and serenely, at a much reduced speed and sound.

"Hey, what's that?" asked Roman as he noticed a living anachronism at the bend in the river.

"It's Huck Finn!" observed Rosie with a laugh

There, going down the river, close to the far shore, was George, punting his way along the shallow edge of the river, on the raft that he had begun to make that morning.

"Shall we go and see him?" Elena asked her husband. "Do you guys want to go and see if he needs anything?"

"He doesn't need nothin'. Just leave the guy alone. He'll figure it out."

"Who is that?" asked Rosie. As she and her husband were out of town guests, it was impossible to get to know the nuances of the locals.

"It's this guy I know from the beach here. We call him '*German George*'. He used to be the caretaker at the farm, but they fired him. Where are you going to get a caretaker these days? However, he and the landowner had a falling out, and he moved up the hill, back with his wife; but then just recently his wife kicked him out, according to him. It was a *misalliance*; he told me she was an Austrian baroness, or some royal blood from Austria," explained Elena, "and he was a sailor."

"And now he is going to live on a raft?" Rosie asked with a laugh, "Is he crazy?"

"Who knows, he probably won't last long. Someone will take him in; there are a lot of generous people around here. I saw him once with this older woman who walks her dogs down by the marina. She's a Christian, maybe she takes him in."

"Who's that?" asked Stanislaw.

"You know that woman with the two dogs, the one that was shaking her fist at me one day – I was driving a little too fast, and she was walking with her dogs, crossing the street. Remember what a bad feeling I had after that? I felt so guilty, although I wasn't really driving *that* fast. I was day-dreaming. She is really thin. Someone at the church told me her story. She's just recently been widowed; her husband died in a plane crash, he was flying his own plane."

"I don't need her whole life story," Stanislaw said with impatience.

"Wait a minute," Rosie said. "This is interesting."

"Well, *her* story *is* interesting. After her husband died in the crash, she inherited a whole pile of money. We all thought she did not have any children; at least that's what we thought. She teaches Sunday school up here at the Church. I never saw her with anyone else, but not too long ago, after her husband had died, her long lost daughter found her. Apparently, this woman had had a child when she was a teenager, and all was kept quiet and secret, and the baby was put up for adoption. The baby was a girl, and until very recently she was living in Vietnam, teaching English. She decided to find her birth mother; when she finally discovered who her birthmother was, she came here to reconnect with her. It was the Sunday School teacher."

"Who was the father?" asked Rosie "That guy on the raft?"

"We're turning in here. It's getting too dark. Roman, flip the bumpers down, will ya, thanks," said Stanislaw as he focused on the boathouse, escaping the conversation.

"Someone said it was some draft dodger from the States," replied Elena her voice trailing off.

"How old is that guy on the raft?" asked Roman.

"He's in his forties. I said *draft* dodger, not *raft*. Anyway, this guy on the raft is a raft dodger, meaning he makes his escape by jumping on rafts and sailing away. It happened at least once before to my knowledge when he ran away to one of the islands and lived with a female pirate, - that's what he told me anyway. Should we go and talk to him before we tie up?"

"He'll be fine. He'll sleep there over night, and then go back home," Stanislaw reassured everyone in his pragmatic way.

"As soon as the rain starts he'll go back home. It would be OK living on a raft in the summer," put in Roman pensively.

"Have you thought about it before?" asked his wife in disbelief.

"Ya, haven't we all?"

They pulled into the boat shed, and finished off the night listening to the sounds of the wharf creaking with the incoming tide, and the ominous clacking of the shrouds slapping and clanging against the metal masts of the moored sailboats.

Chapter 21

The weekend was over, and today was another glorious September morning. Elena walked Clarissa to school. There was a certain nostalgia about Septembers, a feeling of childhood returning, when all the children holding hands, skipped to school, and the chestnuts made toys and science projects, and a certain remembering of friends that prompts one to go out and be spontaneous, to visit people, and if one is lucky, to be invited to lunch - perhaps with the Mayor. One would accept such an invitation of course. However on this day, it was up to Elena to pay her visits unannounced. She had errands to complete; that was true, but without a social purpose in the making, the errands seemed unimportant, even not worth doing at all. She was acquainted with a certain Mr. Locke whom she had met years ago. She thought about visiting him, but decided to wait until after 3:00 when she took her daughter to ballet, it would seem more natural then, for her to drop in and visit. He had moved his law offices from the city to the suburbs, which now, as with London, was becoming one large land mass of people connected and separated by freeways and main roads, whose names bear the connection to the Empire – King Edward Highway, and Queensway, and by the many rivers, (five in all), and bridges, inlets, and numerous interurban transit lines. In all, the traffic going and coming around the urban landscape was often described as "snarled". But it wasn't as pretty as London, it was lacking the architecture of the curving streets with elegant brick and stone townhouses topped with pointed tile gables and iced with thick, white, 'Royal Icing' fascia boards. But what one did not see in the architecture one could see in the beauty of the mountains surrounding what was once considered a village on the edge of a rainforest. The mountains change their elevation by day, when once they may be diminished in height by an onslaught of altostratus clouds, and another day erupting far above the horizon as a frozen skating rink reflecting the dim morning sun. Elena chose to imbibe the landscape. Others chose to move their work, or their homes to be closer to either one. The spot chosen by Mr. Locke for his office had easy access to the freeway, but was only six minutes by car from his home, down a road cut straight through the forest.

She entered the office, which was next to a dance studio in a newly constructed warehouse. The outside of the building was a made of aluminum siding painted white, with small black glass door entrances which gave one the impression that there was really nothing inside. She opened the door gingerly. There was nothing on the inside except for more blank white walls which zigzagged to another door. She stopped to read the emergency escape route map on the wall looking for an indication of room numbers or names. There were many little stick men on the map, all running. She didn't feel the need to run; there was no panic in her demeanor, or anxiousness. This was merely a spontaneous visit to a person of mutual acquaintance to her father. He was interesting, being a criminal lawyer – and successful as well, judging by his large home in the forest, a full time gardener, several cars, his small private airplane, winter home down south, and his new office building; there were plenty of criminals around to keep him in business. Elena followed the chamber walls to another door, and pulled it open.

A desk greeted her, but no one was behind it. There was mail piled up on the already overcrowded counter top. She noticed the business card holder, and indeed there was one for her friend "Edwin Locke, Criminal Lawyer". She searched around the desk for a clue to his whereabouts, and then her eye beheld a bell. Oh how she loved to ring those bells. "Ding," went the half dome of silver. It sounded so nice she rang it again.
Around the corner appeared the white-haired, squatty, short man, with a wide grin and moustache.

"Elena! How nice to see you," he said, always in the same genuine, surprised sounding voice. "It has been so long since your father and I have spoken, I was just thinking about him." Elena directed her glance over the top of the counter to where the voice was coming from.

"Mr. Locke, I am glad you are here. I had seen the sign from across the highway, and thought I must come in and say hello."

"Please, come this way, I'll show you around," he said without hesitation, and turned on his heels, swung his arms around happily, and proceeded up the brand new wooden staircase. It was at one end of the warehouse, and it led up to a floating hallway, or balcony hall, which connected the upper offices together. It was open to the floor below, and the sun radiated in through the windows high above the ground on the outside wall. The ceiling was flat, but there hung light fixtures on long black wires, which brought some dimension to wide open space above them.

"Here is the bathroom," he said proudly, "Have a look in there." Elena opened the door and looked into a tiny 'water closet' and noticed a toilet like any other. There were two rolls of toilet paper on the back of the toilet.

'Hmm,' thought Elena, 'It must not be quite finished yet.' There was barely enough room to go all the way inside, so she came part way out intending on finishing her inspection of the bathroom from the hallway.

"Look up," he said.

She looked up, and there it was, the pièce de résistance. Elena beheld a lowered ceiling made out of frosted glass to allow light in from above, but also to create an ambiance of privacy.

"I designed it myself," said the exuberant Mr. Locke assuredly.

"It's really nice. Great idea; I like the frosted glass."

"Come this way. These are all the offices. And have a look down there." He stopped and pointed to the desks down below, both occupied by secretaries who glanced up.

"Do you notice the windows?" he continued eagerly. "We had those garage doors converted into windows which we can open on a nice day."

"Very New York," Elena remarked.

"Yes, it is, isn't it? Very New York." He hadn't really thought about it before, and maybe it wasn't the intention when he designed his offices, but it sounded very cosmopolitan. How should he know anyway? He had never been to New York. They proceeded down the back stairs, while he pointed out various rooms and their uses. "This is our library; that is another office," he said pointing. "He - is an architect, and rents from me. And here..." at this moment he paused and held out his arm with palm up, "Elena, *this* is my office." Mr. Locke stood aside and with a sweeping gesture of both his arms as though he was about to burst into an aria, motioned toward the glass wall and doors to allow his guest to proceed ahead of him. "I was just going over a case. Do you know what *sodomy* is, Elena?" he asked almost mockingly. She did not reply, only shook her head so as not to engage him in discussion. "Well, the world is full of kooks, and it's my job to sort it all out; you know these guys, the psychopaths, murderers, red-necks, this guy he's a real bad one, I can't disclose any details, but the whole thing is so twisted, so gruesome, you can't imagine; the bestiality, the fraud, the deceit, and what's worse, is these guys seem like everyday people. Now what can I do for you? What brought you here to see me today? To what do I owe the pleasure, and it is always such a pleasure."

"I wanted to ask you a few questions about Wills and Estates – free legal advice."

"Free legal advice? Is there any other kind? I don't mind, but I'm not really the one to ask. But I can recommend someone to you."

He never really concentrated on what she had to say, always jumping to the next topic. He started to shuffle a few papers around and open a little day planner as though he was doing two or three jobs at once. The desk was piled with various papers and books, interesting knick knacks and other tell tale oddities of the legal profession. He now clasped his hands on his lap without speaking, and surveyed his guest over the piles of paper with obvious pleasure. He was not more than five feet tall, and looked as small as a schoolboy sliding down in his desk, save the salient, thick black moustache above the ever present, ever grinning mouth. Elena wondered why he always seemed happy. The heavy dark stained oak desk that stretched nearly the whole length of his office, was long enough to seat four chairs on one side – for his clients. Or were they for his own woes, whereby one by one he hears each case, assesses, decides, and then files away, case closed. Who might be seated where Elena was now - a whole family perhaps; a distraught, frantic woman over fifty, flicking her long curls away from her face in an agitated manner, and her brother, tattooed on his shoulders, wearing a black singlet; a father-in-law, his skin dripping down over his jaw bone; and a daughter, ready to shriek her accusations. They all leaned forward and cursed like a torrent, the 'dirty bastard' (and more), had absconded with their money, they'd been fleeced; and how his lust led to bestiality and perversions – how one night, on a dark country road, leaping from his truck to scrutinize the dead animal he had just struck, his wife tried to run him over.

"Tell me now, Elena, how *are* you doing?" he asked once he had seated himself comfortably in the leather chair. He stared with pupils dilated through his black, heavy rimmed glasses at her, like an owl at a vole before it is eaten. "It is so nice to see you! I would like to see more of you – but you are fully dressed."

"Mr. Locke, am I supposed to act flattered?"

"But it is true Elena; I would like to see more of you."

"I am sure you say that to all the women - I thought that I was special."

"You are special Elena, and if I could have you all, you would be first, at the front of the line, and then there would be your friend Melody, and the rest down the line. Would you marry me Elena?"

"So you are still not married then?"

"I am very close. But I can't make up my mind. I'm serious, what do you say?"

"I'm married, maybe in twenty years."

"Elena, I can't wait that long."

That is not what she wanted to hear. If he were truly in love with her, he would say at least, 'I will wait for you forever'.

"Besides", he continued "I am dating three women at once. Of course they don't know this. A man can walk into any bar, Elena, and meet a lady. But back to the three, of these, there is one that I am particularly interested in – a very nice lady. She teaches Sunday school. You know women, give them a little freedom and who knows where they might go. I want someone a little more subservient - traditional."

"Submissiveness doesn't rule out promiscuity, you know. In fact, I think that a submissive behavior when observed by another man, is more likely to evoke a certain pathos in the observer; which might lead him to entice someone else's wife into some sort of infidelity – like an heroic effort to set a woman free."

"You are aiming this at me, but you have missed the mark. My wife *was* stolen from me, I grant you that. But not because I kept her in shackles – she was free to do as she pleased."

"Mr. Locke, I am sorry to insinuate anything by my comment. I really came to say hello. And here is your picture," she said changing the subject and looking at the wall with documents and degrees lined up. "You look just exactly the same now as you did back then, except that you wore your hair a little longer; it was thicker then."

"You recognized me? Most people say: *That's you*?" he said as he felt his balding head.

"Of course, you look exactly the same," replied Elena, although she didn't remember how big and green his eyes were back then. 'The eyes don't ever change; he definitely looks more subtle and cultivated now - more defined', she thought.

"What does "LSP" stand for?" she asked as she read the initials under his class photo.

"Class president. I was president of the Law Student's Society." 'Good for him,' she thought.

"So Elena," he continued, "tell me how your family is doing? How is your husband, Bert, isn't it? It still troubles me that you don't consider him your friend. I remember you telling me that a long time ago. I have always felt that one's spouse should be one's best friend."

"His name is Stan. I define spouse and friend as two different things. A husband means something very different than a friend, and *they*, meaning spouses, cannot be both."

"I find that very troublesome," said Locke folding his hands in his lap again.

"I have many friends, and I spend a lot of time with my friends; but one gets sick of friends after a while, and there is a time where I just want to be with my husband. I have to leave a friend for a while; if my husband were my friend, I'd have to leave him constantly, and I don't want to do that." Mr. Locke started to laugh, "You really have a strange way of looking at things," he retorted to her argument; but he didn't seek any further explanation. Elena knew that he would ponder that comment for a while, be troubled by it, and then bring it up at a much later date.

"How is your friend, the lawyer that I met, *Doris was it*?"

"I think you mean *Rosie*. And she *is* married. She is very busy with Native land claims. Have you done some work for the First Nations People? I notice that you have a carved mask there."

"Yes, a client gave that to me."

"It is beautiful. What does it represent?"

"Actually I don't know, to tell you the truth, but they were worn for ceremonial purposes, I know that much."

"Sort of like the wigs and gowns judges and lawyers wear? Do you wear a wig, Mr. Locke?"

"Call me Eddie, please, and I will wear a wig if you would like me to – or you could wear a mask," he said grinning.

"Mr. Locke, the innuendo is far over my head. Why do Judges and Lawyers wear wigs and robes?"

"Oh, Elena, I am so glad you asked. Like the Indian's mask, the wig or robe represents some *aspect* of society, *not* the individual. There are many ideas about the robe, but generally it represents *society* too, and the values or morals established; it's a pure metaphor for that which we come to understand through tradition and history. The wigs, or robe, must represent the 'law', and not the individual making a judgment on the criminal." Mr. Locke leaned back in his chair and put his hands up behind his head with his elbows out to the side. And then he looked at his watch. He was done with his edifying.

"Well," he started again after the silence of a moment, "it has been so nice to see you, Elena." She read the social cue. It was time to go; now he was starting to get fussy with the papers piled around his desk again.

"Yes, it has been nice to see you, too," Elena said obligingly. They both got up at once and walked down the hall to the door. "Good-bye."

"Goodbye Elena," he said as he leaned over as if to give her a kiss on her cheek, "Now one for me," he beckoned. "Come on, just one, right here," and he pointed his index finger to his cheek. And then, as if to suggest he was on the verge of a tantrum, in an ingenuous manner he pleaded, "*Please*, I won't let you go 'til I get one!" He closed his eyes and waited. Elena leaned forward, and with her feet not too close to his, she tapped him on his cheek with the end of her rabbit-foot key chain.

"Thank you Elena," he said opening his eyes and smiling, "and have a good day." And with that, fully satisfied, he ceremoniously spun around on the heels of his shiny black oxfords, and strutted down the hall with her good-byes echoing around in his head.

"Good-bye," he sang out without looking back, "good-bye!" Relieved to finally be over with this disenchanting meeting, Elena opened the door and entered into the bright sunshine. She did not get the information that she came for, and now he was 'OFF' her list of friends. "Off with his head," she shouted out in the car, "you are OFF of my list!"

Chapter 22

There was always a rush in September to fulfill every summer dream and desire, each sunny day seemed as though it were the last. One never could tell. When there was a last final fling of summer, a hot spell followed by clear nights that sang themselves into a lullaby; was it any wonder that all were jolly and wont to burst into song? This evening for sure had to be spent on the boat- surrounded by purling conversation, voices lost in the lapping of waves against the hull, a gentle rocking one off to winter's retreat. There was little time to prepare a real fall feast, but Elena and Stanislaw merrily gathered up a variety of cheeses: smoked apple wood cheddar, Weneslydale with apricots, and Dubliner white cheddar, a firm cream colored cheese from Ireland - to represent the literary; some fresh purple grapes, crunchy and sweet, baguettes sliced on the diagonal, and other condiments including olives and a fig spread, thrown into a bowl, and nestled securely into the picnic basket. It would be enough. To drink was a bottle of red wine from Spain. It is said one should always eat a little something when one is drinking wine. Anything, just something to enhance the taste of the wine – the enzymes must mix.

"Elena, you must bring beer, besides the wine. I've just heard from Wilson, a client of mine, and he is going to join us. That makes seven of us, am I right?"

"Who is Wilson?" asked Elena.

"I've told you about him before. He's the orthopedic surgeon, one of my investment clients. Remember? He built the new house on the beach front. His wife died a few years ago? I told him I would like to take him out for a cruise, he's a good guy, and he's an opera fan, I think you'll like him."

"I better bring some opera music then," she said, "and what does he like to drink?" Just to be sure there was something for all tastes, more beer was added to the drink basket, and also a bottle of rum for the latent pirates aboard.

Later on, the guests assembled on the dock, when all was ready, they handed the cumbersome baskets to the skipper, and stretched their legs from the dock, up and over the side of the boat. Immediately after the engine revved, two men, Harry and Michael, sitting in the rear seats of the cockpit, began to sing loudly above the noise, "My Bonnie lies over the ocean, my Bonnie lies over the sea! My Bonnie lies over the ocean, now bring back my Bonnie to me….bring back, bring back! Bring back my bonnie to me!"

Wilson, whose dark visage portrayed a more staid nature, sat next to the skipper and observed the crew. Both Michael and Harry loved to sing. Michael was a devotee of folk music, both Scottish and American, playing the guitar and singing at small local gatherings. The tune and words however, this evening, were lost and mingled with the motor and its wake; but the exuberance still showed on their faces. The women sat up alert, and noticed the scenery, the other boats, the railway trestle and the distant glaciers, which did not seem cold as they were, nestled into the purple grooves of the mountaintops far in the distance.

The happy septet passed the half hour journey enjoyably as they made their way to the destination, just beyond the boundary marker, and in full view of Mt. Baker, the gallant volcano, ever present and ever patient, waiting for its time again. Once in the bay, past the houses, the wharf, and other traces of civilization, the skipper cut the engine and they were left to drift aimlessly, to bob on the waves.

"I'm starving; can we put the food out?" asked Elena hopefully.

"In a minute, just wait 'til I open the wine," said Stanislaw. He was a cogent sort, and she being his wife, had to be forbearing, especially since they were on a boat - with no escape. When he uncorked the wine and filled the glasses, Elena turned on the magnificent music of Gaetano Donizetti, and let play a duet from the opera *Gabriella di Vergy*. Only this could encapsulate and celebrate the end of the summer season. The music was audio fireworks, like a volcano erupting with the voices of ashes and steam, and carried across the rippling waves. For a moment all eyes were on the distant peak.

"Do tell us one your stories, Elena. Whatever happened to the wedding dress?" urged Harry, who delighted in pert and obtrusive personalities and their predicaments.

Before she got started, an airplane flew overhead, as they did, one every ten minutes. Wilson commented remittent, and interrupted the conversation whenever one went overhead.

"See, there it goes again, another plane," said Wilson as he looked up, squinting and frowning. Elena's friend Valencia, the mayor, was always accommodating in a controversial situation, reached over and put her hand on his knee and said:

"We are looking into that Wilson; in fact we have a council meeting about it on Monday night." She was diplomatic and genuinely concerned. All parties had to be considered.

"We pay our taxes, why must we be inconvenienced so that the airline companies can save fuel by taking a shorter route over our neighborhood.

And my health is being jeopardized. I am constantly woken from sleep, and the noise is so incessant during the day, it makes me crazy," Wilson argued.

"I love the sound of the planes coming over," said Elena. "Seeing the planes make me think of all the people traveling, coming and going. Just think of all the refugees finding freedom in our country; and of all the adventures!"

"You are a contrarian, Elena, could you not agree for once that someone else may be right?" asked Michael, dismissing her and sounding bored with her conversation. He was the husband of the mayor and had heard every issue that had come up in council. "Valencia, I'd love hear more of what you think. You are closer to the problem than we are, although I too am bothered by the planes."

"No, I wouldn't want air traffic to completely stop, of course. I love to travel just as much as the next person. Every country we travel to must endure some sort of disruption in the people's lives. I am sure they are countless. If the flight pattern is changed here, it will only affect someone else in another neighborhood. Besides, it's because of airport expansion that we need more airspace, and that the flight paths have been changed to accommodate the more flights coming and going," said the mayor. "In politics it is always about the same thing. The planes come in lower now to save money."

"Yes, that is true," said someone else, "but they don't need to fly so low, and put on their brakes."

"Brakes, planes have brakes?" asked Elena trying to make a mockery of the conversation, "but what do I know, I'm just a seamstress." Elena didn't realize that planes had brakes.

"Elena, planes gear down, and they change elevation by adjusting their wings, it's more complicated than just brakes," explained Wilson, his mood slightly inflamed from his lack of sleep. "It is more than just braking. The noise is unbearable and irrational. I paid top price for my property, and maximized my square footage when I built my house, so I could have privacy. I pay more taxes than anyone I know, and I can't even have friends over for a drink on the deck without this constant interruption."

"Do you like to travel, Wilson?" asked Elena.

"No I don't as a matter of fact. Travel is vulgar. No one really needs to travel. I don't anyway, I have all that I need right here. And I especially wouldn't fly if I knew that it was infringing on other's rights to quiet and their environmental health."

"So you think it is just a matter of people respecting others? Do you not agree that our world is changing and that air travel is increasing and we're becoming more dependent on it?" asked Elena again, to everyone there.

"There is a solution," said the mayor, "and we are working on it. We still have meetings with the air traffic controllers and the airline companies."

"So it is merely about the airlines saving money, do you think?" asked Elena again, "and not about the increased traffic, and a pilot cueing system?"

"It's got 'ta be about a lot of different factors, I bet wind has something to do with it," said Stanislaw who was familiar with wind and tides and their effect on boats in particular.

"And what about turbulence, I don't know anything about flying, but does the changing weather conditions, and turbulence have anything to with the way a pilot adjusts his approach path, or landing path?" persisted Elena. "Does a pilot operate merely on the wishes of the company to save *them* money?"

"You talk like you know the answer. I bet you have been woken up in the night before and cursed the planes," said Wilson still very irritable.

"No I haven't."

"Yes you have, we all have," said Wilson, "Don't deny it."

That noise, and other changes seemed to bother a lot of people; just as did the fact there were more people visiting the beach every summer. Local politics had the same issues - and a '*Not in my backyard*' policy prevailed. Some new residents to the beach did not respect the style of the existing homes and they built larger homes that rose above the flood plain and cast a shadow on the smaller cottages. And what really bothered a very few, if not only just one, were the people who infringed on government property by putting large stones along the city property line and along the road in front of their house so that no one could park or walk close to their property. Now *that* was a criminal offense of enclosure of public domain and creating a hazard. All else was just a matter of personal opinion. People were bound up in their own conservatism and could not adapt – where was Darwinian Theory? Where was Socratic morality and discourse?

"Come on Elena; let's hear one of your stories," insisted Harry tired of politics, "How about the *dis*-closure of the clothes in the garment bag?"

"OK, it's complicated and goes way back, but it involves some of the very people in our neighbourhood who had the minor infraction of 'building up' some years ago.
It was about ten years ago now, and it's mostly forgotten, but a certain acquaintance asked me one day if I could do a small favour for her. She happened upon me on the beach one morning as she and her husband were just getting ready to leave on a three year trip to Dubai. For tax purposes

they had to stay out of the country the whole time, and she asked me if I could possibly store her wedding dress for her, look after it while she was away. It was the one article of clothing she could not bear to part with. I felt quite honored by this request. 'Clarissa won't be needing her closet space will she, not for a few years yet?' she asked me. 'It's only a two by two garment bag, and it can just hang there in your closet.' I imagined a beautiful wedding dress, all poufy and frilly, with layers of lace over satin and tulle, and neatly sealed in a garment bag for such a time down the road when a daughter may want to use it.

'I guess that would be o.k.' I said to her thinking quickly. 'You are leaving in a few days?' I asked.

Then she said, 'Yes, we are leaving in three days; I'll bring it over'.

A few days passed and I never heard from her, until the night before they were to leave, late, just after 10:00, there was a knock at the front door. It wasn't very loud. It was as though the knocker was hoping that no one would hear the sound, and then they could leave unnoticed and relieved. I did hear the knock though, and it was a neighbour from around the corner who was friends with …I'll call her *Petunia*; I don't really want to say who she is. 'I have something for you from Petunia,' the neighbour told me.

'Oh! Is it the wedding dress?'

'I don't know about that,' he replied looking behind him into the dark, 'it's a garment bag.' He was a strong, middle aged man- an Olympian even!

'OK, bring it in. I was expecting it.' He went out to the van and came back in with the help of Petunia's husband carrying what appeared to be an extremely heavy, lumpy garment bag. It was over six feet long and resembled a *body* bag. Both men were looking very sheepish, and I said in a surprised voice, 'Goodness! What's that? I can't carry that!'

'Where do you want us to put it?' asked the friend.

'Take it upstairs, I suppose. It is supposed to go in the closet.'

Petunia's husband never said a word. It is hard to remember that he was actually there. The two men struggled with the weight as they carried the bag upstairs, lay it down on the bedroom floor, and left in a hurry, rushing down the stairs and out the door without even waiting for me to let them out.

    Curious about the wedding dress, I opened the bag only to find it was crammed full of woolens and basketball jackets, and kilts, and mohair sweaters, turtlenecks and capes, long woolen scarves, and a child's wool overcoat. There was also what I took to be the wedding dress. In the bag, laying flat against one side, was a wispy, fine lace dress - flimsy, very plain, and with sheer long sleeves and a high lace collar. I was very disappointed in the dress."

"It was a '*Yofi*' dress," added Nancy, the first of the guests to interject with a comment.

"Yes, Nancy can tell you all the details that I forget," said Elena

"And a Hudson's bay jacket was in there too," she added.

"That's right, the famous replica jackets of the early fur traders – boiled wool," admitted Elena. "I didn't know what to do with all of that clothing. A few days later I decided to pack it all into boxes with mothballs, except for the dress, and return it to her house. Someone was renting the house, so I told them to take the boxes back, and find a place for them for the three years. A few months later I wrote Petunia a Christmas card and sent it to the family in Dubai. I wrote:

Dear Petunia,
I hope you and your family are having a great adventure in Dubai, and that all is well with you. We are all doing well here. I have a bit of bad news to tell you though. Over the holidays we were broken into. Interestingly enough, all that was taken from our house were the woolens from our closet, all your kilts and sweaters etc. were stolen. The thieves left your wedding dress here, thankfully. I am sorry to tell this to you.
Happy New Year to you all and good luck in Dubai.

I never heard a thing back from her, and it's been over five years since they returned."

"Who has the dress now Elena?" asked Wilson, who sat and listened intently to the whole story.

"I do," said Harry, "I dress up in it all the time."

"Was that the right thing to do, Elena? I mean, couldn't you have just told her the truth? A real friend would not do that, would they?" said Wilson.

"I guess I'm vindictive. We've all done something like that before haven't we? It was just a practical joke." Elena asked the group. "I didn't mean any harm by it. I'm trying to be a good person; now, of course, I would have just sent the bag back with her husband and helper that very night."

"Elena, you should have told the guys right then and there to store to their own bag of clothes, you need to stand up for yourself," Stan said. Valencia reached over to offer more wine to comfort Elena. However, at that moment, in a moment of silence, a sudden wave dashed the side of the boat sending wine like a rainbow everywhere. There were growls and gnashing of teeth, especially from Wilson who was seemingly out of sorts. Everyone lunged forward with serviettes and towels to mop up the exuberance.

"Is there a head on board, Stan?" asked Wilson politely exhibiting his nautical vocabulary.

"It's not working," Stanislaw answered.

"What do you mean?" inquired Elena surprised.

"We haven't got it hooked up yet. You have to go off the back end," explained Stanislaw.

"I can't do that. I'm not comfortable doing that," said Wilson tersely.

"Tinkle, tinkle, tinkle," whispered somebody.

"We won't look Wilson. We'll all look the other way," was an encouraging voice. "No I can't possibly, but I really have to go," came Wilson's urgent voice from the top of his throat.

"Here, use this then," laughed Harry as he offered up his wine cup.

"We'll all go down inside the cabin and shut the door," said Stanislaw. "Come on everyone - down inside."

"Man the capstan! Blood and thunder!" Elena sang out quoting Captain Peleg from *Moby Dick*. The six proceeded, one by one, ducking their heads as they went below, rocking side to side in the waves, and trying not to bump into one another. Once inside, Stanislaw pulled the door shut. "Careful of your wine," he cautioned, as there was another near mishap. And then he added emphatically, "*That's* why I tell you never to use glass on boats. Swells unexpectedly knock things out of your hands."

"But these are plastic. We're not using glass," retorted Elena.

"I'm just reinforcing it," Stanislaw said in finality.

"Oh!! Awaaa!!!" A cry for help came from outside. The crew heard a splash.

"Was that Wilson?" Henry asked. Wilson had fallen off the bow of the boat while relieving himself. Everyone scrambled out of the hatch and clambered through the cockpit to his rescue, with arms reaching overboard and voices yelling in all directions.

"Wilson, don't panic," hollered Stanislaw, and threw him the orange life ring. Someone should have warned him too about rogue waves.

Chapter 23

Summer holidays were officially over. It was strange going back into the Dojo. Here was another world; this was where one talked to one's body. 'This strike can kill someone,' she remembered the gentle and ingratiating voice of the old Sensei say, half way between a purr and the growl of a tiger training its cubs. No one dared to move or speak, "Could my hand actually do this? I pray I never have to test it out" – you could almost hear the thoughts of the younger students. The members bowed down briefly as they entered the *dojo*. The Sensei, also sensitive to the student's feelings, could read what most tried to conceal. He had the ability and confidence to be a leader, and he needed to show utmost calm and confidence in order for his students to fully trust him. His demonstrations of a strike came within millimeters of their target - you could feel the space between a fist and your nose like the puff of a bumble bee's breath.

"Come in, everybody line up!" he called out brusquely. He surveyed the group like a bull dog eyeing a cat creeping across the top of a fence. And to the new student, a bulky athletic man of over fifty, he said quietly,

"Just stand in line there, beside the white belt, follow along, and don't worry, you'll catch on."

The lesson began in the traditional way with the Dojo creed – 'Seek perfection of character; endeavor; respect others; refrain from violent behavior'; and so on. If only for the discipline, self-awareness, and physical training, the karate dojo was worthwhile. But it was so much more. It tried one's spirit and made one look at oneself – one had to face challenges that were both physical and mental. One thought about all sorts of things under the duress of the demanding and intense training. One had to tell oneself – "seek perfection of character," and "endeavor," as those two phrases alone helped justify the burning sensation in ones thighs during a prolonged 'horse stance' , or in one's abdomen while prone supported on elbows and toes six inches above the floor, all the while grimacing, sweat pouring form pore you never knew you had, and the Sensei counting, s-l-o-w-l-y in Japanese: "*Hichi, hutchi, ku ju*, and rest…..again….*HAI!….ichi, ni, san.*"

"Remember, when in a fight somewhere, you won't be able to stop and say…my stomach hurts, I need to stop," he said encouraging everyone. The students were thinking – 'I hope I never have to face an opponent.'

"Today we are just going to work on basics," he began. "Form two lines. Face each other. Attacking side, you are going to get your distance for *'yakazuki'* to your opponents chin, stepping forward. Defending side, you are going to step forty-five degrees to the side with a rising block and then *yakazuki* under their arm in the ribs. Remember, no contact, you want to just come within striking distance. Watch me demonstrate. Nick, can you step out here. Everybody else move around so you can see."

His instructions were clear and simple, with no time for questions from his students. What wasn't clear at the start would become evident soon enough. He stepped toward the mirrored wall, and set up a student as his opponent.

"I want to stress here the reason for stepping aside at forty-five degrees. You see, if I step straight back and block when he comes in, I am opening myself up, and he can move forward faster than I can move away backward, and I can't reach him for a strike if I move back. But if I move away at an angle, see how I can block the punch, and still be close enough to strike my opponent under the ribs? Good Nick, thanks, now do five each side, everybody, left foot forward, *gedambarai*. *Hai!*"

The class moved in unison. "Don't forget to kee-ai," shouted the Sensei. The room suddenly felt large and noisy with the sound of 'kee-ais' and shuffling of feet.

When it was all over, the students waited and thanked the Sensei. Each one wanted to get his attention individually. It was important to establish respect and appreciation for the Sensei, and show no fear – it built trust.

A white belt, a short and stanch, fully muscular clean-faced man was the other new member to the club. Although he was only a white belt, it was evident that he had had some other formal martial arts training. His *'kee-ais'* were more like deep black bear grunts, save for his boyish face, he had the appearance of a flat faced bear. The younger members tried to imitate him, causing much smirking and restrained explosion of laughter. The thirteen-year-old twins were only a few inches shorter than the bear, but they could be twisted and flipped aside like a twig in the forest being dismissed by a heavy furry paw. He was seriousness, and it wasn't until the end of class when all the students were running for their shoes, that Elena gave him what he most wanted – a question about himself.

"You've trained before, haven't you?" she asked him as he bent down to pick up his shoes. He was happy to discuss with anyone his extensive background in the military that included basic 'man-to-man' combative moves, combined with a series of varying martial arts including judo.

"I was in the service for ten years and we did a different form of *karate*, there are so many different styles. Do you know the Brazilian *Banderos*?"

"Yes I've seen it," she replied. "It is very different."

"It's really interesting; I did that for a few years."

It was more than she was really interested in hearing at the moment. Everyone was shuffling around, trying to get dressed, and he seemed to be intent on telling her everything all at once. Some people don't read social cues very well, and don't know when a shorter more concise answer would be appropriate. It is like a child retelling the whole story, or relaying the whole movie instead of just summarizing the plot. 'Give the listener a break.' She thought. 'And if they press you for more, *then* elaborate, stay out all night, go for a drink!'

"I just finished my time in the reserves," he continued.

"Lucky for you," Elena said. "I mean, I think it would be lucky not to be called up to fight now."

"You're quite right," he said. "Now it's a different thing. The Taliban are indiscriminate in their actions and killing. They kill everyone, not just military personnel. And you never know who they are. A friend of mine in the reserves is in Korea, and there they know just exactly what the North Koreans are up to. They can watch them. In the Middle East, it is different." The last of the class were shuffling out. She overheard the new-comer speaking to the Sensei now.

"I have these knee problems, and I don't know if I can continue in this. Some of the exercises I just can't do."

"Don't worry," the Sensei replied. "We all have our health problems. Like I've had a broken hip, and I have problems with my shoulder. You learn to work around it."

She could tell the first night did not impress the expert. It wasn't like *her* first year. She had to leave now. There would be more opportunity to talk later if the ex-soldier returned.

On returning home, Elena needed to get out into the fresh air. It was only the second day of fall; as with summer comes the sun, with fall comes the harvest moon. She walked down to the end of the road and turned the corner toward the dyke. The blue mist purred across the open field. Something was in this fall air. Her senses were sharpened. The full moon was higher and much brighter now illuminating the path. The air was filled with mist, she could not see it in front of her, but when she looked across the field in the direction she was going, it was there, thick and blue, waiting, empty but full. The air was empty but full. She walked in emptiness into fullness, but when she arrived the thickness was gone. 'How strange to see, and then not to see it when you were in it,' she thought. The voices of crickets started up as she stood for several moments listening to the night. 'Why was the sensei in my dream?' she thought, thinking about the Sensei and remembering her dream…'there were wolves, hungry wolves ready to tear me apart, and yet I am not afraid of wolves, at least I don't think so. I am not afraid of coyotes either, or am I?' She really was testing herself out there, alone on the dyke, alone on the dark path, where one could disappear into a mist and no-one could see you, no-one would know. She moved along the path more quickly, and again hearing the crickets at once behind her, and also ahead of her, but never with her. No one was around. She was all alone, yet surrounded, making her way in the darkness, following her shadow along the moonlit path. "*Du kannst nicht uber deinen einigen shatten springen,*" she said to herself, in German - 'one can't jump over one's own shadow' - you can't escape who you are,

the crickets kept reminding her. Elena really was a bit scared now, the more she tried to relax, the more frightened she became. But afraid of what? She decided it was time to turn back.

Chapter 24

The weekends now were generally devoted to Clarissa. Although Elena was always thinking, always active, she did not neglect her parenting duties, which still included walks in nature although the weather was impetuous at times.

"Look at the carvings in this rock, Clarissa, What do you think of that?" asked Elena pointing to the unusually large rock more than three feet high and four feet across. "A thought just occurred to me," she continued as she gazed at the impression in the petroglyph of smiling faces. "There are so many civilizations that make monuments to themselves, like the Mayans of Mexico, for example, but their peoples have disappeared from existence, and no one understands what happened to them. There was also the fall of the Roman Empire, and the end of the ancient Egyptians, with their mastabas and pyramids and temples; all built complicated stone structures. What we have to show that there was a great civilization here, is this glacial erratic with happy, smiling faces."

"So, what's your point?" asked her husband, never quite being able to follow her train of thought.

"Why did the Indians carve faces in the rock, Mama? They look friendly," responded Clarissa, tracing her hand through the smooth, wide grooves in the rock.

"I've been thinking about the grandeur of New York City, and how much competition there was between all the financiers and industrialists, and they've all built these incredible monuments to themselves of marble and gold; and it seems that it will not last three thousand years, the way history goes. There will be an obvious decline in *that* empire. But the indigenous peoples, those here on the west coast, the First Nations People like the Squamish or Musqueam tribes still exist today – not in the same numbers as in the past, but they have never built any permanent monuments to themselves, except this, and it was already part of the landscape. And the Eskimo people too, come to think of it, have existed in exactly the same way since their beginnings, and didn't change. I wondered after I came back from New York the first time, why the Native peoples did not progress through time to the degree that the modern world did, and yet they have managed to survive as a distinct culture unchanged basically for 10,000 years – since the last ice age," she concluded.

"I don't know about that. How do you know they are unchanged?" asked her husband. The dog yanked on the leash and wanted to sniff at something buried under the mossy grass, which was covered in purple speedwell, looking like umbrellas on a hillside. She stopped on the path, and waited while the dog made loud sniffing noises, inhaling and exhaling sand and dust, while it prodded the earth with its nose and scratched frantically at the now exposed shell filled soil. Clarissa ran to catch up with her mother and father.

"Unless they built pyramids or temples here which have long been buried, and are undiscovered, I am assuming that the Indians of this area still exist today because they have lived congruently with nature; and I am assuming the various peoples, the ancient inhabitants of these parts who came from somewhere else, lived here, as a part of nature, just as the deer and the bear, and the elk did. They may have undergone changes in their population over time, but up until the white man from Europe came 200 years ago, they existed with what they had, and had a highly developed society. They just didn't ravage the land. They lived in harmony with their environment. One can tell from the legends that they were tied both spiritually and culturally to nature. I think that the first Nations People are going to save the earth from destruction - they are the only people who are knowledgeable about how to live in the wilderness, and how to survive using materials available to them, and out of a spiritual reverence for 'mother earth' have survived."

"That's a subject for an anthropologist," said Stanislaw, "but I know what you mean. But what about the Buddhist monks? Aren't they a culture that has survived for thousands of years in the same way as their leader taught them? Look at the Shwedagon Pagoda. They say it is at least 2000 years old, and the people who come to worship there are still the same practicing Buddhists as have been worshipping there for centuries. Don't they count as a civilization that has endured; or the Christians for that matter? Their culture is also 2000 years old; wouldn't you say that is an enduring culture of people?"

"I would have to think about that. The difference is, is that you are talking about specific religions, and I am talking about an isolated group of people who have lived for ten *thousand* years the same way. What I am really talking about is why did the native peoples not build monuments to themselves? And yet they managed to survive. That's all. Just a thought," she said in a lighthearted way. "I just thought about it as I passed the "Happy Petroglyph".

They continued on their walk, now past a home of a prominent figure in the community, the local physician. He and his wife supported keeping the community the same as it was when they had first arrived over a decade ago. They went to community meetings to fight against development and the railway, and the usual controversies which bring change to a small village. But the doctor was very well liked, especially amongst the young mothers who were patients of his. He understood their problems, with their husbands always working, and they themselves always over tired from raising children, and chronic lack of sleep. The women told him everything, and confided in him, and trusted his council. He had a soft voice and a gentle touch. And his wife, too, was respected. She worked right alongside her husband at his office, setting up appointments for him, and keeping his patient's files in order and up to date. She knew what ailed everyone, on account of her working so closely with her husband.

There was a rustling in the woods beside the railway tracks behind a sign that said '**NO DUMPING**'; and on the subject of bears and deer, one may have thought that a bear was in the woods. Instead, the good doctor emerged from the shrubby undergrowth with an empty wheelbarrow pushed out in front of him. He stopped for a moment to pull out a stick that was jammed in the axel of the front wheel, and looked up in time to notice the couple. Elena had just stopped to tie up her shoelace, and noticed as she was getting up, the words in bold print on the garbage can by the doctor's gate which read: '**Do not put your dog waste in our garbage can**'. Elena gave a vigorous tug on the dog's leash.

The three all said a quick hello as they were passing. The afore mentioned doctor was clearly busy at his yard work, and they in turn were in the middle of a discussion which needed no interruption of small talk. And so they resumed their walk and their conversation turned to other topics, as with the natural chit chat of husbands and wives they discussed the price of houses, which homes were newly painted, and what they would do that weekend, or what they should make for dinner. And so it went, with Clarissa prattling along the way, sometimes in front of her parents, sometimes behind, but always observant and gathering ideas for her next drawing.

Chapter 25

"A thing of beauty is a joy forever," Elena said out loud as she observed the birch tendrils floating in the breeze. 'I wonder who said that?' she thought to herself. It was one of Romantics to be sure – Keats, Shelley, - Was it, *Ode to a Grecian Urn*?' She used to know all of them. It was not to say that she did not still appreciate and love that which comes from the mind of a genius, she just could not place the quote. But that she loved and appreciated the beauty of nature and the poet's interpretation of it; that was what connected her to the great artistic minds and heroes of the past. Then, if she were in the company of certain family members, she digressed into ephemeral thoughts that were educated and lofty – until she spoke them out loud and bored everyone: 'Let's get on with the here and now,' they would say; or 'That's way too deep for me'; or 'Some of us have to work' - *that* was the other way out of a serious conversation. She had best keep her thoughts to herself. Sometimes she would call all the people she knew on the telephone until she could find someone at home to go out for a walk with, or to go for a coffee. There were so many coffee shops; the neighborhood was beginning to resemble Budapest from the turn of the century. Coffee houses abounded then, but they were on a much higher level, where groupings of intellectuals, politicians, artists and the aristocracy gathered in their leisure time; instead of the gathering of the unemployed and destitute. Here one needs coffee to help one on the steady run of getting to and from work, not for the relaxation and socialization aspect of it.

"Doesn't anyone work around here?" resounded a voice from the neighbor's yard.

She looked out the window to speculate on the weather, when she noticed something unusual in the front yard. Under the Riverbirch, and no ordinary tree was this, attracting the throngs like ladies to a department store sale, the creatures inhabited the tree, from domestic cats to squirrels, bushtits, and raccoons, wasps, and who knows what else; while displaying every season something new - catkins in spring, bright green leaves in summer, and then yellow, gold, and amber in fall. Then, like a curtain opening on stage, the bare branches revealed a prospect distinguished by a pure white bark. But there, almost hidden from view, under the dangling branches of the tree, sat a crow, seemingly a baby, and the sound of a frantic mother overhead.

'There must be a cat outside', she thought and ran downstairs to see. She opened the door quietly, and stood on the porch; her Siamese cat ran past her, with wild eyes and hair standing up on its back.

"Did the crow try to get you?" she asked the cat in a tender high voice. The cat answered her back by crying and looking up. Elena came back in the house for a moment and called upstairs to someone to come and get the cat and put it away in the laundry room while she went back outside and looked around the yard. 'We don't want any disasters to happen here,' she thought.

A crow from above was on her in an instant, swooping down over her head, and cawing loudly as it shot past her and careened back into the tree. She covered her head with her hands and ran for the shelter of the porch. She knew about '*Corvus brachyrhynchos*' – the sometimes mean and cruel bullies of the neighborhood - but she had to reassess the situation before she made any judgment. In spite of her general distaste for the birds, and her former lesson in "leave nature alone", she was curious about the situation. 'There was no harm in looking', as they say. Clarissa came out onto the porch.

"What are you calling me for, Mama?" she asked.

On a previous encounter with another world of birds, Elena had come across a lone duckling darting this way and that way, down a dirt path, peeping its little neck out, crying for its mamma. She thought she would save it from the coyotes, and caught it in her jacket, put it in the basket on the front of her bicycle, and took the little duck home with the intention of returning it to the lagoon the next morning. She put the duckling in a box with a skein of wool, thinking it would keep the duckling warm. Unfortunately in the morning, when the family excitedly ran to the box to look at the fluffy, yellow duckling; it lay stiff and cold, tangled up in the wool, with the yarn wound around its little neck. In essence she had killed the baby duckling. She cried, and cried, as did Elena's whole family; and her gut ached with regret; and her heart was filled with remorse, and compassion for the little creature. Now a new little drama was revealing itself.

The baby crow had hopped a little distance further away from her and flattened itself down in the longer grass to hide. Its feathers were rumpled and dull, it no longer had the luster of a well preened fowl, but strangely it had shining, blue eyes. Its mother was satisfied with this lair and went quiet; and our observer came back out of hiding and non-chalantly unwound the garden hose from the rack by the front porch. She turned on the tap, and carefully, without her usual hurry, began to water the garden closer to the house. This gave her a chance to observe.

Everything was dry, the ground was hard like a stale loaf of bread, and the yellow tea rose seemed to call out, "Water *me*, water *me*." With the hose still flowing, Elena gradually and cautiously made her way over to the other flower bed to see what had become of the young fowl; 'Just to look,' she thought to herself. There it was!, all pressed down in the grass, just as its mother had warned it to do. She held the hose over the newly planted palm; it too needed water, and could take the weight of the giant water drops on its tough and spiky leaves. She held the hose steady in one spot and looked around the garden at the *'mahonia aquafolia'* – the native Oregon grape. It had shiny sharp leaves and dusty blue berries that hung elegantly from the jagged branches. She stood still for a moment, admiring the silver globules of water, and the sound that they made falling on hard leaves. Ahh! The young crow heard it too, and like the children after the Pied Piper, it hopped in the direction of the falling water with its wings outspread, and it neck curved upwards. It held open its beak under the spray, and stood like a figurine in a fountain statue, while droplets fell into its open beak, and rolled sparkled across its wings. But *there* was the problem. One wing did not hang right; and the disfigured bird was missing feathers from its mantle on the back of its neck. This was the transfiguration of the common crow: the baby crow, little black beauty, with blue eyes staring into Elena's, its wings splayed out for balance, was coming to drink from the fountain of a human hand.

"Mama, what is wrong with the bird?" asked Clarissa quietly walking up to her mother and reaching to hold her hand.

"I think that it is sick. See how it drinks the water? Its mother is cawing like crazy again."

"When a bird dies at someone's house, it means someone we love will die soon."

"Where did you hear that Clarissa?" asked her mother surprised.

"It's a song we sing when we skip. 'A little bird came: hop, hop, hop; my love soon lost his head, pop, pop."

"You sing that when you skip?"

"We turn the skipping rope and have to jump *in* on *hop*, and *out* on *pop* – that means the person is dead."

"Oh! I think we should leave the bird alone now. We are distressing its mother. I don't think it is going to die," ended Elena.

The next day, in the back yard, lying next to the reflecting pool under a tree, next to a fern, Clarissa found the bird dead. She was about to climb in her favorite tree, and suddenly looked down at the black ruffled feathers. The crow had somehow managed to find another source of water, although it was too late to save itself. For three days afterward the mother's caw and call for its fledgling haunted the neighborhood; and then it too disappeared.

"Mama, Mama," cried Clarissa out loud as she ran into the kitchen. "The bird is dead. I found it under my tree!" Clarissa could not find her mother. There must be a proper burial, but first she wanted to draw the bird. I t is easier to get to know a thing if you draw it, and Clarissa loved all the animals she met, feeling a special kinship with the ones that shared her back yard. But she was eager to sketch her new subject before someone came and took it away. She was born with a natural talent and desire to draw, like any child given paper and crayons, but her mother encouraged her a great deal by her sincere interest in her youngest child's propensity towards art and her compliments to her colourful drawings and her imaginative images. Because her siblings were much older than her, this child was left to entertain herself quite often, and she would fill her days sketching the birds and animals that surrounded her. As she grew older, she was encouraged to enter her drawings in contests, and consequently, the walls of her house were filled with framed sketches covered in winning ribbons. She drew birds of every kind, dogs and horses and cats, and these also found their way into the homes of her grandparents as gifts.

Chapter 26

October had presented itself with a dusting of snow on the distant peaks. The weather had turned cool during the day. As Elena drove along toward her home, a black cat, like a warning flag, ran in front of her car. She winced at the same time and came to a sudden stop.

"Did the cat make it?" asked Clarissa from the seat beside her.

"I think so; cats have nine lives, and that must have been its eighth because it ran across the road the other day in front of a car when I was walking past. Cats take many risks. They never give up a chance to do something."

Elena drove a little slower and now and rounded the bend in the road. This time the leaves from the giant maple were scuttling across the road like clouds in front of the full moon. She put on the brakes and let them finish their journey; some were smaller and were running to catch up with the bigger leaves. She watched until they had all crossed the street.

"What are we stopping for now?" asked Clarissa puzzled.

"The leaves, the leaves, can't you see the leaves? We have to let them go."

They drove further along the road. A squirrel scampered across the road now too; everything seemed to be in a hurry, 'But for what?' she thought. As they got out of the car, the two could hear the voices of everything that the wind had touched. The River Birch bent over by the wind, was nearly touching the window of the house. It was making a mellifluous sound, as a rushing stream, pouring its yellow and brown leaves out of a jug and onto a rocky shore. The squirrel appeared again, this time with a nut in its mouth, and hastily pawed at the ground with its tiny claws, releasing the nut into a mossy bed, then proceeding to pound at the ground like a pianist with fingers springing off piano keys, it covered the nut with leaves and dirt, to claim for its future use.

"Mama, it's so windy! Let's go inside," urged Clarissa and she ran inside ahead of her mother and disappeared into the parlour and began fill the candle holders with candles. Elena went to the woodpile, and filled her arms with firewood. She loved having company for dinner, and today she contentedly chopped and sifted and made preparations with the determination of a cat pouncing on a mouse. Her pleasure in domestic affairs was greatly enhanced by music, especially opera, and today the "Anvil Chorus" from Verdi's "*Il Trovatore*" beat out a rhythm in the background.

Elena went first to the fireplace and lit the crunched up paper and kindling. Next was the kitchen. She began to peel and slice the apples for a pie. "Make my favorite apple pie, won't you love?" was what Stanislaw had told her earlier, "Remember, the way to a man's heart is through his stomach!" She turned on the oven, and combined with fireplace, the kitchen began to heat up. She measured the flour and the lard, and began in earnest to prepare the dough for the pie shell, first the flour, then the lard, and then the water. It took a lot of strength to cut in the lard to produce such a delicate and flaky pie crust, with a vigorous motion from her arms and hands, she worked her magic - the less time it took to prepare the crust, the better the crust turned out. Elena sprinkled the rolling pin and pastry board with fresh flour and patted half the dough into a circle. The rolling out took no time at all; it was lifted off the board into the pie plate, and the same procedure was begun with the remaining dough. She rolled it out fervently and lightly, without taking too much time. She added a generous spoonful of cinnamon to the bowl filled with sliced apples and sugar. "*La zingarella!*" she sang out loud with the stereo. At last, she topped the apple pieces with dots of butter and carefully manoeuvred the smoothly rolled out round of dough to the top of the apples piled high in the dish.

"I think they will like this," she said thinking about the guests that would be coming to dine later that evening - especially the bachelor, as she knew he would appreciate something home-cooked. There was a knock at the front door.

"Hi," Elena said as she opened the door and wiped the flour from her apron.

"Good day, are you the lady of the house?" asked a complacent man of about forty-five years old.

"Well I do live here, but judge for yourself if I am a lady. I am a woman, as you can see."

"Do you do the cooking and the food preparation here? Are you the main cook in the household?" he asked again seriously.

"Yes, I will say that I do most, if not all of the cooking. Why? What would you like?"

"I have some wonderful meats here. I have steak, and prawns, and chicken" he continued as he turned and looked out toward his vehicle parked in the driveway.

"I don't need any, thanks. You see, I don't have a freezer, and my fridge is very small."

"We have different sized portions, depending on what your needs are. Are you ever obligated to have people over for dinner but you really don't want to do all the cooking and you are not sure whether they can appreciate your good cooking anyway, and all the time that goes into it? Whether you are having a party or just serving small numbers - do you ever have large dinner parties..? Everything is individually wrapped, in single portions." The salesman did not give her a chance to answer - he thrust a frozen chop instead of his foot, into the doorjamb as a joke. She had to think quickly. Stanislaw had invited a close friend for dinner, a bachelor; she wanted to impress him with a home cooked meal, it wouldn't do to serve him something from the freezer, something pre- prepared in another kitchen. No, it was simply against her principles.

"Just a minute, please, I am *not* interested in buying any of your products. But if you would like to step in a minute; I'll show you my fridge." He knew he could get her to buy, once he engaged her, 'the hook' as it were. He followed her into the house, bandy-legged and happy-go-lucky, as though a sale was always so easy. "We just can't store anything; I shop everyday like they do in Europe. My fridge is like the ones in Paris, they don't have big fridges there," she argued trying to convince him of her lifestyle. She led him to the kitchen, fearing that by this time the crust would be eaten off the top of the pie by the dogs. She slid the leaded glass door open and he followed close behind her, hoping for an opportunity to make a sale.

He was curious about the fridge, but did not know why he allowed himself be led into her kitchen after all. It was dark in there, coming in from outside, and a large dark shape came swiftly across the floor towards him. His heart beat in his throat. A dog quickly ran over to him and jumped up with its paws pushing into his abdomen. He wasn't sure what to do, but the dog started to gnaw at his forearm while the woman yelled at it to get down. As his eyes started to adjust to the light he could see another giant dog, stretched out on a sofa.

'They must be ready to skin it and eat it,' he thought as he pushed away at the animal that would not let go of his arm. The dog on the sofa jerked its head up. It was a magnificent beast; like the ones seen in paintings, with elegant features – almond shaped eyes and elongated snout. He did not have enough time to determine the breed, nor enough voice in his throat to make another sound.

In the meantime, Elena had had started to say: "See, this is my fridge, and we don't really have a freezer. I mean, we have a freezer but we only use it to freeze ice."

The dog would not let up, and then the Borzoi gracefully jumped down from the sofa with one continuous bounce from its illustrious, silky coat, and trotted over to sniff the newcomer and join in on the action. The salesman was speechless, for once, with fear in his eyes, and a frozen package in his trembling hands; he tried to get the door open behind him without turning around. And then he managed, like a clogged drain, "Guh-guh-guh." He tried to talk, but only a stutter came out. Elena, laughing with restraint, tried to show compassion toward the pushy stranger by opening the door for him, and nudging the dogs back into the kitchen with her knee. As they too tried to get through the door in a hurry, thinking of their escape to freedom, she stepped on a paw by accident whereby the dog's yelping made up for the loss of voice in the salesman. She eventually slid the glass door shut behind them. At the end of it all, when the dogs suddenly realized that the man, who smelled like meat, was leaving, they began to bark furiously and jump on the glass door, not letting the meat out of their sight.

"You see," Elena began above the commotion, "I don't really have room for extra meat in the fridge... Sorry about the dogs."
He was out the door without a word, and turned and got into his van. 'That's strange,' she thought. 'Well he should have listened to me in the first place.'

"Who was that Mama?" asked Clarissa suddenly appearing in the kitchen again.

"Just a salesman," Elena said as she remembered her pie on the counter and hurried it into the oven. Next she needed to get out the roasting pan for the beef, peel the potatoes, slice the green beans, and quarter the squash. The colours of the dinner were out of a still life by an 18th century Dutch master. She wanted to show her guests how home- prepared food looked *and* tasted; Hookers Green were the beans, cadmium orange was the squash, burnt umber the beef, and zinc white were the mashed potatoes – how wonderful on a blustery night in October.

"It's going to be a sumptuous meal," she said to Clarissa, "set out a tablecloth of vermillion to match the wine, and use the white candles in the tall crystal candle holders, the ones we used last time." On the sideboard she placed a cake covered in walnuts, brown sugar and cinnamon. They would drink from a huge pot of tea, in cups of varying sizes and designs that were meant for a *Mad Hatter's* tea party. Elena knew that the tea would last long into the night, but only after Bacchus was satisfied.

Chapter 27

Now the inevitable rain came, and the immigrant children from warmer and sunnier climates always asked their teachers: "Teacher, when it stop rain?"

'*This* is our winter,' Elena thought. "I love the winter, in winter!" she admitted to her husband when everyone else was complaining about the weather. This is the rainy coast, of dark dripping cedar and misty moss, of overhanging oysters in clear, cold water; this is the land of the black and shimmering; this is the land of thick-furred black bears who escape the world wrapped in their dens. And this is the place where people, covered and covert, recede into *their* lairs, their routines, their work and their relationships. Very few people walked the beach now, and the night observed fewer and fewer of the ramblings of the former patron's of sun and sea.

On this typical autumn evening, John, like many others, was standing at his stove. He was frying some chicken again, and steaming broccoli and rice. The hot oil spattered up and he pushed the slices of meat back and forth in the pan, warmed by the flames, and thinking of his past, triggered by the aroma of the meal. She could see him at the stove as she looked up from the path, noticing movement from within the house. She had just walked around the corner, and into the lane, when she could smell the smoke from a wood burning fireplace. It hung like a thick and seducing paralysis over the house. She knew he would be alone, and it had been a long time since the impassioned piano episode. The steps were slanted and slippery. She grabbed the railing with trepidation; and felt the cold shock of water seep into her woolen gloves. The railing was not smooth, but her hands showed her the way, for her eyes were looking inward. Quietly, she tapped on the door. He glanced up from the stove in the direction of the window, but could not see out for the reflection.

"Someone knocking on my door; someone ringing my bell," he sang as he reached over from halfway to the door, and turned off the gas on the stove. In a few steps he was at the door.

"Well hello!" he said in a slow voice as one awoken from a sleep, "Elena, I'm surprised to see you. Would you like to come in?"

"Hi John... I just thought I would stop by and say hello. I have a book you might be interested in, since our last visit - although I don't have it with me. You are right in the middle of dinner, I see."

"You are just in time. Sit down. Would you like some? It will be done in a minute. Here, I am just having a glass of wine," he said encouraging her. She sat down. There was something that she wanted to say. There was a reason she wanted to see him again.

"I would have liked to get to know you. But after the last time I saw you, well, I know that it was not right. I'm surprised that you are still here."

"Don't worry about last time. A man will always try to get what he desires. Besides, you seduced me," said John always grinning.

"Me? I don't think so. I was an innocent bystander. You are still living here I see, and are you all alone? You never did finish your story. What happened to your wife, and your girl friend?"

"I haven't been married for years. After my marriage ended, I tried to lay as many women as possible. It's so easy to find willing women," mused John.

'Who does this guy think he is?' she was asking herself. 'Is it really true, or is he incredibly lonely and lacking in courage, so he is making up a story to make himself appear desirable?'

"Well then, where are all these women?" she asked him outright.

"I played around until I found someone that I felt I could commit to. I pursued a woman from Austen." He paused here and continued to stir the chicken without speaking. Then he added sentimentally, "She played in the symphony there. She played the cello; and she moved in with me. But she was much too young for me, and alas, she wanted children. Of course it had to end. It was beautiful, thrilling… exhilarating – the music and all." He looked over at Elena with his usual confident smirk. "And here I am."

"I think that you are hiding something from me," she said.
He, having returned to his cooking now with his back to Elena, pulled two plates down from the cupboard, held them for an instant above the counter, as if in deliberation. Then turning toward Elena, he set them on the table.

"Would you like some? I've made enough for two."

"Is there any garlic in it?" she asked politely.

"No, why, are you allergic?"

"No, not really, but I don't really care for it, and my husband, he knows that I never eat it, and that if he could smell it on me, then he might ask."

"Your husband. Always your husband. I think that YOU aren't telling me the truth; I don't think that you *have* a husband," he said looking at her from under his eyebrows.

"Yes I do, and that is what makes me different, of course; I am married. Anyway, he isn't here this week, so I suppose I can stay for a bite to eat."

"Here," he said pushing the plate closer to her, "I always wanted to see you eat, you always look so hungry."

"So," she continued as she readily ate the dinner, "I think you are hiding the truth from ME!"

"What do you mean?" he asked casually as he picked up his wine glass and sipped from the edge, while looking over the rim at her. She had that funny feeling in her stomach like hot tea poured over honey.

"What I mean is that 'truth' is the most important thing, and unless people can be frank with each other, they cannot develop any sort of relationship. There is so much cant'. And I don't mean 'c- a- n- apostrophe – t-,'" she spelled out. "But that too, I suppose. I mean, that unless one can really share one's true thoughts - what is really on one's mind, then the friendship, or love, or whatever it is, can go no further. And I think that is what happens - people guard what is really foremost in their mind, and they walk away from people."

"Hmm… ya," he said as he was staring at her. He wasn't really thinking about what she was saying, he was thinking of the bedroom. "Are you going to tell me the truth first, or shall I begin?" he asked her.

"I am going to begin by telling the truth. There are many attractive people in this world, and sometimes one feels an attraction to a stranger. But for me, because I am married, it stops me from being with other men."

"And me," he broke in, "I don't care about that, I enjoy sex and I will take if I can get it. It is fun for me. Pure pleasure..."

"Well, that is where we differ. I will never give in to a man who cannot and will not be committed to me, and me alone. That is the price one has to pay for devotion and loyalty! *Let me not to the marriage of true minds, admit impediments, love is not love which alters when it alteration finds* – Shakespeare."

"Come here, come over here, you'd better be telling me that on my lap, I'm very hard – of hearing. Look, your blushing"

"Obviously your values do not get rewarded. Look at you. I wasn't finished with the truth. You are attractive, nice looking, you're in excellent shape, I can see that, you've had an interesting life, from what I know of it, and you are retired and have some money, from what I can see."

"Well, go on, so far you are correct," said John enjoying the attention.

"Why are you single?" insisted Elena, "doesn't everyone want companionship? Isn't love the only unifying, cohesive thing that holds the world together? I think that was *Gandhi* who said that."

"Never mind *Gandhi*, I know what I want. What is wrong with wanting companionship and commitment? But I also need something more. Buddha spoke of love, too; maybe Gandhi studied him. However, Buddha said that the highest form of love does not require love in return. I'm not there yet," said John, and looked into her eyes, waiting for a response, there was too much talk, 'Forget the talk,' he thought, 'let's get into bed and get this over with. I'd like to screw her brains out right now, but a gentleman doesn't tell a married woman that. I have to be a gentleman, or I shall send her running, this frail, naive thing.'

"Although, I shouldn't really be saying this, alone here with you," she continued, "but you seem like an interesting man. And you are attractive, to me. And I don't want to admit that. But if my husband were attracted to another woman, I would be... extremely angry and jealous. I pretend to myself that it is not possible for him to find another woman attractive. And then I am satisfied, and think that it is OK for me to like another man, because that is just the way *I* am. But what is YOUR problem? What is *your* truth?"

"They all wanted me, Elena, the girls, the football scouts, Uncle Sam ....the boys. Would you like some more wine? I would; here have another glass. You look thirsty."

The rain had started to beat against the window pain, and the wind had forced the smoke from the fireplace to meander sleepily through the house. It crept along the floor and up the dark wooden stairs to the bedrooms. It curled itself around banister, and seeped into the kitchen like a path through the woods.

"Here, let's take our glasses into the infamous parlour, I have to fix the down draft." They picked up their wine goblets and with a little hesitation, Elena unbuttoned her long, wool, dark green coat and left it hanging over the back of the kitchen chair. She followed him into the living room, to the chesterfield where she had sat and listened to the concert, some months ago. She tugged her burgundy velvet skirt down over her knees, and she pulled self-consciously at the bra strap underneath her fur-trimmed sweater.

"Relax; I am not going to accost you again. Now where were we? What was your question? Something about truth?" he began.

"I wanted to hear from you the truth. And why did you stay here, by the way?"

"Oh yes," he said as he set the bottle down on the coffee table and settled into a chair across from her. "I am here to write. The winter climate is a change of pace from Mexico, and I like this place; the soft, wood paneling on the walls and the old furniture is warm and comfortable, and makes for a good work environment. And it is dark, and very quiet here in winter - sort of what I imagined Majorca to be in winter." And with that he glanced up at her, to see if she caught his reference to Chopin and George Sand and their retreat to Majorca.

"I want to write too," Elena said quietly looking down at the floor for a moment.

"Then why don't you?" John asked her rhetorically.

"So if you like women so much, why can't you be with just one? It would save you a lot of time and trouble," continued Elena.

"You have to have a willing partner," he said rather sardonically.

She felt an awkward sense of sorrow that perhaps his wife or partner did not freely commit to a full relationship. The memory of what her minister had said to her and her husband in their pre-marriage course came to her: 'Sex was to be enjoyed within the sacred relationship of man and wife.' She didn't remember any rules attached, except that sex was to be 'enjoyed' - within the marriage.

"I want love, and to be loved. I want a lasting committed relationship," he continued.

"So what is the problem?" she asked again.

"My wife couldn't love me. Did I mention that to you?" he asked in bitter rhetoric. "I was a Marine in Vietnam," he added without expecting an answer. How easy it was to talk to a stranger. "I've killed the Vietnamese with my bare hands, strangled them in their sleep... I've eaten insects, just to survive...Do *you* know what that's like? Don't talk to me about love and devotion, and duty. I *did* my duty," he added emphatically. And then in a more quiet dispassionate whisper: "I'm beyond duty. Do you think that some tight-ass bitch from an upper class New York is going to accept that?"

There was silence. There was nothing more for her to say just then. She was almost sorry that she had asked him about his truth. Could even *she* love him? - in another time or place perhaps. But he would have to be *very* good to her.

"Would you like another glass of wine?" he asked, and not waiting for her to answer, he got up and went into the kitchen. Elena wanted to relax but she sat up expectantly. John returned with another bottle of red wine, and an opener.

"Here we go, this is a nice bottle of French that I have been saving in the cellar," he said cheerfully as he returned from the kitchen. His mood had changed from andante to allegretto, like a Beethoven sonata. "I love this one.

The burgundy color matches your skirt. We should dance." And he opened the wine and called, "Minstrels, the music!"

The flames from the hearth leapt up and reflected off her glass. 'What a pretty pattern,' she thought, trying to concentrate and stay alert while the crackling fire soothed her, and she slid a little more into her chair sipping the wine.

"You are not going to run away from me now, are you?" he asked her.

"No, but don't go falling in love with me," she sighed. "I'm married you know, and one man is enough."

He poured the wine and then got up to put some more wood on the fire. He bent over and carefully put a log on the bull shaped andirons. His forearms were sinewy and golden.

"I *am* falling in love," he said… "with this place." And he stood for a moment staring into the flames. Then, lost in silence, in front of the flames, he squatted down breathing in strength from the heat like a pyretic satyr; and poked at the fire with the iron prong.

"So what was the real reason that you and your wife divorced?" asked Elena.

When a thing is long and complicated, it is impossible to respond with any genuine, coherent explanation – unless of course, the answer to such a question is well rehearsed. One might find oneself sounding trite, cynical, or ignorant.

He stared at the fire a brief moment more before answering.

"Transference," he said "that's it."

"Pardon me?" she quietly said feeling the wine warming her inside, and suddenly not wanting to go.

"I said '*trans*ference'. My wife recommended that I seek help, 'psychiatric' help, after the war, *after* I tried to strangle her in her sleep."

"Just a minute, I haven't gotten past the transference."

"I was suffering from what they call 'post traumatic stress syndrome', and my wife insisted that I seek help from Veteran's Affairs. Which I did, being a reasonable, intelligent, thinking man - I took her advice. But I fell in love with my therapist – a woman, by the way. And that was the end of that. Now I've gone on about myself, tell me about you, and your husband. I haven't heard much from you yet."

"I *am* going to run out on you now. I am a complete stranger; and I'm leaving you in the lurch in your time of need," Elena suddenly said surprising herself.

"Oh, so that's it! I tell you everything, and you just say nothing?"

He rushed over to her at once, took the wine glass from her hand, and as she stood up to leave, he pressed up against her, looking at her deep in her eyes, and searching. She answered back, unafraid with an unblinking look as hard as the teeth on an excavator:

"Don't try anything."

"You are a shrewd little witch," he said to her half smiling. "Just one little waltz; just put your arms around me here. That's it. Just this time, I promise I'll be good." And he, putting his arm around her waist, he waltzed her into the kitchen.

Chapter 28

The days fell into line, as if marching towards Christmas and the New Year. There was another war overseas, this time it was in a desert, a cold and barren, harsh, rocky landscape. The circumstances were different, but the young soldiers were the same. Put in a situation, it is 'do or die'. As in a sporting competition, the player becomes stronger, more competitive, more determined than in practice, to win. It was like that in karate. If you were not ahead, not defending yourself or attacking your opponent, you would lose. After a match, or sparring, one becomes immediate friends again with ones competitor. It was all in the sport. A sort of reverence and respect for the fighting nature of man, the insuppressible nature of one's self at its base level - the driven instincts of one to compete and survive. But nothing like that except in sport every really happened at this seaside community - except what one hears in the news, or the latest traffic report, or the weather.

The power had gone out for the second time in a few weeks, and knowing that it usually took a few days for the electricity to be restored, people headed up the hill to eat in the smaller cafes or pubs. On the night of this windstorm, John walked down to the Marina Pub, along the winding dyke trail, hoping to spend the evening there in the company of his new found friends. The marina kept a generator and the pub was always cozy, with dim lights and a fire. He opened the door and struggled to close it behind him on account of the wind. The pub was already very full. He looked around the dining area, nodded to a few people he recognized, and sat down comfortably at an empty table. Across from him sat the woman whom he had seen many times recently out on the spit, walking her dogs. She was sitting with two other women.
He ordered his meal and his usual beer from the waitress, and in no time, the ladies caught his eye.

"Won't you come and join us?" one of them said in a loud voice as he stared over at them. No one was really paying any attention to him; people clearly had been here for some time, keeping warm and drinking.

"Ya, I'd love to, thanks," he said with a smile and getting up from his chair, he extended his hand and reached over the small round table and introduced himself. "I'm John. I think I've seen you around the beach" he said to one of them.

"Yes maybe, I'm Cheryl, and this is Mary and Louise."
"You have dogs, don't you?" John asked Cheryl.

"Oh yes, I left them at home tonight though, they're pretty good about sleeping through these wind storms. How long have you lived at the beach for?" she enquired right away.

"Just about six months now. I came up to look after my mother's house, and I decided to stay for a while. I'm retired," he said in his heavy Texan accent.

"But not *tired*, we hope" one of the women said laughing.

"No, not *that* by any stretch. Does one of you ladies care to dance?" asked John answering the challenge. It was a romantic notion, but no one knew how to take it. It just slipped out, 'How else does one get a woman to stand up and look you in the eyes?' John thought.

"Not just yet, let's wait 'til after you've had your dinner," said Mary.

"I don't think I've ever seen anyone dance here before," added Cheryl.

"Well, we could be here all night if the power stays off, so we will need some kind of entertainment," stated John.

"What kind of dancing do you do, John?" asked Cheryl, "coming from down *south* and all," she added, trying to emulate his accent.

"I went to a private school, and we had to learn to be gentlemen. We learned to dance, - waltz, foxtrot, - 'Cha, Cha, Cha'," he added with emphases moving his arms. "And I get to lead, be in control. Just thought that I would let you ladies know that."

The evening slipped on, and the fire kept getting brighter as more wood was piled into the great stone hearth, and the wind coming in through the opening door fanned it with gusts of damp air. Before long, the three women were relaxed and having a good time, until one of them leaned over to stroke the face of John, the long lean Texan, and knocked over a tall glass filled with beer. The waitress was there quickly enough and wiped it up, including the small amount, which had run over the side of the table onto John's leg. When the waitress leaned over to dab at his leg, he leaned back in his chair, and protested abashedly that it was nothing at all.

"I really would like to hear about where '*You*' are all from, why don't we go around the table, and one at a time, tell your birthday, and what brought you here to the beach. And I'll start, since it was my idea," decided John. The ladies agreed, making jokes about their ages. Then John continued, clearing his throat, and looking to see that he had everyone's attention. "J my name is John, and I come from Texas. My birthday is October tenth, and I drive a Lexus."

Louise continued under protest,

"We won't reveal our age, but we *ladies* all first met in the dorm at university."

"Well, how did you ever all end up down here?" asked John leaning far into the table as if he were ready for an arm wrestle.

"Serendipity," one of them answered.

The bar was getting distinctly louder, and when John's dinner arrived, he ordered another jug of beer for the table. The rest of the pub was full to capacity, and people kept coming and going, opening and shutting the door, probably looking to see if any lights were on up the hill yet, or if any boats had broken from their moorings. And someone was always coming over to the table of the three ladies, and the 'long, lanky, Texan' as John was dubbed by one of the women. The rain railed against the dark windows, and at times the room seemed to shake over the pylons, which projected partly over the water. A tarp had come loose from the top of a boat, and blew up against the window like a phantom from the lagoon. A few people let out a startled shriek and a '*Woo-ooow*' as it slashed at the window, and tumbled across the deck, disappearing into the blackness below. The music seemed loud too, to compete with the noise from the wind and the rain, and coincidently, a famous song, "Have You Ever Seen the Rain?" played wildly over the speakers. There was a flicker in the generator power, and then the music was turned off to conserve the energy. The waitress and the bar tender came round to the tables to replenish the candles, and then there were questions about how long they would be staying open, under the circumstances.

Again there was a gust of wind that was felt by all, and before there was time for the local members of the yacht club to reach any sort of agreement, a loud, excruciating crack was heard; and a thud and groan made its way inside.

"What was that?" sounded a cacophony of voices from around the room.

"I hope it wasn't a boat," sounded someone uncertainly.

Everyone ran to the windows pressing their faces and cupping their hands against the glass. Everyone except John, who remained seated and examined the backsides of the women. He all but licked his lips at the sight. 'To imbibe,' he thought to himself.

The liquor was having its effect on him. He began to fantasize. In front of him was a bevy of beauties, paraded before him as though he were looking at a women's fashion catalogue. The Marina crowd wore tight blue jeans, not unlike women practically everywhere in America – although he preferred the feminine shape of women in dresses and skirts like in Mexico. But the majority of women had on fancy tops, like the various colors of the *plumeria*, or colourful sweaters that just met the top of their pants, revealing the shape of each buttock, enhanced by the fancy stitching on the jeans' pockets. One of the three he had been sitting with wore a most becoming sweater made out of periwinkle blue wool. It had a peplum bottom made of pinstriped gauze with flecks of silver and indigo. He remembered that from the front; the sweater opened down into a v-neck, which gave him the advantage to see the slight curvature of her smooth white breasts. From the back view it accentuated her waist. The others wore sweaters and tops of various styles and colors which captured his imagination and desire. One of the ladies wore a sweater of red cotton, loopy, knit, with a ruffled high neck line and a black strapless camisole underneath. Another wore a leopard print short sleeved, scoop neck, silk, sweater which enticed one to rub and stroke it like a cat alluring its owner to affection. John was suddenly jolted out of his ephemeral pleasure.

An awakening noise from outside was easily distinguished above the din of the bar; it had sounded as though a boat had come loose and crashed against the dock. But in truth, it was like an avatar, in the form of a tree, an ancient fir, which had been blown down and flayed its massive weight along the edge of the wharf near the banks of the cove to shake things up.

"This is rather exciting," said John, and he sat there bemused while the storm and the fallen tree stirred up great emotions. A few of the men grabbed a flashlight from behind the bar and went out to see what had happened. It was closing time now, and the manager announced to everyone, it was time to leave. The three women returned to their seats.

"Have you all got rides?" John asked them.

"Oh yes," Cheryl replied.

"Cheryl has her cabriolet, her horse drawn buggy, only enough room for two!" said Mary in a mischievous, singing voice,

"That's what I call her old mustang convertible," added Mary.

"Could I get a ride then? I actually didn't bring my car tonight," explained John.

Just then the men returned from outside with one other. It was German George, of the raft, all covered in rain and mud, standing in a yellow rain hat and jacket. The men were talking to him at the door.

"We should leave... Which one of you ladies could oblige me with a ride?" asked John again.

"Come with me, you live down here anyway," offered Cheryl.

"Thank yee kindly, ma'am," John said as he stood up for the ladies to get up from the table. He motioned eloquently for the ladies to go before him, and they walked out to the hallway to retrieve their coats and hats. It was unusual for a man in this part of the world to treat the women with such manners, and so the three were impressed and felt very privileged to have the gracious Texan help them with their coats. There was certain gentility about him that seemed different from the other men, but in reality, he was just charming.

"Hey Cheryl," someone called just as they were ready to go. A man came over to where she was standing, and in hushed voice he said, "Cheryl, do you think you can put George up for the night? He said he has stayed with you before. He is quite drunk, and the tree just fell into the boat shed where he had been living, apparently, for a few weeks."

"I don't think so, not tonight, it just isn't suitable, I have guests tonight, Martin, I am really sorry, I'll see what I can do after tomorrow, give me a call."

"Cheryl, before you go, you're Cheryl Bordeaux, aren't you?" said John urgently and overcome with apprehension and alarm at his fleeting chance to make her recognize and acknowledge him. "Aren't you even going to shake my hand?"

Cheryl looked at him from her sad big blue eyes with eyelashes thick in black mascara,

"John, let go of my arm," she replied. "When did you realize it was me? I was waiting for you to recognize me." She fumbled for her coat in the crowded coat rack, and he suddenly seized her again by the wrists.

"Cheryl, I knew it was you," he said as he burst into laughter, I wasn't sure that I would recognize you but when I heard you speak, I knew it was you. A voice never changes, you know Cheryl. I've seen you around, I've been watching you, but I wasn't sure until tonight." Someone was trying to reach past John into the cloak closet, and he let go of her for a moment. Then before she could move in any direction, he moved over her and said in a deep whisper, "I need you Cheryl, kiss me. I want to kiss you again."

"Not now and not here. We must talk, I'm not the same girl I was thirty years ago. And I'm their children's Sunday School teacher," she continued with her protests looking at the patrons of the bar reluctantly leaving. "They all know me, I can't be here in the bar, kissing a total stranger."

"But *I* can," said John and her lunged at her, pulling her into the closet and kissing her. "You still taste the same," he ended.

She pushed him away and stepped into the hall, adjusting her hair and her coat.

"Cheryl, there you are! What are you doing?" asked Mary.

"Goodnight John," Cheryl managed in a stifled voice and she turned and stepped down the steep stairs leading to the outside of the pub, holding onto the smooth iron railing as she went down into the dark corridor.

"Are you giving George a ride?" asked Mary following her down the stairs, "Is John going with you?"

"Mary," began Cheryl as they opened the door into the windy, rainy night, "John knows me, and I can't talk now... he doesn't know *anything*. I've got to get out of here."

Cheryl began to cry, and Mary put her arm around her shoulders,

"I'll stay with you tonight, Cheryl. Where is Louise? I'll tell her to meet us at your house."

Cheryl climbed into her car. She was unable to drive; to begin she could not get the key in the ignition, and then there were the thick streaks of rain on the windshield, like the tears running down her cheeks, all which greatly impaired her vision, leaving her physically and mentally swamped in her seat. All she could think about was her daughter and the family she should have had. Cheryl was overwhelmed with the latest of life's events unable to manage her emotions, overcome with an outpouring of sensibility in regards to her own unenviable state. Mary came back a few minutes later with Louise and the three wet women climbed into a waiting taxi, half laughing, and half crying like cats coming in from a storm. The door to the pub swung open and shut as the last of the revelers left the building. John had been left standing in a daze in the upper hallway. He put his thumb and index finger to his forehead and closed his eyes, as if to focus his thoughts. He braced himself against the wall with the other arm like a cottonwood straining under the force of a gale. Before long he had regained his strength and holding onto his past memory of emotions, he was once again walking down the familiar, deserted road.

"*So I best be on my way ... in the early morning rain,*" he sung unwittingly to himself. And then as he walked and thought over the events of the evening, he sang louder shouting out to the wind, "*and with a dollar in my hand, with an aching in my heart, and a pocket full of sand...so I best be on my way.*"

Chapter 29

"Who will it be this year? Whose turn will it be to leave the party early on account of too much to drink?" somebody always asked. It was tradition in this part of the world, amongst a group of friends, to celebrate New Year's Eve. Elena and Stanislaw had their last argument of the year, but the first in a very long time. As they got ready to go out, the usual ironing of slacks and scurrying to and fro, matching socks and tying ties, Stanislaw announced to Elena his condition.

"Elena, there is something I must tell you," he began when the final moment of opportunity struck him. Elena felt the inside of her stomach go hollow as bath water is sucked down the drain. For a split second she thought he might have a mistress. Thoughts can rush through one's mind faster than the speed of light, and she thought about the times she had spent alone, while her good husband was in meetings or with clients. "Elena, my words are worse than the devil himself; just speaking them is more than I can ever want to say, but I have *cancer*, and I've known for some time now."

The news hit Elena like smoke from an oven fire when one opens the door - Elena couldn't breathe or see, so great was her shock on hearing his words. When she recovered her senses, her reaction was more unpredictable than Stanislaw's timing of this dreadful news:

"Stanislaw, we will overcome this," she said in a most matter-of fact, optimistic voice, "you've always been healthy; you will be cured. There are more and more discoveries every day. That is why they say *living with cancer*."

Not to seem insensitive or callous to all those who have been touched by grief and sadness - it is hard to describe how or why people act as they do under stress or terrifying circumstances; it is usually that part of life which is unrehearsed. But Stanislaw held in his own genie lamp all the emotions the world has ever felt, ready to be released from the infinite depths of the brass - fear, anger, anguish, remorse, apprehension, denial, guilt and sadness. Then he continued steadily with his often rehearsed statement,

"I wanted to continue to live as though I didn't know; *no one* really knows when one is going to die – every moment of my life has been filled with great joy - everyone wants to live a little bit longer - like our babies sucking at your breasts and wanting 'just a little bit more', this is life Elena. We have time later to talk... But Elena, it's confirmed. You can't see by my outward appearance."

"You are not going to die," she continued stubbornly, and in answer, Stanislaw started to yell,

"You are not listening to me, Elena. And oh, how I love to hear my own voice say your name - I need comfort, not contradiction. Love,.. love, compassion ...closeness, assurance, - and you are denying me the right to wallow in my feelings, as childish as it sounds, I'm terrified... lost, I can see it coming like a monster, and I'm terrified, and I have nowhere to hide." He bent over in the chair and started to sob. He had kept his secret too long, to protect his family from worry and further strife; and now he had spoken, his emotions let loose, like the opening of the starting gates at the race track, where stallions stampeding full force, their hearts ready to burst, surge down the course, such was the power of his suffering. There was much to discuss, days and days of discussion and planning - if Stanislaw was lucky enough, to share this new part of his life.

"You must go out tonight," he finally said, looking up. "You must see the others and don't let on," he continued in a decided manner recovering himself before Elena could speak. "I have a year, - at least," he lied. Tonight he needed to be alone, to think alone; he was somewhat relieved, - spent, like a child who, after throwing a tantrum, settles down into a whimpering exhausted sleep, Stanislaw needed to rest. Now that the worst was over, he could think; his secret was out.

Chapter 30

Once again, as on every December 31st as far back as anyone alive could remember, in fact as far back as Julius Caesar had dedicated the day to Janus, the two faced Roman god, who looked forward as if into the future, at the same time as looking back at the events and histories of the past, people gathered together in celebration of new beginnings. Here at the local Legion, acquaintances gathered to look back and to look forward, and embrace new beginnings amongst friends and acquaintances they loved; and so too the friends of Stanislaw and Elena gathered, in a place that had history and memories, not only amongst this group, but also amongst all those who served in the military, and before them. At the door to the Legion, one had to sign in, or identify oneself, like going to another kingdom, say the magic words and the door opened. It was an inconspicuous door, though it was heavy with time, and the wooden slats originally snug fitting tongue and groove cedar over a hardwood core, had absorbed the moisture from many years of winter, and one always had to tug hard to pull it from the door jamb that was reluctant to release its swollen captive. Once inside the hall, dim lights and general merriment greeted the participants. The interior of the building itself was distinguished by the flags at the front of the dining hall; and by the photos of World War II airplanes on the wall; and by picture frames filled with medals of Honor, bravery and distinction. It was denoted by the very elderly, the one or two, who still made it out to celebrate, wearing navy suits with brass buttons. And it was marked by the ladies, who wore ball gowns and dress gloves that came up to their elbows, disguising their well worked hands. Some even wore a tiara, fitting for the occasion, but possibly too good for the surroundings, which were humble and comfortable, but rustic. In truth, it was a shabby place, but then its patrons were just regular people who wanted a place to go and be together for that mutual celebration of the passing of time.

Elena looked around the hall, now it seemed everyone looked old to her. Actually, they looked like fish in an aquarium. Some had the face of an eel, bald headed and all lips. Others looked like an octopus, with a large bald head and half hidden eyes. She recognized some of the men, there was the local butcher, the postman, the high school principal, the lawyer, the inventor, the musicians, the ambulance driver, and the dentist - and characters of all social status and description. Put in a room together, beer in hand, you couldn't tell the pauper from the prince. And these people knew how to have fun. And they could dance the 'white man's dance' – by counting their steps and following a pattern, every once in a while, by accident, men letting their partners slip from their hand, and let fly into the crowd a bright red dress. But the year was coming to a close, and why not let go? There has to be endings and beginnings, and endings; Elena was discussing life and literature with someone at the table,

"Is there such things as a happy ending?" someone asked.

"That depends where you stop – in life there is ultimately one beginning, and one ending; but we have to break our lives down into chunks of time and events, don't you think?"

"– isn't that what this New Year's celebration is all about?..Tomorrow we will be swimming in the ocean, washing away our past and our cares, and starting anew."

"Ya, ya, and the days will be getting longer again too," someone else said bored with the conversation. The lights flickered as if to warn of some endings.

The band answered with a ballad of *Robby Burns*, and a chorus of revelers began to sing: *"Should old acquaintance be forgot, and never brought to mind...?"* Amidst the din of the bagpipes and the singing of *Auld Lange Syne,* the Scottish tradition that kept on going, long after the *Clarkes* and the *Grants*, the *Bruces* and the *MacDonalds* had married into other clans and ethnic groups, there amidst the uproar and celebration, the sound of a passing fire truck could faintly be heard. But not one of the revelers prickled with apprehension; no one seemed to notice, and the party carried on. Streamers flew and couples kissed and swayed to the music. The lights flickered off again, and this time the electricity could not redeem itself. More candles were lit, the Legion, in true military fashion, was prepared for anything, and the candles burned more brightly with gusts of cold air from outside; and people moved their heads closer to the flames to talk, as though the darkness had affected their hearing. Elena had had enough to drink; she could not stay a minute longer. No-one but she knew of Stanislaw's condition, and a melancholy, which she could not control, started to overcome her.

"I am walking home," she announced to her friends, "I'm going to write my resolutions, and go to bed! The power might still be off at home... I think I should be there - and Stanislaw might need something for his flu. I will catch up with you all ..." No one was really listening; she did not need to make excuses. The tradition was to stay awake all night, and continue the revelry at someone's house, long after the Legion had closed its doors, until the first light of day, and there was still one merrymaker left standing. They would keep themselves awake by drinking strong coffee mixed with rum and brandy and liqueur, in tall glass mugs, etched in holly leaf and ivy designs, and topped with whipped cream and a maraschino cherry for the occasion. They would drink these hot, trickling with richness; and dance and sing and listen to their fellow musicians playing the guitar, the fiddle and the ukulele. Each guest in turn would talk about the past, 'the year in review' as it was called, and look to the future, and talk about what they might do, their goals and their plans - and the first light of day in the northern hemisphere in winter, was at least fifteen hours after sunset the previous night – there would be time for everyone to evoke nostalgia.

Elena did not want to miss that part of the New Year, but this night was different from all others. Snow had been falling for some time now, and it coated the rooftops and cushioned the ground, hiding familiar forms from view, save for the candle flames which perforated the powerless night. She trudged through the silent, sympathetic snow, until turning into her own yard; she reached forth a tremulous hand to open the glistening, frozen, wrought iron gate.

Chapter 31

Late on the following morning, New Years Day, a small crowd was gathering along the north shore of the beach. The temperature was five degrees below the freezing mark. People were hopping on the sand to keep their feet from freezing. Some thought that the water was far too cold to jump into. For the onlookers, the sight of the swimmers standing on the edge of the shore made them feel colder than they were; others, who were already undressed, could not wait for the countdown to plunge into the icy waters whose temperature was warmer than that of air. They were anxious to warm up, somewhat. The truth is truly in the eye of the beholder; it has been said more than once, 'It is all about perspective.' And even the mountains seemed different today – they were further away due to the cold haze in the atmosphere, but their icy tops were reflected in the water's edge, making them appear close to the near shore; and even the salt water had frozen just enough on the edge of the tide rippled sand to leave a slight film of frosty white ice., joining the mountain tops to the sea. Many people were on the dyke path above the beach now, revelers from the night before. People were drinking hot chocolate, and rum, and others had thermoses of coffee or tea. The jingling laughing like icicles breaking could be heard above the shout from a much deeper voice below the on the sand, calling to attention the crowd and trying to get the new Year's dip under way. He was the local community events ambassador, always seen about town at the country fairs and pancake breakfasts. He was dressed in nothing but his swimming trunks, and was trying desperately to quiet the boisterous multitude. He had a broad hairy chest, and his muscular thighs, calves and forearms bore resemblance to a possum, white and pink leathery skin covered in bristling coarse hair. And then, the beard on his face was clipped very close, but the hair on his head was long and black, and tied into a ponytail at the nape of his neck. He did not seem to notice the cold.

"Everyone, I would like to have your attention, please," he shouted up at the spectators. "I would just like to say, that for over twenty years we have had this celebration. It only started with a few, including myself, but here with us today, one of the original, fledgling swimmers who swam almost every day of his long life in this ocean…" At this point he held up high over his head like a trophy, an urn that he was holding. The crowd was becoming more restless, and cold, and some child in behind the audience was talking loudly and shouting, "I can't see, I can't see."

"Our good friend, sadly ..." He tried to continue but the onlookers at the far end of the group could not really hear him and suddenly, from out the throng, a stronger, louder voice began to chant, "Five, four, three, two, one...." And hundreds of nearly naked amphibians rushed past our eulogizing hero, and into the deep, and briny startling water. There was an abundance of shrieking and laughing, and cheering and groaning. Like a teacher who had lost control of his class in front of an ice-cream stand, the swimmers were doing what they had longed for to be over, and our almost fur clad announcer, finished off his elocution by opening the urn graciously and reverently, and swirling its contents, those of a man, a community figure, the 'Unofficial Mayor' of the village, into the ocean, along with and amongst the swimmers. No sooner had the once-renowned swimmer, caretaker of the village, ubiquitous gardener, taken his final swim; the nonplussed eulogist dunked himself and was out of the water, lost in the crowd amongst the towels and blankets which seemed to cover everyone there.

"You would not believe how warm you feel once you are out of the water," someone was saying.

"The water doesn't seem that cold compared to the air, but now that I am out, I feel so warm," remarked someone else, "things are sometimes not how they seem." The onlookers did not dare to remove their coats; the crowd slowly dispersed, and the village, now fully awake, filled the streets and began to forage for friends and greet each other. "Happy New Year," could be heard echoing through the frosty air. John too had come down to watch the swim. He stood at the back of the crowd, keeping to himself listening.

"Did you see the house on the way down the hill?" someone asked.
"No what house was that?"
"The house by the marina road. There must have been a fire there last night." "Someone must have died. The house is surrounded by yellow police tape."
"Which house was it?"
"You know the old one, behind the trees?"
"Someone said it was the lady with the dogs."
"Which lady? Everyone has a dog."
"Who are you talking about?" someone else asked.
"The house where the fire was last night."

John had overheard the questioning. He didn't know if the weather was changing or the words enveloped him, but suddenly he was overcome with numbness and cold and could not see. The clouds above him started to swirl and make him dizzy. He turned away from the crowd at the beach, and with long strides he walked away, in the direction of his home. He was troubled. As he came closer to the main street, he could smell the smell of cinders. Changing his mind, he picked up his pace, and walked quickly in the opposite direction of his house. He stopped on the street corner near the restaurant where he had eaten many times. He hesitated a moment and then moved on. The owner was standing out front of the entrance, sprinkling salt on the sidewalk.

"Happy New Year!" the owner of the restaurant said to John.

"Hi, Happy New Year to you too. Did you happen to hear about the house that burned down?" John asked him. The man took his cigarette out of his mouth and held it by his side for a moment.

"Ya, someone died last night, and there was a fire, that's all I know."

Around the corner came another man out for his morning walk.

"Hey, Walter! Happy New Year! How's it going?" he asked casually.

"Chuck! Happy New Year to you too! This is John. John, Chuck Chatsworth."

"I've see you around," Chuck said coolly to John.

"Pleased to meet you," John said extending his hand. Chuck held out his thick leather gloved hand and looked at John with a cold stare,

"Sometimes I see you, and you don't see me," he said ominously.

"John and I were just talking about last night. There was a fire, and a death up the road. We're trying to figure out what happened. Sad way to start the New Year," said Walter.

"Oh yes, it sounds terrible. The circumstances are horrible. I've just been there. It's all taped off. Seems like foul play. The police have interviewed witnesses, but they aren't closer to arresting any suspects. As a matter of fact, they questioned *me*! Seems like they wanted names of people for questioning. They might have to subpoena a few of the locals who don't want to get involved. I think I know who it was. Her name was Cheryl. She lived alone – a real nice lady."

"I think I know who you mean now. You said foul play, do you mean murder, then?" asked Walter.

"I was thinking more like suicide," said Chuck.

"Someone told me she was a drinker. Maybe it was an accident," said John solemnly.

"Whatever it was, what a tragedy," said Walter.

"What about her dogs? Where are the dogs," asked John; his voice now trembling.

"Apparently she had them put in a dog kennel for a few days over the New Year. That part was taken of," said Chuck. He leaned closer to Walter and added in a half whisper, "They found her dead on the ground, at the bottom of the stairwell."

It was easy for the men to speculate on what had happened because they did not know the lady in question personally. It was easy to wonder and speculate. John felt sick inside. He said goodbye to the men, and continued toward the hill in measured, deliberately unhurried steps. The words 'dead on the ground' started to swim in his head. He began to lapse into a flashback, Ohio, Kent State, his time in Vietnam; with the song pounding merciless in his chest and his throat, like a bullet and a scream, *"What if you knew her, and found her dead on the ground? How can you run when you know?"*

As if caught off guard by the sight, he found himself amongst a crowd at the smoldering scene. Stumbling upon it unawares, his legs could not move with the shock of the grim sight. He could smell the smoke long before he could see the house behind the snow- covered hedge. His thoughts swarmed like a wasp nest disturbed by an intruder. 'What had happened the night before was a blur – was he responsible, could he blame the alcohol, had his lack of discipline killed Cheryl?'

Police cars were everywhere. A small gathering of people across the street was standing and talking quietly. John's breath clouded his vision and when he regained his stamina, he crossed over to the other side.
Looming up in front of him was the ghastly sight of what once was the three-storey house, burned half way up one side with the trestle of the roof a blackened skeleton hanging limp, yet frozen, ready to collapse. Beneath the cold grey cover of the sky, and hidden in the singed branches of the great green cedars, the once majestic house stood like an ice-covered castle. It was a frozen embryo of death. A solid waterfall covered the ruin, thick and permanent, and caught in time. The icy hand of providence preserved the scene with the spray from the fire hose turned to ice. John turned away – no arctic temperature could make him feel colder and more deathlike than he felt now. 'How could this be?' he thought to himself. The lines of poetry he had composed during his first winter in the north came into his head like a prophetic dream:

> *I walked along and witnessed winter's wreck,*
> *While wind blew icy threads around my neck,*
> *And steps seemed slow to ponder earth's bare floor,*
> *Where once tall grass and meadow flowers were.*

The aging poplars moaned and grieved to send,
The last their whirling dropping leaves to end,
And distant peaks shone forth new glistening coats,
Just tinted rosy by the sunset's stroke.
I trudged along, now back turned to the wind,
My bearings lost amid nature sublime,
 Each element showed all its might and force;
 Earth, water, air and fire take their course.

He slowly turned away, and walked on, down the road, not wanting anyone to think that he had just come to look.

Chapter 32

John found himself the next day boarding a plane for Vietnam. He had only his knapsack, which he had packed in a hurry, and his travel guides bought at the airport, and a name. Of all of these, the most prized possession he carried was the name of the young woman who was his daughter. He slept most of the flight, changed airplanes in a daze, and arrived not knowing what he would do next. 'To die of the cold, or to die in the heat; they were both the same thing,' he thought, but he could not have waited any longer. The once strange and exotic images now looked familiar and comforting – he remembered them well, their image buried for years, the graceful and form fitting dress of the women, the flaps of their tunic dress blowing in the wind, the soft flowing curvature of their bodies swimming through his mind – it was all coming back. He noticed the white *Ao Dai* uniforms of groups of school girls crossing the road, and wondered if his daughter was nearby, teaching. Once out of the taxi, he was moved forward into the crowd, beyond his power to resist. His heart palpitated and he opened and closed his hands unconsciously. The humidity wanted to lay him flat, but he continued down the main street, surrounded by bobbing and moving, the conical hats, and the incessant honking of scooters' horns. 'Were they honking at him? Did someone know him here?' he asked himself. It was impossible for anyone to know him; but everyone seemed to stare. Some pretty young women smiled and giggled as he passed. His salient figure seemed to move in slow motion, - carried along by the heat itself.

He stood still for a moment amid the frenzy and chaos, the beeping horns and the revving of engines; beautiful women with long shiny hair flying out behind them from the backs of their scooters, with brightly colored silk scarves wrapped around their necks, and white flashing teeth, all smiles, passed before him; and myriads of men in white shirts talking on cell phones, acknowledged him with a nod, all busy with their lives.

"Hey, you play American football?" an old man with missing teeth called out to him. He didn't stop to answer; he had heard the question a lifetime ago, same place, different circumstances. Somewhere out of a café came the mellifluous music of Mozart. It made its way to him, and moved him to introspection.

"Piano Concerto number 21, in C sharp major," he said out loud to himself, wanting to hear some English spoken. He knew the piece well. He stopped right there in front of the café, witnessing three eras melded into one: 17th century Europe, the Vietnam War, and the present. And he stood there, still, and listening, wiping the sweat from his brow and his temples. The salt slid into his lips, and tears began to stream down his face mingling with the sweat, so that the two could not be distinguished one from the other. He was back. A pineapple vendor was calling to him to buy: "Mister, sweet and juicy pineapple for you, you look like you need it."

"No thanks, partner," he said in a distracted way; and looking up from the voice, he strode through the crowd, and the world stood still around him like a patch of smooth water on a rippled sea.

Epilogue

Two days later, after a dissolute and somewhat disjointed New Year celebration, yellow tape continued to surround the old house on the hill, still partially covered in ice. No one seemed to speak much more about it; one woman had died, a wealthy widow, whose daughter had just reconnected with her, but was currently out of the country. The police continued their investigation. In spite of the destruction of the house, forensic specialists were on the scene gathering specimens for DNA testing. Several people were called in for questioning surrounding the mysterious circumstances of the woman's death. Anyone with information about the incident, or who had any connection with her were requested to call the police. Names were given to the police by some members of the community. Mr. Chatsworth put forth Elena's name - his love of justice perverted to spite: 'If I can't get her for stealing a tree, or letting her dogs run wild, I'll innocently suggest my suspicions of some hanky-panky on her part, some connection to the other parties in question...That will shake her up – teach her to have more respect for the law,' he was heard telling his wife.

Of the dozen or so contacted as witnesses, and sought after for further questioning in regards to their whereabouts on New Year's Eve, only a few were of any significance. Of course the local physician was called in for questioning, as the deceased had been a patient of his. Furthermore, for various reasons, others included (not yet incriminated) were: the criminal lawyer and Andy of the beach as both had a liaison with the Sunday School teacher; the derelict raft builder, as the Sunday School teacher was his benevolent mistress from time to time (he had to be subpoenaed); John Lees who was the father of her only daughter and who had secretly left for Vietnam; and Elena Beaufort – for her esoteric relationships and her timid yet eccentric behavior.

Made in the USA
Lexington, KY
10 August 2012